Arms of Freedom

Kathleen Neely

Other Books by Kathleen Neely

The Street Singer

Beauty for Ashes

The Least of These

In Search of True North

What Readers are Saying

Arms of Freedom had me up two late nights reading! I cried in a couple spots of the book. The writer wrote such emotion into the pages. Your mind could visualize it like a movie. – Tammy Karasek, President of ACFW Upstate SC

I absolutely loved *The Street Singer* by Kathleen Neely. This novel is a true love story on so many different levels. The author does a wonderful job creating a beautifully flawed heroine, Trisha, who rises above societal expectations and norms to follow her heart and do the "right" thing. And Rusty? What a beautiful picture of sacrificial love. A wonderful read. I couldn't put it down. –Carol James, Award-winning author

The Least of These: From the prologue's poignant quote of Matthew 25:37-40, "'Lord, when did we see you hungry?" to the last sentence in the epilogue, the reader is taken on a journey to the land of the homeless. Here we are introduced to sights and sounds of a culture deeply hidden in the day, coming out at night like zombies to roam a bleak landscape. No one seems to care, because they are invisible, until Scott Harrington, in an act part selfish, part humanitarian, draws back the curtains. We witness Scott's struggle between using these human beings to further his ambition as a writer or allowing himself to feel their pain and take on their cause. Stella, the feisty, hard-working owner of a cafe proves the perfect foil to Neely's Scott. The twists are just enough that you don't see them coming. The ending is satisfying and the supporting characters are well-rounded. A beautiful book by Kathleen Neely, that delivers a punch to the heart. –Suzy Parish, Award-winning author of *Flowers from Afghanistan*

Dedication

To Sandy, my sister in Christ;

Thank you for being my go-to person

for ideas, help, and encouragement.

FOREWARD

Arms of Freedom was birthed during a time of racial tension in our nation; a time when social injustice and protests were forefront in the news. Many publishers safely avoided manuscripts with any mention of racial issues—perhaps a wise decision from a business perspective.

However, failure to look at our past denies us the opportunity to learn from history. Our fear of offending can push major historical offenses into a dark closet. I chose to illuminate those offenses by launching this book. Following the Civil War, the period of twelve years known as Reconstruction was perhaps the most brutal period of racial terrorism. The contents may be hard to read. I confess that I often wrote through tears.

In the end, I hope your takeaway is this: Regardless of race and ethnicity, all people are created in the image of God, a one-of-a-kind miracle, loved by Him, and created for a purpose. We are called to unity, to be perfectly one (John 17:23). May we join together in raising our arms of freedom to the Savior who released us from the captivity of sin.

So if the Son sets you free, you will be free indeed. -- John 8:36 NIV

Kathleen Neely

1

Lights peppered the skyline of New York City as the plane began its descent. Miriam Gentry managed to doze between Heathrow and LaGuardia. Dalton Designs' corporate jet had not been available, so Miriam's assistant, Lacey, had arranged for them to board the commercial jet. They slipped unnoticed into their seats before other passengers entered, thankful for the privacy dividers provided in first class.

The speaker crackled with audio feedback followed by the pilot's words, smooth as velvet in his British accent. "Thank you for flying with Global Airlines today. We'll be touching down in LaGuardia in the next ten minutes. The weather in New York City is sunny and 72 degrees. At this time, please turn your electronic devices off, return your seats to their upright position, and keep seatbelts securely fastened." The rehearsed words arrived polished and melodic despite the amplification.

Miriam scooted forward in her seat to retrieve her sunglasses and ball cap. The photo shoot in London had been exhausting, and a few weeks ahead with no assignments sounded like heaven. She craned her head to look down upon the city emerging below. "Who's picking us up?"

Lacey's seat clicked into place as she moved it upright. "I asked for Rudy. They'll allow us to de-plane first.

We'll be picked up at the gate, then a transport will take us to the car."

Miriam had gone through three assistants before finding Lacey. The first one didn't want to travel with her and assumed an assistant could arrange everything from the office in New York City. That clearly didn't work. The second one thought her job was to give the orders instead of taking them. The third one liked to talk to the press. Lacey was a keeper. She effectively managed every detail of Miriam's life, a necessity since she'd become the *Face of Dalton* three years ago. As Dalton Designs grew to giant proportions in the fashion industry, so did Miriam's modeling career.

The wheels touched down with a slight bounce, and she felt the pressure of speed as it taxied on the runway. "Good. I'm bone weary and ready to be home."

~~*~~

Miriam welcomed the respite of the Manhattan townhouse after being surrounded by people in a frenzy of activity day and night for the last three weeks. Photographers, designers, models, stylists, make-up artists. Merely thinking about it fatigued her. The new line of clothing would launch next month, and an air of secrecy bordering on paranoia kept the designers tense. With the competitive market, everyone wanted to showcase something unique, something announcers would namedrop at the Grammys or Oscars or some high-brow social event.

Nellie, Miriam's live-in housekeeper, had her own quarters, but magically appeared on the penthouse balcony with breakfast. After placing the tray on a table, Nellie quietly disappeared back to the kitchen. Miriam had no need of live-in help, but when she set out to hire someone to come in a few times a week, the agency had Nellie, sixty-something whose husband left her in need of a place to live.

8

Something tugged at Miriam's conscience, a kinship to abandonment. The agency told her that very few opportunities surfaced for live-in help. So Miriam hired her. The split bedroom floor plan allowed privacy for each of them.

Bypassing the breakfast, Miriam reached for the cup of green tea. London had been difficult with too much food and too little exercise. Miriam refused to sweat in a public gym where photographers competed to capture pictures for any scandal magazine willing to pay their price. She scanned the breakfast, quickly dismissing the toast. No carbs today. Instead, she opted for the celery sticks, spreading them with unsweetened yogurt.

The morning routine included HIIT – high intensity interval training in her private exercise room. Jump rope, crunches, push-ups, squats, and sit-ups. Thirty-second rest intervals kept the cardio intense. After the HIIT routine, she'd pull on the gloves to meet another opponent—a heavy boxing bag. Her mother loathed the punching bag. Eleanor deemed it the most unladylike method of weight control. But Miriam found it to be a sweet release of frustration. It had become various people at different times in her life, usually her father, although the bag wore her mother's face a time or two as well.

Energized, she showered, dressed, and began to brush her silver, blonde hair. The hair always gave her away in public. Her stylist called it diamond blonde because it reflected light like the facets of the gem.

The time had come to fulfill her daughterly duty. With a press of the intercom, she spoke. "Nellie, will you please order a car? I need to see my mother. I'd like to leave in thirty minutes."

Nellie's voice responded through the speaker. "Yes, Miss Miriam. I'll call you when the car arrives."

~~*~~

Eleanor gave Miriam an obligatory hug when she entered, a little shoulder squeeze that didn't require touching faces. Her mother loathed touchy-feely. "When did you get back?"

Light poured in from the floor-to-ceiling windows high above the city. Her mother's not-so-subtle eyes traveled toward her midriff, hips, and belly, before craning her neck to the buttocks. Nothing got by Eleanor. She'd know if an extra pound went on. Miriam set her handbag on the entry table and walked past her mother into the living room. "Last night around seven. It felt good to sleep in my own bed."

She sank into the feather soft sofa across from her mother's chair. Eleanor took her seat, lifting her legs onto the ottoman. "Did you watch?"

Less than two minutes. She wasted no time asking. "Watch what?" Miriam knew exactly what her mother was talking about, but feigned ignorance.

Eleanor's face stiffened with annoyance. "The pageant. It aired last night."

"No, Mother. I stopped watching those years ago." Ten years had passed since her last beauty pageant, and her mother still couldn't get over it. She had Miriam enrolled in her first pageant at age seven. Initially, it felt like playing dress up, a step into a world of make-believe. It didn't take long for the tedium to set in. The girls in the pageant longed to be kids—playing, giggling, and running around. But the moms—take any soccer mom and multiply the determination by a thousand, and you still haven't reached the fervor of a pageant mom. The girls had to sit prim and proper like little princesses until their turn arrived.

"You had every possibility of winning state and going on to Miss America. I don't know why in the world you had to quit after all we put into it."

"Really, Mother?" Even when Miriam was a child, Eleanor didn't want mom or mommy. She wished to be called mother or Eleanor. "All we put in?" Miriam laughed out loud. "You mean weeks teaching me how to walk correctly when I should have been learning math?"

Eleanor's eyes narrowed. "And don't tell me that hasn't benefited you now."

Miriam crossed her arms at the chest. "Singing and dancing lessons when I couldn't carry a tune and had no sense of rhythm?"

Her mother stood and headed toward the kitchen. "I don't want to argue. You made your choice. I'm just saying, you could have won." She re-entered with two bottles of sparkling water and set one before her daughter. Eleanor thrived on the competition. It was all about the win.

"Are you aware I made the list of top ten models in the world?"

Her mother waved a dismissive hand. "Barely. You were number ten. Be careful or you'll be off the list next year. There's always someone younger and prettier coming up."

Clearly, that level of competition didn't excite her as much as a crown and floating confetti. Miriam's anger reached the surface. "I earned over $15 million dollars last year. You're living in Manhattan because of me. When will it be enough to satisfy you, Mother?"

"I said I don't want to argue."

Finishing her water quickly, she stood up to go. She had fulfilled her responsibility and a driver waited at the curb. "I'm leaving for Pittsburgh tomorrow. I wanted to stop and see you before I go."

Her mother's sharp eyes softened for a moment. "Will you see your father?" They'd been divorced for five years, but Eleanor had not gotten over her husband leaving her for a woman fifteen years younger.

"No." The word forcibly spit from her mouth, leaving a sour taste behind. A bitter herb too pungent to swallow. Eleanor was aware of the wall that had been erected between

11

father and daughter, but never asked why. Miriam wanted to believe she didn't know. Her knowledge and silence would be indefensible. "I'm visiting Nana."

A scowl replaced Eleanor's moment of nostalgia. "Of course. You're always visiting Nana. You should see your father. Marriage didn't work for us, but he loves you. At least call him."

Miriam offered no response. That would not happen. Ever.

Eleanor lifted her chin and put on her wounded look. "I'd have gone with you. I still have friends there, too."

But she didn't. Her friends were pageant moms. Competitors. All of their energy went toward pageant preparation. Her mother had obsessed with the best of them. At fifteen years old, Miriam said no more pageants. Her mother begged, pleaded, and cried. Then she threatened, playing the guilt card.

"Where would you be if I hadn't rescued you from an orphanage? I pushed you to make something of yourself."

It was clear why her mother had chosen her over the others at the orphanage. Silver blonde hair and bright blue eyes were exactly what she needed for a pageant daughter.

Where would I be? A question she'd pondered a thousand times over. If she'd had a normal childhood. If she had gone to school instead of the sham her mother called homeschooling. If her childhood hadn't been spent parading around a stage in high heels and make-up. Where would she be today? *If* is a complex word.

~~*~~

The Roswell House Assisted Living offered the best nursing care in Pittsburgh. Miriam had vetted them carefully. She parked her rental car and strolled the brick path bordered by fragrant lilacs. Another garden area could be seen through an ornate wrought iron rail. Miriam scanned the wheelchairs to see if her grandmother was among the other elderly residents enjoying the sunshine, but caught no glimpse of her. Either way, she had to enter and sign in.

"Hello, Miss Gentry." The receptionist greeted Miriam as she signed the visitors' register. "I believe Miss Lillian is in the great room."

The staff knew her by name. She suspected she was Nana's sole visitor, even though her father lived a mere five miles away.

"Thanks. I'll find her."

The great room served as an area where some residents liked to interact with people. For others, the lounge became a place where they could sit in solitude without being alone. Miriam was glad to see Lillian among the social group. She shared a table with three other women, with her oxygen suspended on her wheelchair. Nana had the ability to walk, but it taxed her heart.

"Hi, Nana." Miriam leaned in close and planted a kiss on her cheek. Her grandmother reached for Miriam's hand and held it in her own silky, translucent hand, as delicate as a bird's bone. Blue veins protruded, forming their own unique topography.

She turned toward her friends. "I believe you've met my granddaughter."

An overlap of greetings sounded around the table as Miriam tried to remember each name. Her grandmother attempted to push the large wheels of her chair backward. "Excuse me, ladies. I'm going to go spend some time with my granddaughter."

Miriam helped her steer the chair clear of the table, then pushed her back to her own room. When she settled her grandmother and covered her legs with a lap quilt, she reached into the oversized tote bag. "I brought you something." She lifted the picture out and held it high. The framed painting portrayed the front porch of her grandmother's home, two rockers with the familiar flowered cushions, and Buster, her long-deceased cocker spaniel, curled on one of them. "I painted it from an old photograph."

Her grandmother took the picture and held it an arm's length away. Tears beaded the rims of her eyes. "Oh, Annie. It's beautiful."

Annie. Only Nana still called by her real name. Dalton Designs had insisted on the name change. Peter Dalton claimed Miriam had more zing, something people would remember. He was right. She had become one of those famed celebrities known only by her first name. With *Miriam* splashed across the cover of a magazine, it needed no explanation.

"I'm glad you like it. Sorry it's been so long, Nana. I've been away on a photo shoot for most of this month."

"Where did they take you this time?" Her grandmother spoke with her eyes fixed on the painting.

"London. Muggy and rainy." Miriam exhaled an audible sigh.

"It doesn't sound like you enjoyed it." Nothing escaped her grandmother's notice. It never had. Her wise eyes wore a question.

"I'm just tired. Everyone thinks it's a glamourous lifestyle, but it's exhausting. The glamour died long ago."

Nana's heart had weakened over the last two years, but her mind was razor sharp. "So why are you doing it?"

Miriam fidgeted with her tote bag, hanging it over the back of her chair. "What else would I do?"

"What else would you like to do?"

Another weary sigh escaped. "I have no idea. I don't need the money, but I can't sit around doing nothing."

Nana's eyebrows arched as she looked at the painting, a suggestion written in her eyes.

"Paint? I'm not sure I'm good enough to actually sell paintings. I certainly don't need any more myself. I've run out of wall space."

The aged hand wrapped itself around hers. Silence stretched between them as they examined the picture. "I can see Buster's soft fur. It makes my skin long to feel it again, to stroke that thick coat. His eyes are looking up right at me, like he's waiting for me to bring him a dog biscuit. And my old rocker, why the cushion has shadows and fringe making it look so real. I see dew on those hanging fuchsias and can almost breathe in their fragrance." Her eyes pivoted from the picture to her granddaughter. "You're good enough, Annie. Don't question yourself."

Her art instructor told her she had talent, but of course he'd throw compliments her way. He knew her as Miriam. Knew her fame and no doubt, her net worth. The internet offered no privacy. "I don't know, Nana. New York's a competitive art hub. That world would eventually be the same stressed lifestyle as modeling. I can barely step outside my apartment now. I need a disguise so people won't rush me for autographs."

"So why do you choose to live there?"

Typical Nana. Always asking logical questions, tactically throwing in words like *choose* to remind her that she had a choice. The circumstances of her life were the results of her own decisions. "That's where Dalton Designs is located." Not exactly an answer, but it was the best she could come up with.

Nana's eyes drilled hers for what felt like an eternity. "I have something for you. I've been waiting for the right time. Maybe this is it." Lillian wheeled her chair in a circle and over to the drawer of her nightstand. She opened it and pulled out a metal container with a key inserted in the lock.

"Nana, I don't know what you keep in there, but it's not really locked if the key's left in the keyhole."

She swished her hand to dismiss the concern. "If it's not in the keyhole, it'd be loose in the drawer. I don't have a lot of options." She leafed though some papers and retrieved what she looked for. Then turned and handed it to her granddaughter. "Do you remember my house in South Carolina? The one where I lived before your grandpa died?"

"Vaguely. I was only about five or six when that happened."

She nodded her head to the envelope in Miriam's hand. "Open it."

Miriam lifted the prongs on the clasp and pulled a page from the envelope. Her eyes widened in surprise as she scanned it. "This is the deed. You still own the house?"

"Your dad wanted me to sell it. Actually, he pressured me. I grew weary of hearing him yapping about it, like he thought he'd get the money or something. I finally told him I'd disposed of it."

Nana, telling a lie? That was so out of character. Miriam barely suppressed a chuckle. "You lied? Shame on you, Nana."

"I did no such thing. I signed the deed over to you years ago and kept paying the taxes. It's sitting here waiting for your signature. It's written in my will that the house goes to you, but I signed this over so there will be no question in case my old ticker decides to quit."

Miriam's eyes widened. "To me? Why in the world would you do that?"

"Because I knew you were the only one who'd value it. My son would have sold it faster than a freight train, and your mother—can you imagine your mother in Hickory Falls, South Carolina? It's yours, Annie. You need only sign the papers."

Her head reeled with the thought. "Do you mean it's been sitting vacant all these years? Is it falling apart?"

"No, child. I've had a property manager who rented it out and sees to the maintenance."

Why did her grandmother want her to own a house so far from all she'd ever known? She knew no one in South Carolina. She barely remembered being there. "What in the world would I do in Hickory Falls?"

16

A smile filled with Carolina memories and a touch of mischief wrinkled her grandmother's face. "Live. Paint. Make friends. Mow grass. Plant tomatoes. Sit on the wraparound porch and sip sweet tea. All the things I loved and miss."

Miriam's head flew up to see Nana's face. "It has a wraparound porch?"

Her grandmother laughed. "That's the part that caught your attention? Go see it, child. I promise you'll love the house. Maybe even fall in love. Might be time for settling down."

Miriam shook her head. "No, Nana. That's never going to happen. When you live like I have, you can never trust romance. Unless it's someone with his own big bank account, and in my experience, those aren't the kind of men I'd want."

"You overthink things. It's doubtful people in Hickory Falls would even know the name Miriam. Maybe it's time to go back to your roots and be Annie again."

"Nana, I've been on the cover of People, Glamour, and Vogue. Even the rural south has seen those."

She ignored the concern. "The house sits right on Main Street. I've had more offers than I can remember. Most people are wanting it for commercial use. It would be a great setting for something like … let's say, maybe an art gallery?"

An art gallery. In small town USA. A place where no one knew Miriam. It all had such appeal. "But how could a small town support an art gallery?"

"It's been over twenty years since I lost your Grandpa. I sometimes regret my decision to move, but your dad's my only child, and you were the sweetest little thing. It seemed right at the time. I suspect the town's grown some. Even so, it sits between Greenville and Asheville, an easy drive to Charlotte and not too far from Atlanta. People will drive for good art."

Was it possible to live there without people recognizing her, knowing her fame and fortune? Another thought inched its way into Miriam's head. "Nana, would you come with me?"

A look of longing fleeted across her face. "Oh, I'd love to set my eyes on the old house again, but I'm afraid my weak old ticker wouldn't cooperate. I feel secure having a nurse right here when I need one."

Miriam's rising excitement couldn't be stifled. "I can hire a nurse, a live-in, someone full time. I'll look for one specifically trained in cardiac care."

Her grandmother rested her head on the back of her chair. Quiet surrounded them, both lost in a world of dreams, weighing the cost of chasing them. Lillian broke the silence. "I'm growing tired, Annie. Will you help me to the bathroom, then into bed? I think I'll nap for a while."

Miriam helped her stand and walk to the bathroom, rolling her oxygen with her. A slow amble back to the bed served as a reminder of how weak Nana had become. With her grandmother tucked in for a nap, she leaned close and placed a kiss on her cheek. The delicate hand lifted and rested on her shoulder. "You go see it first. The thought of that trip makes me tired. If you aim to settle there, I'll think about it. But I best tell you this—those walls hold secrets. Secrets that need to be set right. That's another reason why I wouldn't sell the house."

That didn't sound like her grandmother. She hadn't shown signs of confusion as many elderly people had. Perhaps her oxygen level was low. "Secrets? What do you mean by that?"

"Small towns are steeped in history. It's not all pretty."

"But these are secrets you know?" She remained skeptical about her grandmother's clarity. "Can you tell me?"

"I know some. I suspect there's lots more. Wait till we get down there and I'll tell you what I know."

We? Nana might actually come. How had a routine visit with her grandmother turned into a long-distance move?

2

The elevator soared to the 24th floor, headquarters for Dalton Designs. Miriam hoped Peter Dalton would be in. She had no appointment with the world-renown fashion designer, but if he was in, he'd see her. She was certain of that.

Valeria stood to greet Miriam. "Miss Gentry. What a pleasure to see you today."

"Thank you. Is Peter in?"

Valeria buzzed to let him know, then took Miriam to his door, rapping gently before she opened it.

The brightly lit office showed the flashy creative side of its occupant. An ultra-modern black stone-top table with sleek white legs served as a desk. Behind it, an abstract geometric pattern of huge rectangles, circles, and diamond shapes formed a wall in red, yellow, and black. Opposite the wall were grand windows allowing light to spill in while overlooking the city.

Peter stood and opened his arms—arms clothed in a magenta silk shirt with jeweled buttons. "Miriam, what a pleasure." She held herself back from a full hug, so he kissed her cheek, emitting the overpowering scent of manufactured spice. "Come and sit over here." He led her to a seating area with swivel chairs in red and yellow resting on chrome pedestal bases. A glass and chrome table sat between them, and a framed Picasso on the wall complemented the geometric shapes. Magazines with Dalton Designs fanned the table top.

"To what do I owe this visit?"

"I'm quitting." She threw it out there with no idea what the reaction would be.

Dead silence. When he'd recovered, he released a condescending snicker. "What's the problem, Miriam? Whatever it is, we can fix it."

She shook her head. "The problem is—I'm tired. I don't want to do this anymore."

"So, take a few weeks off. Or more. We're done shooting the new campaign. We can all afford to kick back a little."

"I'm quitting, Peter. I'm not kidding. I'm done with modeling."

His eyebrow rose as all semblance of a smile disappeared. "I'm afraid you can't do that, my love. We have a contract."

"I know. That's why I'm here. I have one more year on my contract. I'm here to ask if you'll release me."

"And exactly why would I do that?"

Miriam turned on her million-dollar smile. "Because I came to you first, asking nicely."

Her smile failed to soften him. "That may be so, but this is business. Big business. I'm afraid I can't accommodate your request."

She leaned forward, uncomfortable in the scooped-out seat that refused to stay still. "Peter, please, I need a change. I'm asking you to do this for me. What will it take? Can I buy my way out of the contract?"

His head shook slowly. "I can't, Miriam. We work way in advance. I have some things coming up that need you. We've signed contracts for venues promising your presence."

Annoyance surged through her. "How can you promise my presence?"

An eyebrow arched again. "I can promise because you're under contract. Remember—the paper you signed?"

Silence hung between them, leaving only the noise of a sound machine with fake ocean waves. Miriam must have looked like a lost puppy because Peter relented slightly.

"I might be able to amend your contract. Cut back on your appearances. Keep your shoots to a minimum."

"I want to move out of the city."

"No problem. We'll set your schedule way in advance. You'll know when you're needed."

Miriam felt the shift in Peter's response. She may as well go for broke while on a roll. "And please don't pair me with Rocco anymore." The sleazy photographer loved to brush against her in the guise of establishing a pose. His hands knew no boundaries.

"Come on, Miriam. He's the best."

"He won't keep his hands off of me. I don't want to work with him."

Peter's smirk showed amusement. "No promises, but I'll see what I can do."

~~*~~

Peter proved to be much more understanding than her mother.

Eleanor stood in stunned silence before erupting. "You've got to be kidding me! You're among the top ten models in the world."

"Which you reminded me can change by the next list. Remember—always someone younger and prettier."

The reminder of her own words brought a glare to her steel gray eyes. "You make millions each year. What exactly do you think your art will make?"

Miriam exhaled a deep sigh. "It doesn't matter. I don't need more money."

"And what about me?" Angry arms moved from her hips to cross at chest level.

"You don't need more money."

22

Eleanor freed her arm to flip her hand dismissively. "That's not what I meant. What am I supposed to do?"

"Whatever you want, Mother. Get a job. Start a new hobby. Find a husband. You'll think of something."

"And why South Carolina. It's filled with hillbillies. Your eloquent diction will soon be a twang. You'll be saying y'all and eating catfish."

"Don't be offensive, Mother. I like the town. And the climate suits me." She didn't bother telling her mother that she'd only seen it from the internet, a website whose sole purpose was to make it look appealing.

"This is all Lillian's doing. We moved her out of that backwoods town years ago. Even the name rings full of redneck. Hickory Falls? Really?" Her facial muscles tensed. Miriam could see her rage simmering, rising to the top, ready to explode.

"I have to go. Remember, I'm still the face of Dalton. I'll be back in town often."

Miriam made her exit before the volcano fully erupted. Her mother had been known to throw things in anger. A book once sailed through the air, barely missing Miriam, when she failed to master dance steps. The worst occurred when her father left. A dozen kitchen stoneware dishes took flight, crash landing in every corner of the kitchen. The memory brought a twinge of guilt. She could have invited her mother to come, but there would never be anonymity with Eleanor around. No fresh start, only a lateral move while she found new ways to shove her daughter into the limelight.

~~*~~

Miriam said goodbye to Nellie, leaving her a nice severance package. She kept the Manhattan penthouse, and kept Lacey on staff. Both would be needed when she came back to the city.

23

Eleanor always assumed Miriam would fall flat on her face without her intercession. Maybe she was right. Miriam had never stepped foot in a classroom. She had no idea how she'd fare. The guise that Eleanor had called homeschooling served to satisfy the state's requirement of standardized tests. They only prepped for exams, spending more time on the strategies of test taking than math or English. All other time was spent preparing for the pageants. Walking. Public speaking. Singing. Dancing. Piano. When she'd failed at the other talents, her mother brought in an artist and they tried speed painting. Another failure. Miriam loved painting but couldn't master speed painting for an audience. She continued to paint which her mother dismissed as a useless waste of time. The best they managed to come up with for the talent portion was dramatic reading. Miriam memorized and read poetry, the only part of pageant life she enjoyed.

~~*~~

The window at the hotel looked out onto the flight path of jets taking off from Pittsburgh International Airport. She'd grown up a few miles from here. Her father still worked as a pilot with Pittsburgh as his hub, which didn't matter since she had no intentions of seeing him. He had destroyed any chance of a father/daughter relationship when he chose to change it.

She saw her grandmother in the morning and they sketched out their plans. She would move into the house, give it a thorough cleaning, and paint walls that had faded over the years. Even though Miriam hadn't actually seen the house, she'd spoken to the property manager and viewed a virtual tour of the interior and exterior.

She'd begin her search for a live-in nurse and set up the downstairs den for her grandmother's bedroom. A medical transport would return Nana to her beloved home in Hickory Falls.

Miriam decided to spend two more days in Pittsburgh before catching a flight to Greenville, the closest airport to Hickory Falls. A fresh start required more than a change of location. First, she applied a store-bought dye to her hair. The non-descript light brown looked natural despite the do-it-yourself kit. A stylist in a ten-dollar, no-appointment-needed econo- shop cut her hair to a mid-length bob with angled sides and a wisp of bangs. Her New York stylist would be aghast. A trip to the mall supplied her new wardrobe of jeans and t-shirts. The designer dresses and spiked heels all remained in New York. Sandals and sneakers became her new norm.

Miriam's eyes were naturally blue, but tinted contacts had enhanced them for the camera. She tossed them out and purchased clear ones. She didn't intend to wear them on a daily basis. Her eyeglasses had little use over the past few years. She tried them on, liking the look with her short, angled hair.

She had resisted using a pseudonym when Dalton hired her, but she lost that battle. They were insistent, so she became Miriam.

A new reflection stared back from the full-length mirror. With her face scrubbed clean, void of all makeup, she wore cut-off jeans, an army green V-neck cotton top, and white slip-on canvas shoes. A fringe of wispy bangs nearly reached the top of the glasses perched on her nose. Miriam was gone. Annie Gentry had returned.

3

Annie found Greenville's airport to be delightfully small. She picked up her luggage and located her hotel pickup van. She'd stay in town one night while she purchased a car and saw to the property deed transfer. Annie stopped in the county tax office and signed the papers prepared by Lillian's attorney. Transfer of the deed occurred without incident. The property manager met her with the keys. She slid them onto her keychain along with the fob for her new silver Toyota Camry, ranked among the most popular cars of the year. Nondescript. Exactly what she wanted. Something that would blend in, just like Annie Gentry.

A rush of adrenaline stole Annie's breath when the house came into view. It sat proudly on a corner, displaying its grandeur. Main Street intersected with Larkspur Road. The house fronted on Main Street which made it perfect for an art gallery, if and when Annie ever got one up and running. Larkspur was to the right with an antique shop on the opposite corner.

Annie's Main Street neighbor was Hickory Falls Hardware Store. The name filled the front drop of a royal blue canvas awning. A narrow black wrought iron balcony graced the second floor, directly above the awning. While small quaint businesses filled most of Main Street, Larkspur appeared residential with homes lining both sides of the street. The silver Camry turned left onto Larkspur, and left again into her driveway. Annie's detached garage, tucked out

26

of view behind her new home, shared an access driveway with a yellow clapboard house.

The private L-shaped drive entered on the side of the garage, requiring a right hand turn before reaching the car stall. Annie stopped short of the turn when she noticed her garage door open. Had the property manager neglected to close it? Then she saw movement through the side window. Closing her car door quietly, she stepped toward the garage, holding tightly to the fob that featured an ear-splitting alarm. Her finger rested on the button, ready to press it if necessary. A man faced the workbench, his back to her, searching through the drawers.

Her hands sprang to her hips. Had people been looting the unoccupied property? "What are you doing, and how did you get in here?"

She had intended her clipped voice to startle him, but he turned his head, in no hurry to move. "I'll be with you in a moment." He continued to shuffle small tools around until he came up with the object of his search. He proudly held up a spool. "Got it. Cord for the weed eater." He closed the drawer and walked to meet her.

"How can I help you?"

Was he really asking her to explain herself? "For starters, you can tell me how you got in my garage."

He shifted the spool to his left hand and held out his right. His blue polo shirt matched the color of the awning over the hardware store, with Hickory Falls Hardware stitched in black thread over the pocket. Light brown hair jutted out from beneath his visor cap shading an easy smile.

His hand reached forward. "Seth Walker. That must mean you're the new owner."

Annie looked at the grass-stained fingers and relaxed slightly. He must have been hired to do yardwork. She accepted the handshake, feeling the rough, calloused hand of someone who put it to good use. "Annie Gentry. Yes, I'm the owner."

"It's my pleasure, ma'am. This is a mighty fine house you got."

Really? *Ma'am?* From someone near her own age.

"Needs a little touch-up here and there, but it's got good bones. Glad to see it'll be occupied again." His eyes roamed the backyard. "Your family here yet?"

Annie bristled at the assumption. "I'm the family. It's only me. For now."

A lopsided smile and a nod of his head brought flecks of light to his hazel eyes. "No kidding. Big house for one lady."

She had no intention of sharing her story with a complete stranger. "I like old houses." That's all the explanation he'd get. "Did the property manager retain you to keep up the yard work?"

"Naw. I've been doing it for a long time. Couldn't let it grow out of control now. Besides, I take care of all of this." He waved his hand toward the lot behind the hardware store and the one on the other side of it. "Easy to keep going when I get the tractor moving."

An idling tractor behind the hardware store showed signs of fresh cut grass clinging to its wheels.

"Well, thank you for taking care of it."

He hooked his thumbs in his jean pockets. "It's been empty since Polly Grainger died. She was the last tenant who lived here. Sweet lady. I helped with the grounds and some maintenance, but it sure can use a little sprucing up. I reckon you're already aware of that."

Annie was anxious to get inside her new home. She needed to end this conversation. "Well, thank you, Seth. I better get unpacking."

"Let me put this away and I'll help you." He started walking toward the tractor as she called after him.

"That's not necessary. There's nothing I can't handle."

28

He gave no indication he'd heard her. His slow, easy gait strolled to the riding mower and cut the engine. Then he lifted the weed eater from the grass, and carried it to her garage. When he reached the car, she had the trunk up.

"As you can see, I don't have much. Most of my things will be shipped here later this week. I'll be fine."

Seth picked up the largest of her suitcases and a duffle bag, completely ignoring her. "Around here, neighbors help neighbors." He carried them to the small back porch. "If you toss me your key, I'll open this for you."

With a deep breath, Annie lifted out the smaller suitcase and her tote bag. Her keys were still in her hand. Should she be wary of this stranger? One look at him told her he was exactly as he appeared—a slow, southern, country boy. She tossed the keys toward Seth and accepted his help. This didn't happen in New York City. Not without an extended palm waiting for a healthy tip.

They had no sooner closed the screen door when the front doorbell sounded its Winchester chimes. Annie looked through the sidelight window to see a woman standing, holding a covered plate. She couldn't be much over five foot tall.

Seth, who had no view of the front porch, chuckled. "Two cents says that's Iris Flannagan. We heard rumors of someone moving in. She's probably been sitting at the window watching all week."

Annie opened the door and the lady extended her gift. "Welcome. I'm Iris Flannagan, your new neighbor. I live over yonder in the red brick ranch smack up behind Arty's Antiques. Course, there ain't no Arty anymore. He was the owner's granddaddy who's long passed."

Annie's 5'8" frame looked down on Iris's head of white curls with a hint of silvery blue, perfectly rounded to match the curlers that had probably formed them. "Thank you, Ms Flannagan. I'm Annie. And what's this I'm holding?" She nodded down at the covered dish.

29

"Oh honeychile, there ain't no Miss or Mrs. amongst neighbors. I'm just Iris. This here's my double fudge chocolate cake." She leaned in conspiratorially and whispered. "Its real name is 'better than sex chocolate.' But we can't let Seth over there hear that, can we?"

As if on cue, he walked toward them. "Morning, Iris. How you doing today?"

She flashed him a smile showing crooked front teeth. "I'm so good if I had a tail, I'd be waggin' it."

"That so? What's all the whispering? You telling Hickory Falls' secrets already?"

She waggled a finger at him. "Now hush your mouth. Don't go giving me a bad reputation in front of this lady." A chuckle followed. "I'll be doing that myself in due time."

Annie listened to their banter, still holding the plate. What in the world would she do with a chocolate cake? It would be rude to refuse it. "Well, thank you for the cake. I better go put this away."

Iris gave no indication of leaving so Annie retreated to the kitchen. Her new neighbor hollered in after her. "Don't worry if your fridge is stuffed too full. It don't need no refrigeration."

Stuffed full? She didn't even know if it was turned on. Annie set the cake on the wooden farmhouse table. It was part of the furniture she'd purchased from the deceased renter's estate. They were happy not to move it, and she was thankful to have furnishings in place when she arrived. Annie rejoined them, still standing in the foyer. This was all new to her. People in New York didn't come calling bearing cakes. Should she invite her to have a seat?

Seth saved her from the decision. "That was very neighborly, Iris, but I think Annie has some unpacking to do. We best let her get to it. Why don't I see you safely across the street?" Annie gave him the slightest grin, a silent thank you that he acknowledged with a wink. He held out his hooked arm and Iris slid hers through it. Seth moved slowly as they stepped down the porch stairs. Iris looked over her shoulder. "I'll come again when you ain't so busy."

~~*~~

As Annie walked through the empty rooms, she saw the truth of Seth's words. Most every room required a fresh coat of paint. The dining room wallpaper had to go. Yet despite the flaws, the house held great charm. She arched her neck backward to stare at the high entry ceiling. Gold and silver merged to form pounded metal squares, each with a floral center. At first, she thought they were all different, but then discovered the pattern. It was a work of art.

Her hand caressed the intricate woodwork. Every nuance matched the 1835 era. High ceilings, a stained-glass transom above the front door, and a porch that wrapped around the Main Street and Larkspur sides. It was a masterpiece that needed a little pick-me-up. She could hire painters, but for the first time ever, Annie had a sense of ownership. She wanted the project of fixing this house up, returning it to its original glory. Something she could baby and take pride in. She might even stop her HIIT routine if painting and stripping wallpaper provided enough exercise.

A baroque stairway, flared at the base with volutes on each side, led to four bedrooms. The three-piece bedroom furniture perfectly matched the house. A high-back bed with an ornate maple headboard. An oval beveled mirror stood behind a deep-well dresser. The trifid feet of the nightstand matched. So totally opposite from the modern décor of her penthouse. The master had an en suite, probably added sometime over the years. Skinny metal front legs supported a sink across from a vintage claw-foot tub.

Annie walked through each room, looking for the best natural light for her studio. She chose the last one at the end of the hall. The nauseating pink paint would have to go, but the corner room offered three windows. One had a side view

31

toward the hardware store and two provided a view of the back of the house. It overlooked her own grassy yard, homes on Larkspur, and mountains in the distance.

In addition to the four bedrooms and the bathroom, the hallway had two closed doors. She tried the first and found a linen closet, deep and empty. When she turned the knob of the last door, it stuck. She tugged and pulled, but it wouldn't budge. That's when she noticed the lock. A glance at the ceiling showed no pull-down attic stairs. This must be the door to a walk-up attic. She went downstairs to retrieve her keys, but then decided the attic was a low priority.

Seated at the kitchen table, Annie began a grocery list. The chocolate cake stared her down. What in the world did Iris think she'd do with a whole cake? Looking at the cake dish reminded her of Nana. She always had something baked, and in those days, Annie ate it, unless her mother's watchful eye was nearby.

A knock on the backdoor startled her. She looked up to see Seth standing there. Really? Was he going to make a pest of himself? Annie opened the door to find him holding a plate covered with foil.

"I'm sure you haven't had a chance to grocery shop. I threw a few burgers and veggies on the grill and figured you could use one." She stared at the plate he held. He stretched it a little closer until she reached for it.

Red meat and chocolate cake. What would Eleanor say? That thought brought a sudden laugh. "Thank you. I haven't eaten and I don't think a double fudge chocolate cake would be a good dinner choice. Will you take some?"

He reached to scratch his head. "Well, I've tasted Iris's chocolate cake, so I won't say no to a piece. But you know it will freeze well?" Seth phrased it as a question.

No, she didn't know anything about cooking or storing food. "That's a thought, but let me share some with you first." She went to the cupboard before remembering that all of the cabinets and drawers were empty. "I guess I have nothing to cut it with, or to send it on. My things are coming in a few days."

"No problem." He reached for the plate she had set on the counter, opened the foil, and retrieved plastic silverware and a napkin. "There's extra napkins so you can scoot a piece of cake on this one and I'll take it with me. I guess you're fixin' to make a run to the Piggly Wiggly."

Piggly Wiggly? Was that some kind of farm, or maybe a barbeque place? "What's Piggly Wiggly?"

The slight, lopsided grin returned. "That would be the only grocery store in town, unless you want to drive about 25 minutes. Folks around here all know what the Piggly Wiggly is. Where you coming from?"

She wouldn't get tangled in a web of lies. Best to be honest, while skirting the whole truth. "New York City."

"Wow. The big apple. This has to be a culture shock for you. What brought you to the deep south?"

"Actually, this was my grandmother's house. She kept it and rented it out for years. I'm an artist. I took art classes in the city, but I wanted a small town, somewhere I could relax and paint. The city's too busy."

"Well, you came to the right place. There's some beautiful country around these parts, just begging to be painted."

"When I get settled, I'm going to move my grandmother down here. I'll be looking for a live-in nurse if you have any recommendations."

He nodded thoughtfully. "Well, let me think on that. I know a few nurses, but I'm not sure I'd trust them with my grandma. I won't make a recommendation lightly."

"I appreciate that."

He took the cake she offered, folding the napkin over it. "I think I made a good trade here. I better let you have your dinner while it's hot."

"Thank you for this." She motioned toward the plate.

33

Seth was right about one thing. Hickory Falls was a culture shock.

~~*~~

Lacey answered on the third ring. "Hello, Miriam. Tell me you've had your fill of country bumpkins and are coming back full time."

Annie laughed. "Afraid not. I've barely started, but I need your help."

"That's what I'm here for."

"It's a little unconventional. Will you do a shopping trip and equip my kitchen? I have no idea what I'll need. Do an online order with next day delivery."

"O—kay." The stretched-out word showed her confusion. "So, what do you have?"

Annie scanned the kitchen. "Nothing. I have empty cupboards and empty drawers. No dishes. No pans. No silverware. Nothing."

"And the budget?"

"I have no idea what it costs to equip a kitchen. Use your judgment. And Lacey, nothing fancy. No designer dishes. No fine china. Make sure to order common everyday items."

"Okay, this could be fun. Do you want to see the order before I place it?"

"No. Do your best to have it here by tomorrow. Oh, and throw a few bath towels on that list, and queen-size sheets. Don't go economy on the linens. You know what I like. And remember to send it to Annie Gentry. No mention of Miriam."

"Will do. When will you be back up here?"

"In about three months. Peter bought me a little time before the next shoot."

4

Sunshine sliced through the haphazard slats of the blinds, laying a striped pattern of light on the hardwood. The night had been restless. New bed. New room. New noises. Crickets chirped when she tried to fall asleep. Birds twittered merrily long before Annie wanted to rise. It was a pleasant sound, not like the traffic noise of Manhattan. The mattress, softer than her firm bed in New York, yielded to her body. The same mattress that felt foreign last night, now cocooned her in softness. She wanted to stay and bask in the luxury of idleness, but too many tasks awaited. With great reluctance, Annie swung her legs to the floor and made her way to the shower.

With nothing in the house to eat, except for the double fudge chocolate cake, Annie dressed and walked across Main Street to The Coffee Grinder. The delightful scent of cinnamon and coffee mingled in the air. She strode to the counter, wearing the visor cap on her cropped brown hair. An old habit. She had reached for it instinctively, forgetting that she no longer had to hide her former trademark blonde. Annie scanned the choices, then ordered a skinny vanilla latte and a yogurt fruit cup.

She had planned to take her order back and eat in the house, but loved the ambiance of the little café. The rounded bare-bulb lights strung throughout, the chalkboard menu in a rainbow of colors, rows of flavored syrups, and the rich aroma of coffee. Three young men sat at a square table drinking coffee. All three wore visor ball caps, shabby and impossible to read the monogram. One man had his long legs stretched out, scuffed work shoes resting on the fourth chair. Their voices were loud and their laughter contagious. Annie relaxed at the sound of it.

She chose a round table close to the door where she could watch the morning activity on Main Street. A glimpse of her reflection flashed from the mirrored glass behind her seat. It still took her by surprise when she saw the short, brown hair poking out from under the ball cap, eyeglasses perched on her nose. The hand wrapped around her to-go mug had nails that were trimmed and colorless. Gone was her French manicure. She had clipped each nail with rebellious abandon as she said goodbye to her alter ego.

Twenty minutes passed. There were many things on her to-do list today; giving the kitchen and bathrooms a thorough cleaning, putting her kitchen in order, making paint decisions, and a trip to the Piggly Wiggly. Annie made her way back across the street. She'd need to stay focused so she could bring her grandmother home.

~~*~~

During the first full day in her house, five boxes arrived with Lacey's order and three neighbors visited. Myrna Mansfield brought a homemade loaf of bread and an invitation to the Baptist church. Ruth Sutton brought a welcome basket with three jars of preserves and a tract from the Methodist Church. Darlene McIntyre brought a baby on her hip and an invitation to the Presbyterian Women's Bible Study.

Hickory Falls, population 2,036. Would they all stop by? In between visiting with drop-in neighbors, Annie unpacked each box, setting up her new kitchen. A feeling of independence spurred her on as she rearranged dishes and mugs. She stood on a chair to clean higher cabinets and store things that would get infrequent use. Some people would find this tedious. Eleanor would have hired the job out. But it held a novelty, almost like a teenager moving into that first coveted apartment.

A few times throughout the day, her mind drifted to the locked attic door but Annie had no time for exploring. By early evening, Annie flopped onto the rocker on her front porch, more exhausted than a HIIT session. A half-dozen pedestrians traipsed up her sidewalk to say hello. She had stopped trying to remember all of their names. Seth waved to her from the front entrance of the hardware store as he pulled in the sidewalk displays. She could see Nana in this place. See her rocking on this porch and visiting with neighbors. She should have stayed. Instead, she moved to be closer to her only child, and he ignored her. But if she had stayed, Annie would not have known her. She had to get her down here. It was the right thing. This is where her grandmother belonged.

~~*~~

After a better night's sleep, Annie came down to her newly equipped kitchen and opened her freshly stocked refrigerator. Her eyes looked beyond the kitchen to the dining room window where she could see The Coffee Grinder across Main Street. She forced her longing glance away and set up her own coffee pot, then found an online recipe for an egg-white veggie omelet. With her new skillet and spatula, she followed every step perfectly, yet somehow her omelet became an egg-white scramble, not at all like the beauties Nellie had created. After eating it, she soaked the egg-scorched pan, then turned to the empty boxes left from yesterday's delivery.

The boxes nested nicely and Annie began to drag them toward the stairs. She would store them in the attic in case she had need of them later. And she'd finally steal a minute to look around that locked space. She picked up the keys and the boxes and headed upstairs.

Annie set the boxes down and began to finger through the keys. The property manager had given her the house keys on a metal ring. Front door, back door, and garage. Another key had been slipped on the ring separate from the cluster. Would that be the attic key? Separated to keep it from renters? She tried it first.

The key turned in the lock, but the attic door still required a strong arm to open it. Years of dried paint scraped the door jamb. The bottom rebelled against the threshold, clearly in need of a carpenter to sand it down or re-align it. She propped it open, hit the light switch and immediately met years of stagnant air. A musty smell caught in her throat activating a gag reflex. She coughed, then hoisted the cardboard boxes to shield her nose and mouth. As the still air began to dance in its new freedom, the disturbed dust mites floated in dull light beams. She'd have to deal with this sometime. She'd take the boxes and drop them upstairs. The attic needed a good airing out before she could look around. With the boxes held high in her arms, Annie climbed the steep wooden stairs.

The dim light cast shadows, enough to know that the room wasn't empty. Annie plopped the boxes down and felt along the wall for another light. Instead, she found a string dangling from a single bulb mounted on the ceiling. She tugged the string and the room came to life revealing a lightly-cluttered attic. Sheets covered surfaces in their attempt to protect them from years of dust. Her initial inclination was to leave this for another day. Or another year. Low priority with all she had to do.

Yet something compelled her to stay. A few boxes and a storage chest. You would expect those in an attic. But a large section of the room held an air of familiarity. Children's furniture had been stacked against one wall. A wooden table, four chairs, two turned upside down to nest on the other two, and a bookshelf. A carpet, about six-foot square, spread out on the floor in front of the furniture. Why was everything so familiar? She had only visited here twice when she was around five years old. And she was certain she'd never been in the attic. Eleanor would not have allowed it.

Annie opened an old chest that sat on the carpet. She lifted the dusty lid and saw the toys, mostly wood and metal. A toy tea set, a sorry looking stuffed teddy bear, and wooden building blocks with faded alphabet letters. A smaller chest sat beside it. She picked up a yo-yo, the string discolored and stiff, marbles in a cardboard box, a metal spinning top, void of color. These were definitely old, perhaps antiques. She lowered the lid, puzzling over this discovery. Another box held two items, both wrapped in cloth. She lifted one and removed the flannel to discover a baby doll. An image formed in her mind. She had seen this doll. She was certain of it. She could see a vision of the doll sitting on one of the wooden chairs. She knew she'd find another when she unwrapped the other flannel—one with red, curly hair.

As she unpacked the second doll, it all came back to her. A picture. She'd seen the items in a painting at Nana's home, the home she had in Pittsburgh before she moved to Roswell House Assisted Living. The painting mirrored Andrew Wyeth's style of down-home realism with rustic details. The table and chairs on the same carpet where Annie stood today, the tea set in the center, and two dolls seated with teacups before them. The gritty window in the background of the picture with its yellow-gold curtains matched the window a few feet away. The gold had faded to a drab shade and held years of dust, but it was the same curtain. The same window. That meant a child's play area had been in this attic. Why would anyone set up a playroom in an attic? Or perhaps this space served as an artist studio, the dolls and tea set staged for a picture. But another thought marched to her brain. Her grandmother's words. *Those walls hold secrets.*

Annie turned and pulled the string, extinguishing the upstairs light, then made her way back down the steps to the other light switch. She shoved the scraping door closed, still baffled about the set up. Who had painted the picture that hung in her grandmother's kitchen? The locked door and separated key indicated that renters had no access. Had her grandmother locked this area away when she left over two decades ago?

~~*~~

Bells jingled when Annie opened the door to the hardware store. She was met with the paradoxical look of a vintage mom and pop business with aesthetic charm. A shabby chic blend of cluttered organization with weathered wood flooring polished to gleam. Quaint, unlike today's mega home improvement centers. She breathed in the unique scents of leather and wood. Seth looked up and waved from his stooped-over position where he unloaded a box of various styles and sizes of screws. He slid each packet onto the metal prong extended from a pegboard.

An older gentleman stood behind the counter at the register. The blue of his apron matched the blue of Seth's shirt. Both had *Hickory Falls Hardware* stitched on them. Annie moved further into the store toward the counter.

"Y'all must be Annie. I reckoned you'd be by here sometime, what with movin' into an old home. I'm Charlie, and mighty pleased to make your acquaintance."

"Hi Charlie. Yes, I'm Annie." She smiled with pleasure at the unique hardware store. "Nice store."

"I hear your name's Gentry. Kurt Gentry your daddy?"

Her smile faded. Hearing her father's name could ruin an otherwise pleasant day. "Yes. Do you know him?"

"I knew your daddy when he was knee-high to a grasshopper. How's Miss Lillian doing? She still livin'?"

"Yes. She had a heart attack about a year ago. It weakened her. She's in a nursing home but I'm going to bring her down here as soon as I get settled."

His eyes lit up like a sparkler. "Well butter my buns and call me a biscuit!" He slapped his hand on the counter. "Lillian Gentry's coming home."

Annie laughed out loud. Oh, if Eleanor could hear this! "So how do you know my grandmother?"

"I was born and raised here. Folks know folks. Lillian, she was one fine lady."

Annie nodded. "Still is. I'll tell her I met you."

"You do that. I don't reckon you came in to chat. What can I help you with?"

"I'm hoping you can help me with some paint and paint supplies."

He stepped from behind the counter, a visible limp as he walked. A mustard-brown coonhound, stretched out beside the desk, lifted one floppy ear and turned sad eyes toward Charlie, but made no attempt to move. "This here's Useless. He's older than dirt and slower than a Sunday afternoon." Charlie circled around behind him.

"That's his real name? Useless?"

"Yep, and I'd say it's fittin'. You follow me. We've got what you need, and if we don't, we'll get it in, right quick."

He took her to the section where cans of paint waited, stacked in a pyramid. A color mixer wore spatters in a rainbow of tones. Charlie pointed to the stack of color grids. "What color you wantin'? We can mix it for you right here."

She chose neutral shades of ivory and a soft tan. While the mixer shook the cans, Charlie helped her pick paint brushes, a roller, and a roller pan.

Seth stepped around the corner. "How you doing today, Annie?" He didn't wait for her reply. "Have you

41

checked the garage? I think you have some paint supplies in there."

Annie hesitated. Anything in there was undoubtedly old and dirty. She'd rather buy new. "Uh, no, …"

Charlie came to her rescue. "Tell you what. I can see you're aiming to get this started. Why don't I ring these up and when you check your garage, you bring back anything you don't need?"

"That sounds like a plan. Let's do that."

Seth nodded his head in agreement. "Holler if you need some help."

Charlie chuckled. "Looks like you'll be busier than a one-legged cat in a sandbox. You might be hollering for that help."

Annie had no intention of hollering for help, but she found herself loving a town that offered it so freely.

5

The caller ID showed her father's name, leaving a knot in Annie's stomach. She hit *ignore* and silenced the phone.

The wallpaper in the dining room had to go. The dated floral pattern was an eyesore. She didn't want to *holler for help* as Seth and Charlie had suggested, but the room held some heavy furniture. The breakfront proved to be the challenge, but thanks to the hardwood floor, she was able to slide it, inch by heavy inch, until she had enough clearance to place a ladder. Annie prepped the floor by laying a tarp where she'd start. It wasn't large, but she'd finish the first section, then move the tarp. Shopping and prepping the workspace was enough for one day. She didn't want to start stripping paper late in the afternoon. Everything was ready for her to begin bright and early the next morning.

Instead, she made her way to the den. The small room off of the kitchen provided the only option for a downstairs bedroom for her grandmother. When the living and dining rooms were painted and the den transformed into a bedroom, she'd bring her grandmother home. Annie stood in the den's doorway envisioning the bedroom. A pale violet. Not her choice, but it would be Nana's. Then she'd paint a canvas of lilacs for the wall. They were Nana's favorite. And this old carpet would need a good cleaning. Two weeks. Maybe less.

Early the next morning, Annie saw another missed call from her father. Her stomach burned with anger. Did he really imagine she'd want to talk with him? He acted like nothing had happened. Annie deleted the missed call. She couldn't worry about her father. There was too much work to be done.

She slipped into jeans and a cheap T-shirt, then pulled a visor cap over her hair. This time it wasn't to hide, but to protect her hair from paint splatters. She applauded herself for remembering to grab a screwdriver to remove the electrical and light switch plates.

Where should she begin? The seams were tight so there were no loose corners to pull. She wedged the scraper along a seam and loosened it. Holding tightly to the ripped edge, she tugged, hoping a large section would follow. To her dismay, she managed to remove a six-inch sliver approximately half an inch wide. As she repeated the practice a few times, the scraper formed divots in the plaster. If she continued, the plaster would look like a golf ball.

Her eyes traveled up to the nine-foot ceiling. Realization hit. This was a big job. Annie's enthusiasm began to wane. She had seen a ladder in the garage on her first day here. Grabbing her keys, she headed outside.

Annie tried three keys in the garage lock, all to no avail. Nothing was going right. All patience had fled. In a temper, she swatted the door with the palm of her hand.

"There a problem with the door? I don't think beating it will help."

Annie about jumped out of her skin. She turned and found Seth close behind her. All of her frustration of the last hour came pouring out on him. "Is that supposed to be funny? Do you always sneak around and frighten people?"

"No sneaking necessary." He looked down and motioned toward his feet. "Tennis shoes and grass don't make much noise. Something I can help with?"

"Yes, you can help. I need a ladder and can't get this blasted door open." She held the keys out toward him.

Seth stepped by, ignoring the keys, and turned the handle on the door. When he did, it easily slid open. "What size ladder? There are a few in here."

Heat climbed to her cheeks. Embarrassment mingled with annoyance. She knew she had been snarky, but she didn't want to stop being angry. The attempted calls from her father had her rattled. And who would have known the garage wasn't locked? People in New York secured their possessions. "I need a step ladder, high enough to reach the dining room ceiling."

He walked to the back of the garage and easily slid one from behind a shorter ladder. Annie reached to take it from him, but he ignored her as he had done with the keys. She hurried behind as he carried it toward the house.

"I can get that." Did he think she was some helpless debutante because she couldn't open the garage door? Her exercise routine gave her excellent upper body strength.

He kept moving. "Why don't you get the door?"

She stomped in front of him, seething, but she didn't know why. He was being polite. She held the door wide as he dipped the ladder, top first, and carried it in.

"Where do you want it?"

As he maneuvered it inside, Annie realized that the same task would have been quite difficult for her, practically impossible with no one to hold the door. "In the dining room, please." Her frustration began to abate.

Seth set the ladder down and checked the safety catch to make sure the legs were secure. "Anything else you need?" He stole a glance around the room.

"I'll be fine now. Hey, I'm sorry if I sounded snarky. You showed up in the middle of a frustrating moment."

"No problem. It happens." He eyed the wallpaper. "Are you using anything to dissolve the adhesive?"

She held up the scraper. "This."

Seth gave a slight nod, then turned and walked out the door. Confused, she held her hands, palms up, and spoke to no one in particular. "And goodbye to you, too."

Her attention had been turned back to scraping the wall when he re-entered. He carried some large drop cloths and held up a spray bottle of something. "We may need to get more of this before the room's done, but this'll get the job started."

We? Without further conversation, he pulled a little tool from his pocket, something she'd never seen before, but it came to a sharp point. He began making tiny holes in a section of wallpaper, then sprayed a twelve-inch square.

"Let it soften for a minute, then we'll remove it. If we examine the backing, we can see which direction the grain goes. Then we'll know which way to pull."

She couldn't find words, so merely nodded, feeling inept. Picking up a knife, Seth ran it ever so lightly across the top, bottom, and sides of the square, careful not to score the plaster behind it. After a moment, he tested the square. Holding firmly to each end of the seam that he'd loosened, he gently began to lift it sideways. His large hands were amazingly nimble, and she couldn't help but notice the neatly trimmed nails. When the wallpaper showed some resistance, he dropped it back in place. Moving those long fingers to the two top edges, he gently tugged, top to bottom, removing the complete square. Not a shred remained.

A brief smile formed on his face when he saw her mouth fall open. "You need to loosen the adhesive," he repeated. "This grain runs up and down, so don't pull sideways."

"Thank you so much. Would it be possible for me to borrow that little thing you used to poke holes? Or I can buy one if you tell me the name."

To her surprise, he pulled a second one out of his pocket and tossed it toward her. "Why don't you work here, and I'll start at the ceiling?"

Annie had wanted to do all of the work herself. Something she could take pride in. But the frustration of the morning convinced her she'd need help. "I'll be happy to pay you for your time. I guess this job's a little bigger than I thought."

As if she hadn't spoken, he picked up the ladder and carried it to the back corner of the room. It was beginning to get infuriating how he ignored her comments and continued doing what he wanted to do. He locked the legs, without looking back at her. "How about if I give you the same price I'd have given Miss Polly?"

Miss Polly. The previous tenant. The money didn't matter, but she had the distinct feeling he was mocking her. "What exactly is that supposed to mean?" She expected him to respond with annoyance, but instead, his eyes softened. Softened and looked right into hers, like he could see a hidden space deep inside of her.

"Annie, I don't want anything for helping you." He waved his hand around the height of the room. "This is a big job. I know you're capable, but I have a few hours. I'm happy to help."

At that moment, she felt tears begin to sting her eyes. They were a foreign intrusion. Miriam never cried. She had erected a wall protecting her emotions. Years of competitions had kept her from making friends. She had no practice forming relationships. But this was Annie. Newly vulnerable. He was being helpful and she'd taken all of her frustration out on him. "I'm sorry, Seth. I guess I'm not used to people …" She fell silent, not finding the right word.

Seth found it for her. "Being kind?"

"Yeah, I guess that's it."

His eyes still held fast to hers. "My mom used to tell me kindness is like the first spring flower. It makes everyone's day better."

Seth's gaze warmed her cheeks. Was he for real? Annie had never encountered anyone who lived with such overt goodness. Could she relax her protective wall? Experience told her she'd get hurt. Yet something deep inside of her wanted to trust. Was that a foolish Pollyanna dream?

Two hours into their work, half of the wallpaper had been removed. The time went faster with someone to talk to. They chatted about the town, her art, and his passion for golf.

Thoughts of the attic playroom returned. "Did you know any of the previous occupants? Anyone before the last tenant?"

"Nope. I lived in Tigerville, a little bit north. Miss Polly was here when I moved to Hickory Falls."

The child's playroom would have to remain a mystery for now. She glanced at the time. "Seth, didn't you tell me you had a couple of free hours? Don't you have to go to work?"

He kept pulling the strip of paper he had loosened. "No, I switched my schedule. We're on a roll here."

She knew he had been on his phone earlier. "Well, let me make us some lunch."

Glad for the break, she went to the kitchen and pulled out fresh greens to make a salad and cheese and crackers. Then she remembered the double fudge chocolate cake. She retrieved two pieces from the freezer and set them out to thaw. A glance through the archway showed Seth eyeing the paint cans at the base of the stairs.

"Are you doing both rooms?" He followed her to the kitchen.

"Yes, but that should be easier than removing wallpaper. Painting's my thing."

"Yeah, on canvas. Do you have a plan for the stairway? It's pretty high."

"I have an extension rod for the roller."

A knowing look flashed across his face. "You better take a look in here." He picked up a few crackers and motioned for her to follow.

48

Wordlessly, his eyes traveled up the stairwell. It had to be eighteen feet high. They stood, their necks tilted, staring upward. She had been so focused on the dining room that she hadn't thought through this high space.

"Well, how tall are those other ladders?" Even as she asked, she knew she couldn't work that high. The first three rungs on a stepladder reached the limit of her comfort zone. Seth stood behind her slouched form. A touch on the shoulder of her wrinkled shirt and a gentle nudge turned her around.

"Annie, I work with a crew of painters who can do this. I can get them over here tomorrow."

That quick? "How do you know they'll be available?" If these men needed work that badly, maybe they weren't good painters. "Maybe I should call a professional painting company."

He dropped his hand from her shoulder. "Trust me— they're good. I'll help and make sure you get a quality job."

She took a step back and eyed him skeptically. "And your boss? He'll let you skip work to come over here and paint?"

He shrugged, appearing unconcerned. "It's slow this time of year."

"And you *will* give me a bill? I can't let you do all of this without paying you."

"You worry too much. Now, I recollect you saying something about Miss Iris's double fudge chocolate cake?"

~~*~~

Annie had two e-mail accounts—one with Dalton Designs which Lacey managed to keep full, and the other was her personal account which typically remained empty. Today, however, an e-mail waited. Her father. Her pulse throbbed as she clicked it open, ready to close it immediately if it held no importance.

49

Tried to call but no answer. What's going on with your grandmother? I thought she sold the house years ago. Now she tells me she's given it to you. Please return my call. The equity in that house should be my inheritance, which you clearly don't need. We need to talk.

His inheritance? Not one word about how his own mother was doing. Did he know she planned to come south? She touched the trash icon and deleted the message. *No, we don't need to talk.*

6

The three painters and Seth worked swiftly. In the span of two hours, they prepped and taped the space, with tarps covering all furniture. One coat of paint had been applied to the stairwell and the living room. Annie declined their help on the dining room. She wanted her fingerprints on some of the upgrades. After a lunch break, they began the second coat. Annie needed something to occupy herself so she'd stay out of their way. Still puzzled about the attic, she wrenched the door open and climbed the steps wearing a dust mask she'd found in the garage. This time she started with the boxes and chest. The chest held old linens, musty and dry rotted. She lifted them out discovering framed pictures. Who would leave these behind?

The clothing worn in the pictures dated them. Long dresses for the women, high-neck blouses with poufy sleeves, high-top shoes that laced up, forbidding one glimpse of an ankle. Men in frock coats and top hats. These pictures were treasures of someone's ancestry. There were numerous photos of a family of three—father, mother, and son in various stages of the son's growth. Another picture showed a maid, a young black girl no older than sixteen. She wore a white maid's apron over a drab gray frock that appeared to be a coarse cotton, a contrast to the embellished silks of the other ladies pictured. On her head, she wore a colonial mop hat, an elastic band separating the brim. The pictures spoke of the family's affluence. Fine clothing, domestic help, and beautifully framed photographs.

Annie lifted each picture, searching the faces. How she'd love to hear their story. Was this their home? Would Nana know who these people were? It was possible they were Nana's ancestors. Did that mean they were hers as well, even though she was adopted?

Three packing boxes were stacked on top of each other. Annie opened the uppermost box. The items inside had been carefully packed, cushioned with Styrofoam peanuts and bubble wrap. As Annie unwrapped each item, she found familiar objects from Nana's home. She unwrapped a china tea pot and a Depression glass vase, amber and etched with flora. These three boxes must be items she couldn't bear to part with when she went into assisted living. How did she ship them down here, and who saw to their storage? Annie decided to clean up a few pieces and display them for her grandmother. A touch of the familiar.

She chose the teapot and vase, then shifted the box to the floor and opened the second one. It held framed photos, more recent than the photos in the old trunk. Many were pictures of a young Annie with her mother and father, while others were of her father as a boy. Nana's photos depicted natural settings, not the beauty contest photos Eleanor loved to display.

Would it be good to have a photo of Nana and her grandfather, or would that be too painful? She decided to wait on that one. Beneath it, clothed in a layer of small bubble wrap, she found the doll's tea party painting. Excitement bubbled up at the discovery. Annie carried it to the light and examined the details. The child's table with two dolls having tea was the focal point. She glanced back and forth between the stored objects and the painting, examining specifics. The child's play area was definitely the one depicted in the painting, and the surrounding details showed that they had indeed been set up in the attic.

She moved across the room to where the painting depicted had been the play area. A cot with a pillow and folded blanket showed years of dust. She resisted touching it and sending a spray of residue into the air. Beside the cot, a black bookcase held shoe boxes packed with children's picture books and chapter books. She immediately recognized some of the titles. Tom Sawyer and Black Beauty. Father Tuck's Nursery Tales and Little Darling's Lesson Book were among them. The lower shelf held a stack of black and brown leather books.

Annie ran her hand across a cover, feeling the embossed pattern. Edges turned slightly showing cracks in the aged material. The narrow depth surprised her when she lifted it. Each book was about a half inch thick. She opened the one she had lifted, and discovered it was a journal. The first line had 1875 centered across the top. Annie opened another. 1873. She pulled them all out, checked the dates, and placed them in order. Six journals ranging from 1872 to 1877. She had wished she could hear their story. Maybe she'd be given the chance.

"Annie."

Seth's voice, calling from a lower level, shifted her attention. She poked her head in the stairwell and replied. "Coming." She reached for the smallest of the boxes she had carried up and placed the journals in it. On top of the books, she added the painting, the teapot, and the vase. She passed her bedroom on the way downstairs, leaving the box beside her bed.

An unmistakable scent of new paint met her. The men were folding the tarps and closing the ladder when she went down. Seth met her at the base of the stairs. "I wanted to get your A-OK before we wrapped it up."

She'd been so preoccupied with the journals that she hadn't paid attention on her way down. She looked at the living room, then upward to the expanse of the stairwell. The fresh paint made an immediate difference. "It's beautiful. Thank you so much for orchestrating this so quickly."

Seth turned to the waiting men. "Good to go, fellas. Thanks for a nice job."

"Wait, Seth. Don't let them leave."

She hurried to the kitchen and opened a drawer, pulling out an envelope, then retraced her steps. "Who do I pay?"

The man closest to her held his hands, palms out, in a stop sign gesture. "That'd be him." He pointed to Seth. The three workers carried their supplies and left Seth to deal with the payment.

"Here." She held it out to Seth. You've been reluctant to tell me an amount so I checked online prices for painters." The envelope held $1,200.

His paint-splattered hand opened the envelope, glanced at the contents, and rifled through the bills. He took seven of the $100-dollar bills from it and handed her the envelope with the balance. "I don't want anything for helping out, but I do have to pay the men. This will do."

"Seth, I did my homework. Four men at the suggested rate of $50 an hour. They were here five hours." She extended the envelope back to him.

He waved her away with a grin. "Then you've already miscalculated."

That comment hit a nerve Seth had no way of knowing. Annie's love of literature, poetry, and art had helped her succeed in the midst of an appalling homeschool experience. But math and science were an abysmal failure. A fleeting moment of panic always accompanied a task involving math. Her mind raced to re-do the simple calculation, but in the presence of another person, she couldn't think mathematically. She switched her thinking to logic. She had calculated and he had returned money. Therefore, her miscalculation must be high.

She glared at him. "I added extra since they came so quickly. Please. Take it."

He tucked the seven bills into his pocket and ignored the envelope she held out. "Really, this is good." He left her standing there as he picked up the remaining paint pan and left. Annie exhaled a big sigh. Seth Walker was a stubborn man. Stubborn and generous.

Annie looked toward the dining room and the stairwell. Paint or journals? She couldn't wait to dig into the journals, but duty first. The living room looked beautiful while the dining room had the blotchy plaster left from peeled wallpaper.

She started with the painter's tape, edging the woodwork. She no sooner finished taping when the doorbell rang. A peek through the sidelight showed Iris Flannagan. Annie opened the door and Iris handed her a dish. The warmth of the fresh baked cookies penetrated the paper plate.

"I saw Seth and his workers over here and figured I best make you some cookies to feed them. Looks like I'm too late." While she talked, she craned her neck trying to see what had been done.

"Thank you, Iris. They did a little painting. The workers are gone. Would you like to take those to Seth?"

Without invitation, she stepped further into the entry. "Oh my. They sure spruced up this room. You best keep them cookies. Looks like they'll be back to do your other room." She pointed toward the right.

"No, I'm painting that one myself. The men did what I couldn't reach on the stairwell walls."

"Well honeychile, if I were you, I'd be butterin' up to Seth Walker. Ain't a young lady in Hickory Falls who ain't trying to catch his eye. You take these cookies over and share with him, or better yet, invite him in for coffee and cookies." She eyed Annie's wrinkled clothes and visor hat. "And you might wanna get gussied up a little."

Best to take the cookies and end this conversation. "Well, thank you, Iris." She turned toward the door hoping Iris would get the hint. They were on the porch when she had another thought. "I guess you were neighbors with Polly Grainger for a long time. Did you know any of the previous owners?"

"Oh my, yes. Polly lived here along about ten years. Before then was Mr. Clive something or other, can't remember his last name. Before that was Lillian and Michael Gentry. He passed and she moved up north where her son lived. I lived way down on Sycamore Street when me and Lillian went to school together. I knew her best of all the folks what lived here."

Annie tried to take advantage of the pause to get a word into the conversation. But Iris barely came up for air before she continued her trip down memory lane.

"Lillian grew up here 'cause this is where her ma and pa lived. When she married into the Gentry family, she moved down to Aiken. They lived there for a lick of time, but when her pa passed and her mother got ailing, they moved back into this house with her."

Annie hurried to speak when Iris paused for a breath. "Lillian is my grandmother. My last name's Gentry."

Iris's mouth dropped open and she fanned herself with an open hand. "Oh, Lord have mercy. Why didn't you say so? That makes you like family in these parts."

"My grandmother is in an assisted living facility. I'm planning to bring her down here to live with me. As soon as I get settled in and the house is ready, we'll arrange for a medical transport. She has a weak heart and needs oxygen."

She shook her head. "My, my, my. Lillian's coming home. I can see us sitting here sipping our sweet tea. You tell her I'll be brewing a pitcher for her when she gets here."

"Thank you, Iris. Make sure her tea is decaf. She can't have caffeine. I better put these cookies away and get back to work on my dining room." She looked at the traffic turning the bend from Main Street to Larkspur. Poor Iris must sit there with nothing more to do than look at neighbors. "Can I help you across the street?"

Sunshine lit her face and she held her arm out for Annie to take it. "I'd be much obliged. Why you're just as nice as your grandma."

The highest compliment. Maybe Annie had begun to break down a few bricks from her protective wall.

~~*~~

Hours later, the dining room had two coats of paint. Annie cleaned her brushes and paint pan, then carried them to the garage. She looked at the handle, cursing herself for not turning it the last time. She rotated the handle as Seth had done and the door rose easily. She could get used to living in a safe neighborhood.

After a shower to clean any splotches of paint off of her skin, Annie walked across Main Street to The Coffee Grinder. She rushed home with her latte and curled up on the porch rocker with the first journal.

1872—My name is Charlotte. This is my first diary and I can hardly wait to write in it. Ma got it for me for Christmas, but I waited a whole week until the new year started.

That's as far as she got before the click of flipflops on her sidewalk announced a visitor. The lady with the baby on her hip, only this time she was alone. She stepped slowly up the sidewalk where green moss crept between each concrete section.

"Hi, Annie. Do you remember me? Darlene McIntyre?"

"Hi Darlene. Yes. You have that adorable little girl."

A smile filled her face. "Selah. She's our joy."

"Would you like to sit a spell?" As she said it, Annie recognized the southern flare of the statement. Sit a spell? Miriam would never use that phrase.

Darlene climbed the two steps and sat on the extra chair, turning it slightly so they were facing. Annie tried to guess her age. A pert little turned-up nose, a slight spattering of freckles, hair a light brown with tones of red threaded through. Natural. Not highlights. She wore khaki shorts and a tank top, but wrapped the arms of a light-weight sweater around her waist. If she didn't have a baby Annie may have guessed she was still in her teens. But perhaps somewhere low twenties. Definitely less than Annie's twenty-four years.

"I was hoping to talk. I hear you're an artist."

Word traveled in Hickory Falls like static through a phone line. "Yes, I paint."

"Can you teach paintin'?"

"Teach? No, I'm not a teacher. I'm not far removed from taking classes myself. I don't have much experience but am hoping to improve. Why do you ask? Who wants lessons?"

Pink colored her cheeks and a smile mingled with embarrassment. "Me."

"That's wonderful, but isn't there someone close who can give lessons? Maybe a cultural center or something?"

"No. Closest place is a good half hour drive, and with Selah and my old car, I don't think I can do it. Besides, they're pretty expensive." The color of her cheeks heightened. "I mean, I would've paid you. I thought maybe it wouldn't be … I mean, I'm sure …"

Annie interjected, saving her from further discomfort. "I know. Some of those places are quite pricey. I'd love to see something you've painted."

"Really? I never show my paintings since I never had lessons. I figure they're pretty amateur."

"Every master painter began as an amateur. That's what my instructor told me."

Annie caught her eyeing the tote bag sitting at the base of her chair. She had the distinct feeling it held a painting and Darlene struggled with a decision. Finally, she reached for it.

"This is a small canvas. I didn't want to tote a big thing over here for everyone to see. People round here don't know I paint."

She lifted the eight by ten and held it to face her. Annie saw the back of the frame. With a deep exhale, Darlene turned the picture.

Monet's La Pastiche the Magpie looked back at her. The snowy embankment, dappled sunlight through the shadows, the imprint of the fence embedded in the snow while the magpie rested on the top, looking at the snow image. "Darlene, this is incredible."

"No, I copied it. I've been getting art books from the library and saw this one. We don't get snow here, least not snow like this, so I thought I could have some by painting it."

"I know it's a copy of Monet's work. Many artists do that when they're learning. But you've done a masterful job. Look at the reflection in the background where the snow meets the gray sky. And the intricacies of your branches. You're very good."

Her hands sprang to her chest, resting on her heart. "Really?"

"Yes, really."

Silence waited for someone to speak as they gazed at the replica of Monet's Magpie. Darlene lifted her hands and shrugged. "So, what should I do?"

"What do you mean?"

"Should I try to get lessons? I don't think anyone would buy my stuff."

Annie's brows both rose. "They'd buy this. Don't underestimate yourself."

The pink returned to Darlene's cheeks as she lowered her head, examining the pattern of her flipflops. "So, someone said you're fixin' to open an art store."

That's why she came. The real reason. Annie blew out the breath she held. "I don't really have plans for that now. What I told someone, and I don't exactly remember who, is that I'd love to open a gallery someday. Right now, I have to concentrate on bringing my grandmother down from Pennsylvania. I'm getting things ready for her. She's not well and wants to come home to Hickory Falls."

"Oh." She began to return the picture to her tote, disappointment etched on her face.

"Listen, Darlene, you've got some raw talent. Natural talent. If you've done this on your own, that's impressive. Don't be discouraged. And stop hiding your paintings. Let people see them. You might be surprised at the reactions. Here's something we can do. Let's get together and plan an art exhibit. Not a gallery that's open all the time, but maybe a weekend exhibition where we display your art and mine. But we should each have a dozen or more paintings, so start thinking about it."

Hope pushed away the disappointment. A renewed excitement found its way to her eyes. "That would be fun. Thank you so much. Could we … I mean … maybe someday we could get together to paint?"

"That would be great. Let me get my grandmother settled in first. I'm looking for a good cardiac nurse who can work full time."

"Nadine Coleman." Her name came without a moment's hesitation. "She's the best and she's not working now. I'll bring you her phone number."

Darlene stepped slowly from the porch and sauntered down the sidewalk, her tote bag dancing from her shoulder. Annie saw a spring in her step that hadn't been there when she arrived. In a town of aging population, she felt a kinship with Darlene. She'd never truly had a friend. There were people she was friendly with, like Lacey, but it didn't count when they were on your payroll.

Foot traffic on Main Street began to ebb as the sun made its descent. Murky shades of dawn settled over the town as the first of the fireflies flicked a light calling others to join in the dance. A glance at her cell phone showed 8:45

approaching. New York City never slept, but Hickory Falls began to fold up for the night ahead. Annie took the journal, along with the now cold remnants of her latte, and moved indoors.

Curled up on the sofa in the freshly painted room, she ran her hand over the journal's aged leather cover, touching the cracked edges. Annie opened to the first mottled page that carried carefully fashioned script. Each letter had been precisely formed; the only mar being blotches from an ancient ink pen. Thin in places and heavily inked in others.

I looked out the window of the upper room.

The journal held the clipped, truncated entries of a young girl, the phrases and paragraphs distinctive to a preteen. Yet within a few pages, Annie saw beyond the written entry. She watched the story unfold.

7

Charlotte

I looked out the window of the upper room. Mr. Pearson would have my hide if he knew, but I'm always careful. He insists the blind be pulled down even though Ma made the pretty yellow curtains. With the blind pulled back a little, I could see across the street to the new frame of the store being built. No one worked on it now because of the holiday. Besides, no one would see me through the edge of the attic window blind. I'd be up here most of the day because of New Year's Day calling. I remembered it from last year. Folks dropped in all day to sip lager or wassail and to welcome in the New Year.

I don't much mind the hiding part. It's the staying quiet that's hard. Once Mr. Pearson used the switch on me when the good Reverend Curtis came calling and he heard my footsteps. When the reverend left, Mr. Pearson came bursting up the stairs, his face red as a ripe tomato, and a switch in his hand. "You couldn't sit still for twenty minutes? I had to lie to the good reverend and tell him I had a critter in the attic that needed trapping."

Ma was right behind him pleading for me. "James, no harm's been done. Leave her be." But he never listened to Ma on my behalf. I got three switches on my bare behind. Couldn't sit for a week. After that, Mr. Pearson had the floorboards bolstered so they wouldn't squeak.

That's why I didn't hear Ma come up until she was all the way in the upper room. She called it the upper room because she said that's where Jesus disciples went when they were meeting up. I think mostly she looked for a name other than calling it the attic. "Hi, precious."

I ran over to her, not mindful of my footsteps, because I knew she wouldn't come up if there were visitors in the house. She kissed the top of my head.

"I brought you some cider and a piece of fudge. You doing okay up here?"

"I'm okay. Is the calling all done?"

She squeezed her grown up body onto my child-sized chair and set my fudge on the table. "We can't be certain. We'll be going out, doing some calling ourselves around 3:00. I'll be sure to let you know when we're leaving."

"Can I be downstairs when you're gone?"

"Not in the kitchen, sweetie. You can be in your bedroom."

My bedroom isn't really my bedroom. Ma told me once how she argued with Mr. Pearson until he allowed me to use the room between theirs and Zachary's. Otherwise, I'd be sleeping on the cot in this upper room. Ma calls it 'my bedroom' but we all know it's the guest room. I can't keep anything in there in case someone comes to the second floor. My clothes and toys all have to stay up here. The second-floor bedroom is neat as a pin.

The good part of hiding days is that Ma always makes it up to me. She'll bake something special or buy me a new doll. Tonight, we'll probably cuddle in the second-floor bedroom and she'll tell me about all the folks who came a'calling.

"I see you've been painting."

I turned toward the easel that held my picture of a snapdragon. Last summer, Ma had snipped two from the yard and put them in a vase. She tried to bring different flowers

63

from time to time so I'd know their names. I painted them today from a magazine picture I clipped.

"I tried to paint snapdragons."

"I see that. You did a beautiful job. I need to go now, precious. I'll be back up soon as I have a chance. Have you done your lessons yet?"

"Yes, ma'am. I mean, yes to my reading and arithmetic. I ain't done my science."

She frowned. "You mean—you haven't done your science. I don't want to hear ain't leaving your mouth again, young lady."

"Sorry. It sort of slipped out by mistake."

"No child of mine is going to use poor grammar. Don't let it slip again."

She acted stern, but she hugged me when she said it. Ma was a stickler for my schooling. I liked our lessons because we spent the time together. If it was a good day, she'd close up the kitchen shutters and I could work at the table. That's the bad part about all of the building going on in town. The more it grows, the less chances I'll have to be on the lower level. Building will keep coming. The town's growing. Mr. Pearson calls it reconstruction.

Ma said we were lucky that Yankee soldiers took over this house during the war for southern independence. Otherwise, it would have burned with the rest of Hickory Falls. Zachary was not much more than a baby and they feared for his safety. Mr. Pearson took them to stay with cousins in Valdosta, then he left to fight against the northern aggression. That's where the really bad thing happened to Ma.

The only reason she told me things a child ought not to know is to help me understand Mr. Pearson. He's the closest thing I know to a Pa, but he told her I am never to call him that. He's not my real Pa.

The bad thing happened on New Year's Day in 1863. That's the day President Lincoln signed the Emancipation

Proclamation. Ma said it threw the south into chaos because it wasn't really a law. The real law didn't come until two years later when the amendment passed, freeing slaves. But the Emancipation Proclamation was President Lincoln's order that confederate states couldn't keep their slaves. Some confederates didn't pay attention because, when Lincoln was out of office, the next president could change the order. That might be what got him killed. Some slaves were confused and didn't know what to do because they feared their masters. Some took off, making plans for a free future and hoping the order stuck. But then there were some that celebrated with all kinds of revelry. That's when a freed slave, drunken and carousing, saw Ma in the yard. He pulled her into the barn and had his way with her. Ma said it was probably retaliating since white slave owners did the same thing to black women for years.

She was filled with shame and didn't aim to tell Mr. Pearson. She feared he'd have taken a gang of armed southerners and hunted down every male slave that ran free. But when she learned she was with child, my Ma had another fear. She didn't know who the pa was. Was it Mr. Pearson or the slave who attacked her? One day when his infantry corps passed through Valdosta, she told him. He said he'd know the minute the babe was born and if it weren't his, they'd take it straight to the Negro orphanage up in North Carolina.

I guess I kind of tricked them all. Ma said when I came out hollering, you couldn't tell what color my skin would be. I was bald as a coot. It was a few weeks before she knew. She told me that by then, she loved me and would never send me to an orphanage. When Mr. Pearson came back, she tried to convince him that he was my pa, but the true shade of my skin started settling in. Little sprouts of black hair popped up, nothing like his light brown hair. They both knew my pa was the carousing slave.

Ma said they fought something fierce. They were still in Valdosta and she wasn't allowed to take me out of the house. Only his cousin knew. When the war ended and they were able to return to Hickory Falls, he planned to take me to the Negro's orphanage in North Carolina. Ma wouldn't budge. She said she would never put a child of hers in an orphanage.

Mr. Pearson said he wouldn't have people looking at me and knowing a black man impregnated his wife. They came to an agreement. If she could keep me out of sight until I was old enough, they'd let me stay on as a house servant. He doesn't like me saying Ma. He fears I'll forget when I'm their house help and call her that in front of people. He wants me to say Mrs. Pearson, but Ma says when he's around, I should call her ma'am.

I returned to the window and could see the townsfolk walking in all their finery, going to do their calling on neighbors. There was a little girl about my age. She wore a long blue dress with layers of ruffles on the skirt. A white sash around her waist matched the ribbon in her yellow hair. Her ma wore one of the new bustle dresses that Ma had told me about. She said they gathered extra fabric in the back and puffed it up so much that a lady couldn't sit. Ma called it foolishness and a waste of good fabric.

Ma must have felt bad about me having to be quiet for so long because the next day, on January 2, I was allowed in the kitchen. It was a treat I only had on special occasions. The kitchen was in the back of the house, and Ma closed up the shutters so it was impossible for anyone to have a peek. The doors were locked, and if someone knocked, I was to scurry up the back set of steps to the upper room.

I shucked the corn while Ma told me a story from Zachary's Sunday School class.

"Pharaoh ordered that all male babies born to the Israelites be killed. Jochebed, gave birth to Moses and hid him for three months."

"Like you hid me?"

"Yes, precious, like I hid you."

"But no one was trying to kill me. Mr. Pearson only wanted to take me to an orphanage."

"Yes, but like Moses' mother, I loved you too much to let that happen." She pointed to the corn. "Keep shucking and let me tell the story. When Jochebed could no longer hide him, she made a basket out of reeds and coated it with tar so it wouldn't sink. Then she placed it in the water near where Pharaoh's daughter bathed. Moses' sister hid near the Nile and watched. When Moses cried, the princess heard him. She knew he was Hebrew, but she saved him anyway."

"Like you and Mr. Pearson knew I was Negro but saved me."

"Here's a very special part to this story. The princess needed someone to nurse the babe. Moses' sister heard this and told her she knew a nursemaid who could help. Guess who it was."

"Jochebed?"

"Yes. God worked everything out to save Moses and to allow his mother to nurse him until he was older."

"Like God let you keep me until I'm old enough that I don't have to hide."

"And like Moses, God has a mighty plan for your life. Tonight, I want you to read Exodus chapter 2. Now, lay those husks out to dry and we'll make some cornhusk dolls with them."

8

Zachary's footsteps sounded on the stairs, heavy as an iron kettle. Not because he was big, but because he pounded each foot on the stair tread, his way of reminding me he didn't want to do this. Ma made him help with my studies. She said, even though he was two years older, I was smart enough to do the same lessons.

He sat in one of the small chairs, his legs stretched out under the table, leaving no room for mine. "We started long division. I don't completely understand it, so we're gonna wait till next time. We can practice your multiplication facts. Mr. Strickland said multiplication is like the reverse of division."

"How many kids were in school today? Were there any girls my age?"

"Yeah. Bess Martindale."

"What's she look like?"

Zachary was always happy to abandon lessons to talk. He helped me to see the inside of the classroom and how it was divided up by age groups. "What did the girls do at recess?"

"Mostly jumped rope."

"What's that?"

He explained about swinging a rope way over your head and jumping through it when it reached the ground. I couldn't quite imagine so I sketched a picture of it. Zachary took my pencil and erased part.

"Not like that." His hurried drawing wasn't neat, but I could see my mistake. And I could imagine jumping rope.

"I wish I could try it. I wonder if I'll ever have a friend."

"Not likely. You'll be hidden a couple more years, then you'll work as a servant. I can't wait for that. I'll get to boss you around and you'll have to do my chores."

"I'd do your chores for the chance to be downstairs."

A booming crash sounded from the first floor, loud enough to be heard two stories up.

"Uh oh." Zachary rushed to the back stairs leading to the kitchen.

I followed him. We stayed hidden in the stairwell, but easily heard Mr. Pearson's angry voice. "Walter Sullivan's a scalawag. I've been commissioner here, trying to put things back together since the north desecrated this town. He has no business in this race. Who wants a public official that didn't support the southern cause? Men lost their lives in the war. Do you think war widows want him running our county? How about parents whose sons didn't come home?"

Ma's softer tones attempted to calm him. "The vote will tell, James. It's a fair process."

"Fair? Look at the number of carpetbaggers soaring down here like migrating birds. They say they're here to help the reconstruction. Don't you believe it. They're here to sway the vote."

"They can't vote here, dear. It's not their district."

Another loud thump. "You can be dang sure some will sneak their way into the voting place. Even so, they're spreading rumors and the scalawags are swallowing their every word. They sing a song of lies about a better south, all the while, taxes are climbing and folks are losing their land."

"Keep your voice down. The children will hear."

His voice didn't lower one notch. "Zachary knows this. I won't have my son live in ignorance to how the

69

northerners are stealing from us. He knows what that slave did to you. Or have you forgotten?"

I heard the anger spill out with Ma's words, her voice suddenly louder. "Of course, I haven't forgotten."

"I guess not. You insist on keeping a daily reminder. That slave ruined our lives, and you keep the girl like some kind of trophy. How do you think I feel every time I look at that black face?"

I could imagine his finger pointed at Ma, him leaning close making her back up. I'd seen it plenty of times.

"It's not her fault."

"I never should have listened to you. She should be in the orphanage, not in my attic. And let me remind you, it's not too late for that."

I heard a slight wince from Zachary and saw him cringe. "You should go back upstairs."

I ignored him, secretly glad that his Pa's words embarrassed him.

Ma tried to bring peace to Mr. Pearson's outrage. "Let's calm down a little. We've gotten off subject. It's a man's right to run for commissioner. I'm confident you'll beat Walter Sullivan. People around here know you."

"I better. I won't have my family following anything he enacts." A slamming door followed, bringing a welcomed silence.

Zachary and I stood there in the quiet. Then he pointed his finger at me, like his pa always did. "Get back upstairs and work on learning your multiplication facts."

I went up and he exited the stairwell. I heard his footfalls bouncing down the other set of steps, followed by another slamming door.

I didn't work on my multiplication facts. Instead, I tore a sheet from my sketchpad and clipped it on the easel. From the pitcher of water Ma always left, I poured a little in the bowl beside my watercolors. Before Ma came up the stairs, I had painted two girls jumping rope. One had light

70

skin and blonde hair. She wore a baby blue dress with a white pinafore. The other girl had dark skin, her ebony hair wavy and pulled into a rubber band. Her frock was a dull umber.

When Ma came up, she carried an apple and a glass of milk. "Hey, sweetie."

The skin below her eyes puffed like welts. That always happened when she'd been crying. I pulled my arms around her waist, leaning my head against her chest. Her arms encircled me. We stood like that for a minute or two. That's how she knew I'd heard.

"He's angry with the new system. Not with you. When he gets upset, he lets things spill from his mouth."

"I'm sorry, Ma. Sorry my being here makes it hard for you."

She took my face in her two hands and tilted my head up. "Don't you ever say that. You bring me joy, no matter how you came to be born. No matter what color your skin is. Do you understand?"

I nodded my head even though it was still in her hands.

"Good. Now you see to your lessons while I go start dinner."

"Since nobody's home but us, can I come down?"

Her chin dipped in sadness. "Not today, precious. Not today."

She left and I bit into my apple while I looked at Zachary's math book. The division looked different and called my attention. Opposite of multiplication. I knew how adding and taking away were reversed. I picked up the pencil and jotted numbers, making my brain reverse the multiplication. Soon I had finished ten problems. I'd have Ma check them to see if I got them right.

I heard Mr. Pearson come home, and I sniffed the aroma of stew. Soon Ma brought my dinner up. Beef stew, a hunk of fresh bread spread with butter, and another glass of milk. I would eat alone while the real family gathered round the kitchen table. I picked up my dish and carried it down the stairs to the bottom step. I sat there and ate. I couldn't hear all of the words spoken around that table, but it made me feel closer. Mr. Pearson's' louder voice was easy to hear.

"I'll be headed out this evening. There's a meeting amongst some of the supporters. Don't wait up. I expect I'll be late."

~~*~~

When Mr. Pearson left, Ma called me down to the second floor. She cautioned me to keep voices low and scurry upstairs if I heard the door.

Zachary jangled his pouch of jacks. "Want a game?"

I always wanted a game. Anytime I had the chance. Sometimes we played checkers or marbles, but Zachary loved the jacks. We sat on the floor in my sleeping room and bounced the little red ball, picking up spiked metal jacks starting with one. Each turn meant we had to pick up one more than before. As we neared the last round, I was ready to win. I needed to pick up all of the jacks with one hand before the ball bounced again. With one swift motion, Zachary scattered the jacks. "You cheated."

"I didn't cheat."

"You did. You only picked up four the last time." He gathered them in his pouch and stomped from the room. I didn't cheat. It's just that Zachary didn't like losing.

Ma came in later and read to me before bed. She continued in Exodus and read about Moses growing up in Pharaoh's household. When she finished, my eyes were already trying to close.

"Sleep, little one. Remember that Mr. Pearson is still out, so you may hear the door open downstairs. It's all right. No need to scoot upstairs unless I tell you."

72

Much later, the sound of hoofbeats awakened me. The position of the moon told me that hours had passed since Ma tucked me in. It had moved outside my window. I heard the screen door followed by his footsteps. He came up and entered his own bedroom where Ma slept. Then my eyes closed again until I woke to sunshine.

9

The following day, a loud rapping on the door alarmed me. I started for the stairs to run up to my upper room sanctuary, but I was too late. The voice belonged to Otis Beltzhoover, the town sheriff.

"James, we got a problem."

"Well, sit down whilst the coffee's hot before you come in with both guns cocked." The sound of Mr. Pearson's movements told me he had poured the coffee. "I got me some fresh cream in the icebox. You want some?"

It was easy to hear the voices. Every sound traveled up this back staircase.

"No. I take it black. We need to talk."

A chair scraped the floor and I figured Mr. Pearson had finally sat to listen.

"There's been a lynching. Cole McGill's dead. Hung from a tree right in front of his wife and kids. The wife told us it was the Klan. I figured you needed to know before word spreads through this town."

I knew from my reading what a lynching was, but I had no idea what he meant when he said *the Klan*.

"I don't know, Otis. You're taking the word of a bereaved Negro."

"They killed her husband. Why would she lie?"

"Exactly. Someone killed her husband, probably had a rightful dispute. She doesn't want you to know whatever it is he did to deserve it, so she tells you it was the Klan, even though we haven't had the Klan working around these parts."

The sheriff spoke with a softer voice so I had to strain to hear. "Maybe not in Hickory Falls, but the Klan's been all around us. You know what they did at the jailhouse in Union."

"Yeah, they saved us from having to house and feed eight blackies. The Klan did what should have been done in the first place."

"That ain't for us to say. A jury put those men there. You hear anything last night? Horses or voices in the wee hours?"

"No, Otis. I was sound asleep with my family."

Sound asleep? Mr. Pearson went out, knowing he'd be late, coming in hours after the house slept. And now he lied to the sheriff.

"Don't go getting off all half-cocked about this, paying good taxpayers' money. The good Lord knows times are tough enough with the devastation the Yankees did. Now they're claiming to help us, but they raise taxes, taking our money first, then when we can't pay, taking our land."

"I hear you, James, but I can't be letting people take the law in their own hands. That's why we have a legal system."

I heard a hardy laughter coming from Mr. Pearson. "Legal system? What court's going to put a white man behind bars for hurting a blackie? None! You'll go and cost the county valuable money that's needed elsewhere. I'm telling you, McGill's dead because of something he did. Could have stolen something. Maybe he even laid his black hands on someone's wife."

"We don't know that, James. Tensions are high and I'm doing my best to smooth them over. It's a new world, and we have to adapt to it."

"Don't tell me you're turning scalawag, Otis? You need to remember what the Yanks did to us?"

"I remember but don't you forget who fired the first shot. It's over. Now we have to make peace with it."

I heard the chair scrape against the wood floor. "You're turning sympathizer. You fell for their lies. If you'll excuse me, Sheriff, I have work to do."

Another chair brushed against the floor. "All right, James. Don't forget about the pledging."

"Yeah, another northern attempt to control us."

"Law's the law. All white confederates must make an oath of allegiance to the United States in order to vote. And if I were you, I'd be encouraging people to make that pledge. You're going to want votes."

"Someone needs to take a pop shot at Grant like they did Lincoln, giving blacks the vote and making whites say an oath before they get theirs back. He's not my president."

"You better watch what you say, James. Those are treasonous words."

The screen door slammed, followed by the rhythmic clop of horse hoofs moving away. A loud crash followed. The sound of a dish shattering. And I'd venture a guess that it wasn't accidentally dropped. Ma went to the cobbler to have Zachary's shoe repaired, and Zachary had left with his fishing rod resting against his shoulder. I figured I better tiptoe upstairs since Mr. Pearson was in a throwing-things rage.

My tiptoe was quiet, but the attic door wasn't. Mr. Pearson came after me, leaping two steps at a time. He grabbed my arm and tugged till I thought he'd break my bone. He held my arm and dragged me until he could reach the switch hanging from a hook in his bedroom. He dragged me back to my sleeping room and threw me up against the bed so I was leaning over it on my stomach. I felt him toss my dress up over my waist and rip my pantalets from my hips.

"Wench!" A voice of raw fury spit out the word.

I heard the crack of the switch before the sting came. One. Two. Three. Four. Five. Two more than he usually did. They hit my bare behind and my back, half covered with the

76

dress thrown askew, and half bare skin. I yelped in pain and that brought a sneering laugh.

"That'll teach you to eavesdrop on me." He yanked me off of the bed. "Get upstairs before I whip you again."

It hurt to climb the steps. I started slowly, holding the handrail so I didn't tumble backward. My undergarments were still pulled down from my waist. I grasped them with my free hand but couldn't pull them up. It stung too badly. I inched my way forward, one hand on the rail, the other holding my pantalets so they wouldn't trip me.

When I reached the top, I went straight to the cot, laying on my stomach.

I heard Ma come home and wanted to cry out to her. I needed her to hold me. To put salve on my wounds. But she saw him first. He was in their bedroom so I heard his booming voice.

"You're going to find out anyhow, so I might as well tell you now. I beat the wench."

"Oh, James." Ma's voice was ripe with dismay.

"She disobeyed and she eavesdropped. The sheriff was downstairs and she made no attempt to hide. I told you, woman, she pulls a stunt like that again, you won't stop me from getting rid of her."

Ma was by my side in minutes. She brought the salve with her.

"Baby, I'm so sorry."

"I tried, Ma, but there wasn't time. The knock came on the door and I stepped into the hall, but he was already in the house. I feared he'd hear me, so I went back into my sleeping room. I was quiet as I could be." The words all came out tucked in my sobs.

"I know, baby. I know." She handed me her handkerchief. "Now hush while I treat these cuts."

She carefully worked on each of the five stripes of raw flesh. When she finished, she pulled my undergarments up, but I cried out with the pain when the elastic hit my waist. She pulled them down and eased my legs out of them. Then she lowered the skirt of my frock to cover my shame.

"Ma, what's the Klan?"

Time seemed to stop as I waited for an answer. Then she said, "Nothing for little girls to worry about." But I had brushed up against her fear. I could smell it in the air.

10
Annie

Annie had been in the house less than three weeks, and it definitely looked lived-in. Only now did she begin to realize all that Nellie had done. The Manhattan apartment never had clutter. Absolutely none. The contemporary décor boasted clean lines, pristine tabletops, and never a dirty dish. Nellie had sanitized every surface until no speck of dust remained. Nana would be here tomorrow, so Annie set about the task of cleaning and organizing the first floor. Her grandmother couldn't venture upstairs. The climb would be too taxing for her.

A box with Annie's painted canvases had been stored in the den, which now served as her grandmother's bedroom. When she painted the walls a pale violet, she moved the paintings to the dining room. Her task today was to adorn the downstairs walls with a few paintings, then store the others upstairs in her studio.

One by one, Annie spread each painting onto the dining room table. From there, she'd choose which best suited the style and colors of her new home.

Ten completed paintings stared back at her. An eclectic mix. She had played around with various styles, trying to find her niche. Some had price tags in the lower right corner, left over from the art show her instructor hosted. She and eighteen other art students had displayed their work. Two of Annie's sold, helping to validate her as an artist.

On a whim, she telephoned Darlene. "Hi. If you have some free time today, I've unwrapped my paintings. I'll be hanging a few, but the rest will go back into storage for a while. Would you like to see them?"

"Oh, Annie, I wish I could, but Selah's sick."

"I'm sorry. Nothing serious, I hope."

"No, probably teething but she's warm and crying. I can't take her out. I wouldn't be able to come until this evening."

A crying infant could be heard in the background. Nana wouldn't be arriving until late afternoon tomorrow. She'd have time to hang pictures in the morning. "This evening will be perfect. That leaves me time to get everything ready today. The canvases can stay in my dining room until then."

Three hours later, Annie stood back and admired her accomplishment. The hospital bed wore a beautiful quilt that masked its unsightly mechanics. Fluffed pillows in yellow, a color opposite of the violet walls, softened the look of the dark power recliner in the corner. Her lilac painting, not quite finished, would hang on the wall facing her grandmother's bed.

A powder room, adjacent to the den, received an emergency upgrade earlier in the week. A plumber reordered the space to fit a shower in one corner. Every inch of the kitchen had been scrubbed clean. All that remained was to hang a few pictures.

Annie worked up an appetite. Weighing in had been a daily occurrence in New York, but she hadn't stepped on a scale since coming to Hickory Falls. What would happen when they called her back for the next photo shoot? She refused to worry about that now. Annie's reluctance to muss up her newly scrubbed kitchen brought a new thought. Hickory Falls had a few places to eat, and she had yet to try them. Maybe it was time.

After hopping in the shower, she blow-dried her hair, a much easier task than her stylist faced when her tresses were long and full. She slid into a pair of shorts that showed off the length of her legs. Not because she wanted anyone to notice. But she had a carefree spirit today. A lightness to her step. Nana was coming. She had made this happen for her. There was a refreshing freedom in no longer being Miriam. They were two different people.

She left the car behind and took a walk down Main Street. As she passed the hardware store, she looked in the window and waved to Charlie. His wave back carried a sense of familiarity. She had friends. She belonged. No one had befriended her solely because of her name. Something new to marvel at.

The past few weeks had been so busy that she hadn't truly explored the town. Today she took notice of each venue she passed. One storefront, Cobbler's Corner, displayed window lettering for shoe repair. Beside that was a bakery with the smell of fresh bread wafting from the screen door. Annie came to an adorable shop called Generally Speaking. The catch phrase beneath it said, A New Kind of General Store. She stopped and looked in the window. With her eyes shielded against the sun, she saw a candy counter, an aisle with bins of something hidden from view, a corner with fresh flowers. It was a delightful eclectic mix. She'd stop in here on her way home to see all that remained hidden from her narrow vista.

"Something interesting?"

Annie turned to find Seth's easygoing gait stepping toward her. "Yes, I can't wait to go in."

"So why are you standing out here looking in the window?"

"I'm famished. I'm headed to Sweet Simone's. I'll stop in here when I'm finished."

"Ah, you eaten there yet?"

"No, this is my first venture out to eat except for The Coffee Grinder. I've become a regular there. The barista even knows my name."

"Margie? She's been there long as I can remember." He shifted, sticking his hands in his jean pockets. "You want company?"

"Um… I … sure."

"I know the menu pretty well. I can steer you to something good."

"You mean some things are bad?" Her carefree spirit teased. Something Miriam would never have done.

The lopsided grin appeared. "Let's say there's some things better than others."

They fell into step and walked to the next block. Sweet Simone's sat on the corner of Main Street and Verbena Road. A scattering of café tables with umbrellas formed an outdoor dining area.

"In or out?" Seth motioned toward the sidewalk tables.

"I don't know about you, but I'd appreciate a little AC."

"I'm so glad you said that. I didn't relish sitting in this heat." They sidestepped the café tables outside and opened the door.

The hostess seated them, and they looked over the menus. "So, what's good and what's bad?"

"Remember, I didn't say bad. You'll be getting me in trouble with Simone."

She laughed. "You mean there really is a Simone?"

"Yep. She fancies herself French even though she grew up a stone's throw from here. You'll find French cuisine on the menu, but they're really fancy names for common dishes. Don't tell her I said that."

They scanned the menu in silence. Seth reached over and pointed. "Beef Bourguignon. A showy name for roast beef with potatoes, onions and mushrooms. Coq au vin—

82

known to southerners as chicken stew. Cassoulet is bean soup with some sausage to dress it up. Look here." He directed her to the breakfast menu. "If you order a blini, you'll get a pancake."

She refrained from telling him she had dined in France numerous times. "I take it you eat here often."

"A few times. I'm going for an all-American steak. How about you?"

"I better do the salmon. I've been hitting Iris's chocolate cake way too much."

Seth's eyes widened. "Surely you don't still have that."

"Still in my freezer. I'm working on it one piece at a time."

He shook his head. "That wouldn't have made day three in my house."

"Well you don't need to worry about your figure."

"Neither do you." He said it with his eyes glued to the menu.

Annie felt the heat rise on her face. She hadn't intended to draw attention to her appearance. That was Miriam's job, and she was no longer that person.

Their meals were served, and Seth slid his napkin to his lap. "May I pray?"

The question stopped the motion of Annie's fork headed toward her plate. She nodded and he asked God's blessing on their food. Nana always said grace before meals and Annie's dad scoffed at her. He once said, "That's what happens when you're born in the Bible belt."

"Uh oh, here comes Simone."

Annie had no view of the kitchen without turning around. "Why is that an uh oh?"

"You'll see."

A young lady with a mass of flame red curls crowning her head sashayed past Annie going directly to Seth. A burst of saccharine sweet fragrance reached the table

83

before Simone. "Seth Walker, where have you been hiding? It's been way too long since you've graced my restaurant." She didn't acknowledge Annie. Didn't even glance her way.

"Good to see you too, Simone." He set his steak knife down. "Have you met Annie Gentry?"

She turned and demurely held out a hand with neon green nails, a color not seen in France. Annie had been there often enough to know. The French typically wore the traditional clear polish French manicure. The offered hand wasn't exactly a handshake, merely a brief connection before she backed away. "Pleasure to meet you." But her expression belied that statement. Her body swiveled back toward Seth.

They talked for a moment while Annie looked her over. Tall, probably mid to late twenties, hips that swayed when she moved. She flashed a wide smile at Seth, an attractive smile, but her teeth didn't have the same brilliance as Annie's. She moved with a trained walk, so familiar, but without mastering the poise required of models.

They finished their conversation and Simone flashed Seth another practiced smile. Then she turned ever so briefly, lost the smile, and spoke to Annie. "It's been a delight. I hope you enjoy your French roasted salmon." With a quick pivot, she glided away.

Annie turned wide eyes toward Seth.

"Yep. That's Simone."

She waited for him to say more, but Seth turned his attention back to their meals.

"If you're looking for something sweet to follow, they have a delicious Mont Blanc chestnut dessert."

"I think I better pass. But feel free to order." She folded her napkin and laid it on her plate. "Unless you'd like another piece of Iris's cake. It's frozen but shouldn't take long to thaw."

"You should know by now that I don't say *no* to Iris's cake."

He stood and pushed his chair in, but Annie stopped him. "We didn't get our check."

"Taken care of."

Surprise mixed with annoyance. "What? I don't want you buying my dinner."

"That's what I figured. That's why I took care of it when I went up for more napkins."

She had left home with a newfound sense of freedom. First came Simone's rudeness. Now Seth was back to his non-communicative ways. "You know, I'm not poor. I can pay for things like painters and my own dinner."

"I figured you could. I horned in on your dinner out. It's the least I could do."

"You know, you can be very frustrating."

His grin came a little wider this time. "So I've been told." He motioned toward the door.

They left Sweet Simone's and strode down Main Street. Seth slowed as they approached Generally Speaking. "You wanted to see the store?"

"I think I better save that for another time. Darlene McIntyre will be stopping by so I should be heading home."

"Sweet girl."

"Yes, my impression, too. Looks pretty young to have a baby."

"Yep."

What did that mean? Did it mean he didn't know or didn't want to say? She wouldn't ask. It would make her look like a busybody.

Seth spoke to half a dozen people on the way back. It appeared that everyone in town knew him. Annie and Seth made small talk when he wasn't running into people who wanted to chat.

"I learned something about my house this week. I had a plumber add a shower to the downstairs powder room. He said it looks like the powder room was added later, using space that had once been a back staircase."

"Doesn't surprise me. Downstairs powder rooms weren't the norm when your house was built. Back staircases were fairly common among families who could afford domestic help."

They passed the bakery and Annie breathed in the sweet aroma.

"Now that the painting's finished, I'm going to have to do a little more exploring. Anywhere around here that sells sushi?"

Seth's step slowed and he took a sideways glance at her. "Around here, we call that bait."

She laughed out loud. "Okay, how about Chinese food? You know, General Tso's, wonton soup, sweet and sour chicken?"

"I know what Chinese food is."

"Sorry. Any around here."

"Other than the ethnic food aisle of Piggly Wiggly, I reckon you'd have to head south toward Greenville or north toward Asheville."

Two ladies walked together and stopped him to chat. He introduced them as the Robertson sisters. "Seth, I got me a problem with palmetto bugs coming in the house. You got any remedies in that hardware store?"

"We have remedies, but if they're getting in, you need to find out where. Otherwise, they'll keep coming."

"I know where they're getting in. The screen door doesn't fit tight. There's a little crack in the gasket. It's no bigger than a minnow in a fishing pond, but they found it."

"Yep. They will. How about I come by tomorrow and fix that gasket for you?"

The sisters looked at each other in question. "How much those gaskets run?"

"Cost nothing if I can patch it up for you."

An audible sigh of relief came. "I'd be much obliged."

"Okay if I come around seven-thirty, before I open the store?"

"I'll have hot coffee waiting."

The ladies continued in the opposite direction.

That was the third conversation during the short walk from someone who needed his help. "So, do you bounce around town taking care of everyone?"

A slight smile formed as he kept walking, leaving her question unanswered. It was becoming a habit.

They were almost to the front porch when Annie remembered the journals. "Seth, do you know anything about a family named Pearson?"

"Can't say as I do. Why?"

"I found journals in the attic. And old photographs. The journal mentions the name Pearson."

"How old?"

"Old enough to wear hoop skirts."

"Hoop skirts." His brows lifted, but his eyes held amusement. "How old do you think I am?"

He teased and she used her most exasperated voice. "I didn't expect you'd know *them*. But maybe some descendants still living around these parts."

"Pearson. Nope. Can't recall any."

11

Annie took two pieces of Iris's cake from the freezer. One for Seth and the other would be offered to Darlene. "Shall I put this on a plate, or do you want to take it with you?"

She waited, but no answer came. Where did he go? She thought he'd followed her as she walked through the entry to the kitchen. Retracing her steps, she found Seth hunched over the dining room table where her pictures were spread out. His focus was on Stormy Sea, a painting of a sailboat caught in an ocean storm, the sails filled with angry wind. They billowed, straining the mast as the captain struggled to control the helm. It was one that Annie's instructor favored. He had guided her painting step-by-step until she captured the emotion on the captain's face.

Seth's head moved from side to side as he examined the details. She opened her mouth to speak but thought better of it. A visceral look showed in the view of his profile. It's how she loved art—to feel it in her gut. He must have sensed her presence because he glanced over his shoulder, a mesmerized look etched on his face.

"You painted this?"

"Yes, those are all my paintings."

He turned back, swept his view over the table, and came back to rest on Stormy Sea.

"You know, that's a terrible way to view art. It should be seen from a distance. A minimum of three feet." She

88

stepped in front of him and picked up the canvas, propping it upright on the breakfront.

Seth stepped back and gazed at the painting, nodding with wonder. Then turned and wordlessly followed her to the kitchen.

"Do you want to sit down and eat your cake, or take it with you for later?"

"I should go since you're expecting Darlene."

He stared at her hands as she picked up the wrapped slice of cake. She extended it forward, but Seth was slow to take it, still staring at her hands.

"What?" Annie half laughed to cover her discomfort.

His familiar smile finally came, moving from her hands to her eyes. "I'm looking at your hands wondering what makes them different that they can paint a masterpiece."

He now held the slice of cake and turned toward the back door. "It reminds me of a Winslow Homer."

She stopped short and swung to face him. "You know Winslow Homer?"

"Sure. He painted marine pictures. Probably did some other scenes as well, but I mostly know his ocean storms." He opened the back door and pushed the screen door. "Thanks for the dinner company and the cake."

She watched him walk toward the back of the hardware store, then disappear. Seth Walker was a puzzle. A slow-moving, God-fearing, do-gooder, man of few words. From all physical appearances and mannerisms, he was pure redneck. But he knew Winslow Homer, a lesser-known master artist. He worked hard, often for free, and seemed satisfied to work at the hardware store, stocking shelves. Probably a minimum wage job. Did he have ambitions beyond that?

Shifting her thoughts back to the present, she returned to the dining room and rearranged the pictures, standing as many as would fit on the breakfront. First thing in the morning, she'd hang a few of them before taking the others upstairs for storage. Stormy Sea would definitely find a place on the living room wall.

A knock on the door announced Darlene. "Hi, I hope I gave you time to finish your dinner."

"Yes, I actually went out today. Explored a little of the town, and ate at Sweet Simone's"

A slight roll of Darlene's eyes spoke volumes.

"You don't like it there?"

"We don't eat out much, but I know Simone. Highfalutin' if you ask me."

Annie laughed. "I don't think she cared much for me."

"That surprises me. She usually gushes all over folks, especially if someone's new."

"She gushed all over Seth, but I got a cool reception."

Darlene arched her brows. "Seth? Oh, that explains it. She wouldn't like anyone that caught Seth's eye. She has her talons ready to dig in, only he's too smart for her. And too good."

"Let me clarify. I didn't catch his eye. We happened to run into each other."

"Well if you do, Simone won't like it. Hope she wasn't wearing that green blouse with the scooped-out neck. My Bobby says you can see clear to the Promised Land."

They still stood in the entry. Annie motioned her toward the right where the dining room waited. "Come on in. I have my paintings in here."

They stepped as far as the archway when Darlene's mouth fell open. "Oh, my gracious. These are so good."

She walked to each one, admiring different facets. "Where do you get your ideas?" The question came as she held Arpeggio, the picture of a piano keyboard with two hands posed to waltz across the keys. Annie looked over her shoulder at the intricacies of the hands. She had worked to make them lifelike. The perfect curve of the fingers showing knuckles at the bend. The definition of lines unique to the musician. The puffy outline of cuticles tracing the fingernails. A slight wisp of hair on the pianist's arms. The tint of blue where veins forged their path. A delicate gold band without adornment circled a ring finger.

"I look through art magazines. I've copied some, but mostly I view bits and pieces of artwork and create my own." She stood there feeling a bond with this near stranger. They were kindred spirits. "Your magpie picture is as good as any of mine. I see your tote bag. Did you bring something else?"

"Yes, two of them."

She pulled out a picture of a tall, narrow house with the focus on a red front door. The garden beside it was protected behind an iron gated fence. "This is Charleston. Everybody paints scenes from there."

"I've seen some of them, but yours is exceptional. What else do you have?"

The last painting was an infant embraced against her mother, seated in a rocker. The picture didn't show the mother's face but focused on the cradled child. "I can't do faces well, so I turned her head so you can't see it full on. Dumb, isn't it?"

"Not at all. I asked my instructor that question when I painted the piano player. He said stay focused on the object of the art. In my case, it was the hands. In this picture, it's the babe. But actually," she paused, thinking. "Actually, it's the love. It emanates from the picture, even without the mother's face."

Darlene gave two gleeful claps of her hand. "That's what I wanted. I'm so glad you saw it."

They would make a good team. As soon as Nana was settled, she would spend more time with Darlene. They'd learn from each other. Who knew where this journey might take them? Annie had a sudden urge to tell her about the journals. About a mother who saved her daughter despite the risk and her husband's wrath. A mother's love. Something

Annie never experienced. One mother left her at an orphanage. Another adopted her with ulterior motives.

No, she wouldn't talk about the journals until she heard what her grandmother knew.

~~*~~

Everything was ready and the medical transport was in motion. They opted not to fly because of Nana's weak heart and compromised breathing. Instead, they were on the road and should arrive within hours.

A beep from Annie's phone alerted her of an incoming text message. Her father.

I CAN'T BELIEVE YOU DIDN'T TELL ME SHE WAS MOVING. SINCE YOU WON'T ANSWER MY CALLS, I'LL BE DOWN NEXT WEEK. I WANT TO SEE BOTH OF YOU. WE NEED TO TALK ABOUT THIS.

She? He didn't even have the courtesy to identify her as his mother. The last thing Annie needed was a visit from Kurt Gentry. He lived minutes away from the Roswell House, yet rarely visited. Now he'd fly here to see Lillian because he wanted to talk about money. Annie couldn't allow that to happen.

She touched the phone number and dialed her father before she could change her mind, bracing herself to hear his voice again.

"Annie. It's about time. I've been trying to reach you."

"I'm aware of that." Did he have any idea what the sound of his voice did to her? Hearing him speak sent a fist to her gut. She steeled herself against the colliding emotions, the urge to run or fight or melt, fading into the ground. She'd done each at some point.

"Listen, your grandmother told me she sold that house. I knew you were paying for assisted living, and I figured the money from the sale of the house was somewhere gaining interest. What happened?"

92

"She didn't tell you she sold it. She told you she had disposed of it. That's because she signed it over to me."

"She can't do that. I've been counting on that money."

"So, you've been tapping your foot waiting for her to die?"

"Of course not." But his voice suddenly lost its fury. That's exactly what he'd been waiting for.

"Nana loves this house. She didn't want to sell it, and she knew you didn't want to live here."

"I'll be down next week. We need to talk about this. With her!"

"No. Absolutely not. Her heart's weakened and we can't upset her. We're not having this conversation with her."

"Annie." His tone turned to pleading. "I follow the news. I know you don't need money or the house. You can buy any house you want."

"Well fortunately, I don't have to. I have exactly the house I want."

"Then you should buy me out. It should have been mine."

Did he always presume to take what he wanted? To assume his selfish desires were somehow his rights? "It was never yours. It was always Nana's to do whatever she chose."

"I'll be down next week. We'll work this out."

"You're not coming to Hickory Falls. The house is in my name and you're not welcomed."

"Annie, I'm your father."

Really? How convenient. When she was thirteen, he reminded her that she wasn't really his daughter. "You're a pilot. You make a good salary."

"I'm in trouble, Annie. Financial trouble."

"Gambling." It wasn't a question. She knew his weakness. "Not my problem. And not Nana's."

She heard his deep sigh. "You always were a thankless child."

93

Annie heard the click as he ended the call. She took in a deep breath to ease the vice that squeezed her chest. Only then, could she breathe normally.

~~*~~

Nadine Colman was indeed available, but she wouldn't agree to a live-in position. She would be here every weekday. All other hours would be covered by a nursing service that Nadine assured Annie was reputable. Iris Flannagan waited impatiently for Lillian's arrival. Annie asked for no visitors on the first day, and a short visit the following day.

A ding notified her of an incoming e-mail from her Dalton account. It had been pleasantly empty for the last two weeks.

Miriam, we've pushed up the next photo shoot due to an unavoidable conflict. We need you in LA in two weeks. Lacey has the hotel and flight details. Expect a ten-day trip.

Two weeks? She'd have to leave her grandmother. She expected to have two more months before she had to leave her. Annie plunked down in the closest chair, her hands clasped in her lap. A glance exposed short, stubby fingernails. She ran a hand through her cropped hair, then removed her glasses. Images ripped through her contentment, setting it on end. Her stylist would be tasked with returning her hair to the diamond blonde, using extensions to correct the cut. The break from her exercise routine and the chocolate cake came with a cost. Two weeks wasn't enough time to correct the damage. While still slender, three or four pounds was enough to erase the svelte physique required by some of Dalton's dresses.

She had no choice but to go to LA. Her contract required it. She sat there; the weight of disappointment heavy in her stomach. Eleven more months. Then she'd be free.

94

12

Lillian slept, wrapped in a soft fleecy blanket and purring like a kitten. If the trip hadn't been enough to zap her energy, the nostalgia of returning to the home she loved stole any remaining vigor. A bead of tears lined her eyes when the paramedics lifted her wheelchair into the house. "Oh, my. Oh my." Those were the only words she found. Annie slowly wheeled her through every room on the first floor. She gazed at the teapot, then at the table where Annie had fresh flowers in her grandmother's old etched vase. When they approached the wall near the back door, Lillian held up a hand for Annie to stop. She gazed at the painting. The colors were muted, but discernable. One doll had red hair and wore a faded green dress. The other had dark hair and wore a dress with an ecru pinafore. The rustic details included the smudged attic window. After a prolonged gaze, her grandmother nodded, and Annie continued around the circle of rooms until they came to her bedroom. A wrinkled hand reached backward and clasped the hand that still rested on the wheelchair handle. "Thank you, child. I never thought I'd see this day."

Nadine Coleman arrived moments after Nana's transport. After her grandmother's homecoming tour, Nadine checked her vital signs and sat talking. Annie listened in, pleased that they appeared comfortable with each other. When Lillian slept, Nadine went to the kitchen table to review her medical history. Annie stood at the bedroom door, watching the rise and fall of her grandmother's breath. The odor of aging lingered in the room. A sweet fragrance that verified Nana was home.

~~*~~

The porch boards moaned in a discordant pattern as Iris and Lillian rocked. Annie tucked her legs up under her on the porch swing, its creaking chains adding to the dissonance. The two white-haired ladies reminisced, laughed, and tried to make up for years of absence.

"Remember old man Robertson? How we would knock on his door and run?"

"You did, Iris. I did no such thing."

Iris chortled. "He was meaner than a wet panther."

"Is he still living?"

"No, he went and died leaving those girls with a boatload of bills. Some for his doctoring and other ones that he ran up delinquent."

"Did either of them ever marry?"

"No. Folks say he never allowed them to have suitors."

Lillian shook her head. "That's a shame."

"Raymond always said he was a selfish coot. Said he could make a preacher cuss."

"Iris, how long ago did you lose Raymond?"

The slouch of her shoulders spoke sadness, so uncharacteristic from the Iris Annie had come to know. "That was back four years ago. Cancer took him hard."

"I'm sorry I wasn't here for you. I remember how you helped me when I lost Michael." She shook her head, trying to shed a weight too heavy to hold. "He was my first thought when I came through that door yesterday. I could see Michael in each room. It's partly why I left. I couldn't bear the constant reminders."

"I know. I still look out back and picture Raymond bent over his garden, pulling out weeds with his bare hands."

Annie listened in silence. What would it be like to love so much that it still hurt twenty years later? An experience she'd never have. Twenty-four years old and she never dated. Her father had stripped her of any desire for a man in her life. Her modeling career began at the age of sixteen. By the time she turned twenty-one, Dalton signed her, making her instantly wealthy. Men wanted her money, her body, or to rub up against her fame. The same things her parents wanted. She was done. In eleven months, that life would be a bad memory.

Nadine came to the porch with Lillian's pills and a glass of water. Early morning air had been pleasant, but the muggy heat began to sneak in. "It's getting warmer out here. Perhaps we should move inside."

"I'm growing tired. Iris, I'd be happy if you could visit me again tomorrow."

An impish smile filled her face. "Nice and dandy, like cotton candy."

Lillian laid her head back and laughed. "Gracious, it's been way too long since I heard that phrase."

"Everyone used to say it when we was in high school."

Nadine helped Lillian to her feet and walked her the few steps to her wheelchair.

"I'll be right back, Nana." Annie stepped toward Iris and offered her arm. With arms linked, she helped her cross Larkspur to her home.

When she returned, her grandmother sat with her wheelchair pulled up to the kitchen table, oxygen dangling from its hook. She was eating strawberries that Nadine had cut. Annie sat across from her.

"Nana, you're so well-spoken compared to some of the older people in Hickory Falls."

"Well, my parents were educated and I went to college, an opportunity many folks didn't have. My daddy

97

was a lawyer, so we had the means. Lots of folks here didn't finish high school."

"I met Charlie from the hardware store. He asked about you."

"Charlie! Goodness. So many people I've forgotten about. Charlie's wife was my childhood friend. I wonder if she's still living."

"I don't know. I've only spoken to him a few times. He's a true southerner. He has a coonhound named Useless."

"Ha. That sounds like Charlie."

Annie wanted to talk about the journals, and to ask her grandmother what she meant about secrets. But she'd had a few stressful days. Best to let that wait.

The following morning, after checking on her sleeping grandmother and speaking with the night nurse, Annie went upstairs to an empty bedroom where she kept her exercise supplies. Weights, jump rope, stretchy band. She didn't have equipment or a heavy bag, so she'd use what she had. An hour later, she wiped sweat from her forehead, realizing how out of shape she'd gotten. Would it be enough? She went online and ordered an elliptical.

After showering and checking again on her grandmother, she walked across to The Coffee Grinder. As soon as she opened the door, she saw the fiery red curls belonging to Simone. Her male companion had his back to the door, but she recognized the familiar brown of Seth's hair and his unchanging blue Hickory Falls Hardware shirt. Simone's eyes met hers with a smug look. Annie gave her a quick wave and walked to the counter where Margie worked.

"Hey, Annie. Skinny vanilla latte?"

"Yes please."

Seth turned at the mention of her name. "Morning, Annie."

"Hi, Seth."

"I hear your grandmother arrived."

News raced through small towns. "Yes, two days ago. She's enjoying a trip down memory lane. I hope to bring her over to see Charlie sometime."

"I'll look forward to meeting her."

Simone's smug face had turned to stone. She placed her hand on Seth's arm and leaned forward to say something. The lean revealed all. Seth would have gotten an eyeful.

"Anything else?" Margie asked as she delivered the latte.

"Not today, thanks."

Annie paid, waved goodbye, and walked back across the street.

Darlene had said Seth was too wise to fall prey to Simone. Maybe she was wrong.

Back at the house, Nadine had arrived, replacing the night nurse. She went to the bedroom to help Lillian out of bed. Annie heard the rushing water of the new shower. Thirty minutes later, her grandmother appeared, dressed and well groomed.

"Nana, it took me a few attempts, but I've mastered the art of the egg white veggie omelet. Would you like one? No yolks. Cholesterol free."

With her grandmother seated at the table, Annie and Nadine worked together to fix breakfast. When they had eaten and Nadine left them alone, she told Lillian about the LA trip.

"I knew this would come, but thought I'd have more time. It's a ten-day trip, and you'll have round the clock nursing care."

"Don't worry about me. I'll also have Iris. I imagine she'll stop in most days."

"Here's my dilemma. No one in Hickory Falls knows I'm the model, Miriam. I want to keep it that way. My plan is to go without announcing that I'm away. Of course, Nadine will know, and some people may realize I'm gone. I think it's sufficient to say I'm seeing old friends."

"Do you have friends that you'll meet up with in LA?"

"Yes, Lacey will be there."

"Then I guess you're meeting old friends. I don't see a problem."

"Thank you, Nana." The fatigue from traveling appeared to have lifted. "I know the move was hard, but now that you're settled, are you feeling okay?"

A tender smile answered first. "I haven't felt this happy in years."

"Neither have I, Nana. Neither have I."

~~*~~

Rain cooled the air, so they decided to have an outing. Lillian wanted to see how the town had changed. Annie pushed her wheelchair down Main Street. They'd stop at the next intersection and turn around. She didn't want to overdo it on their first trip out. Nadine helped with the two steps then left them to their walk.

Annie pointed out The Coffee Grinder. "My favorite morning spot."

"When I left, that coffee shop was a pharmacy. It had a soda counter in the front and prescriptions were filled in the back."

"Hello." The sound came from above.

Annie looked up and saw Seth standing on the balcony above the hardware store. "Hi. What are you doing up there?" Not that it was any of her business.

He leaned over the balcony, his arms resting on the rail. "Did you think I lived in the hardware store?"

"You mean you live up there?"

"Yep."

She considered introducing Lillian but decided against it with the awkward height. She waved goodbye and turned back toward her grandmother. "That was Seth. He works for Charlie. I'll introduce him sometime. Would you like to see Charlie before our walk?"

"I'd love to say hello."

Annie pulled the door open and tried to maneuver the chair. A passerby came to her aid and held it for her.

"Thank you."

She clunked the chair up over the threshold and they were inside. Charlie's face broke into a wide smile.

"Glory be. Is that you, Lillian?"

"It's me. How you doing, Charlie?"

He came out from behind the counter, stepping a wide circle around Useless, who lay snoring. "Why if I were any better, I'd be illegal."

"Look at us. Twenty years older. It shows on me, but you look the same as the day I left."

"And you've only gotten prettier. I told Patty you were coming. I know she'd love to see you."

"Please bring her around."

"Well, afraid I can't do that. She's in Havenbrook. That's a nursing home. She's having trouble remembering stuff. And people. Doc says she's got the Oldtimer's disease."

Annie and Lillian shared a glance, certain he was talking about Alzheimer's.

"She remembered you when I told her. Might not the next time. I can't never tell from day to day."

"I'm sorry to hear that. I was in a nursing home in Pittsburgh until my sweet granddaughter managed to bring me home."

He looked at Annie, then back to Lillian. "You got a good one here."

"Don't I know it! We're off to take our walk. Say hi to Patty for me. I'll stop back in again sometime."

They went to the corner and back again. Even riding in a wheelchair, it was enough to tire Lillian out.

After that, they tried to get out each day. Folks stopped in but Lillian loved to see the town. The end of the two weeks was fast approaching. Three more days until Annie had to leave for LA. She'd been half starving herself and doing her HIIT routine every morning. She hoped it would be enough.

Iris proved to be a Godsend. Lillian loved her visits. If the air was cool, they'd rock on the front porch. On muggy days, they'd sit in the parlor. Today was an inside day. Their voices drifted from the front room, catching Annie's attention when she heard Iris mention the Robertson sisters.

"I heard it was $20,000. It came with a letter from some attorney saying it was an anonymous gift. Words are buzzing all around town. Nobody knows who could'a done it. It's like manna falling straight from heaven."

"That's wonderful. Maybe now they can pay their daddy's debts and medical bills."

"Good thing old man Robertson's not around to know. He'd be headed right down to the saloon getting drunker than a skunk."

~~*~~

The time had passed too quickly. Annie was packed for her early morning flight. She e-mailed her stylist and let her know what she'd be facing. Annie still expected a shock when they saw her, but hopefully the e-mail would lessen the surprise. She placed the next journal in her carry-on. It was a long flight and she was anxious to learn more about the girl named Charlotte.

Her grandmother slept and Annie sat on the front porch, lost in her thoughts. Cicadas sang their night song and storefronts began to dim their lights. She wouldn't find this peace in LA. She'd find frenzied people, hurrying to go nowhere. Competitive models vying to be the next big one. Phony greetings from people wanting their name or picture splashed in a tabloid with Miriam.

A distinct clunk sounded on her walk. Annie looked up to see Seth stomping up to the porch. "Is that noisy enough? I learned my lesson about startling you."

"Hi, Seth. Are you ever going to forget that?"

"I don't know. I have a pretty good memory." He sat on the top step. "How's your grandmother doing?"

"She's so happy. I don't know why she ever left this place."

He swiveled, resting his back against a post, so they were facing. "Works for me. I plan to stay put."

"It's pretty convenient living above your workplace."

"Yep. But I'm fixing to build a house on the property that stretches out behind the hardware store."

"Nice. That should be fun, starting from scratch and planning it."

"How about you? You finding time to paint?"

"Not as much as I'd like. I finished my grandmother's lilac picture and started a waterfall. I'm not happy with it. When that happens, I tend to drag my feet."

"You've got a boatload of talent. I bet you're being your own worst critic."

"I don't think so. It needs something, but I'm not sure what. I can't feel anything when I look at it."

Small nods of his head told her he was thinking. "You ever been up to Crown Peak Falls?"

"No. Never heard of it."

"You might want to take a trip up there. Take some photographs. It's pretty impressive."

"Maybe."

"Pick a day. I'll take you up. It can be a little tricky to find if you don't know your way."

She couldn't pick a day. Not now when she'd be in LA. "Let me think about it."

13

The TSA worker at airport security scrutinized Annie's ID. He looked back and forth, suspicion etched in his brow.

"I cut and colored my hair." She yanked off her glasses hoping he'd see her features in the photo. He studied her face for another moment, then allowed her to pass.

Lacey wasn't there making arrangements for her privacy, but she doubted anyone would recognize her. She slid into her first-class seat and took the journal from her handbag. She hadn't opened it since her grandmother arrived, so she flipped back and scanned the pages she'd read. How in the world did they keep a child hidden for years? How must Charlotte have felt? How could her mother tolerate the beatings? Even as the question formed, Annie knew that women had few options in those days. Did she know her husband had joined the Klan?

The plane took off and Annie settled in to read.

~~*~~

Lacey waited at LAX baggage claim. Annie saw her scanning the crowd, probably looking for the silver blonde hair out of habit.

She sidled up next to her, unnoticed. "Hi. Are you ready?"

Lacey turned and her mouth dropped open. "Are you kidding me?" She squealed, her shock elongating the word *kidding*.

"I told you."

"You told me but seeing it … Wow. Someone's going to throw a fit."

"Maybe more than one someone. Let's go and get it done. Is Peter going to be there?"

"At some point. I don't know if he's arrived yet. We'll soon see."

A car awaited them. The drive to Beverly Hills on I-405 felt like a NASCAR race compared to the pace of Hickory Falls. Lacey jabbered on about changes in Dalton, new models hired, speculation on who Peter would choose to replace Miriam.

They arrived at the hotel where Dalton Designs had a block of rooms together. Annie and Lacey dropped their bags in their adjoining suites.

"We're due downstairs. The lower level is set up for us."

Annie braced herself for the impact, but still wasn't prepared for the frantic reception.

Her hair stylist let out a small scream. "What have you done?" Her hands rushed to touch the cropped hair, flicking it to examine the cut. "I can't fix this in time. Why in the world would you do this?" She didn't wait for an answer but turned to her team. "Someone! Get Peter. Now!"

She turned back and picked up Annie's hands, looking at the clipped nails. Then she ogled her body, eyes traveling the path of her hips, her tummy, and her thighs. "Good heavens, Peter's going to flip."

Annie reached deep inside herself, remembering the power that came with the name Miriam. "Stop freaking. I want to meet with Peter in private. Find me a space."

A few moments later, she was ushered to a closet-sized room where she waited. A mirror reminded her of the

106

transformation and revealed something she hadn't noticed. Blonde roots had begun to emerge, a sign of her deception. It wasn't unusual for a brunette to go for a lighter shade, but not many natural blondes chose to become a non-descript brunette. Had anyone in Hickory Falls noticed?

A rap on the door preceded Peter's entry. He must have been warned because he showed no surprise. No greeting. No questions. No shocked expression. He simply strutted up to Annie, examined her hair, her face, her body. He stepped around her, circling and analyzing from every angle.

He stepped back to the door and motioned to his assistant in charge of the shoot. He entered with the stylist directly behind him. "Let's capitalize on this. Don't go blonde." He fingered a lock of her short hair. Peter spoke about her, but not to her. "We'll keep the picture off the cover. Instead, we will emblaze it with the word *Miriam* with a question mark after her name. Sub-titled *A New Look*. I'll get marketing to work on something catchy to entice people to open it. Repair this cut, make it short and sassy. We'll show that short can be sexy; photos with cleavage and lots of leg. I'll pull some fashions that can handle the extra weight." He tipped her chin, calmly passive aggressive before looking back at his assistant. "Oh, and be sure to have Rocco do the photography. He'll know exactly the look I want."

"Peter?" Her timid voice held a plea.

He turned ice cold eyes her way. Then motioned the others out.

"Peter, please don't do this. I made changes so I won't be recognized. Please allow me some anonymity. I know she can restore color and add extensions."

"This is business, Miriam. You decided to rock the boat."

Miriam had never begged or pleaded or whined. Annie reached deep for some of that spunk. "I won't do it. I have a clause in my contract. I have some rights of refusal."

"For nudity and offensive photography. Dalton Designs doesn't engage in those. We're selling fashions. You, my dear, are merely a conduit to showing them off. And if you refuse, I'll sue you. Imagine the press that will generate."

With that, he pivoted and left the room, allowing the door to slam behind him.

The transition to Annie had allowed the protective wall to crumble, brick by brick. Tears gathered and began their descent, leaving their mark on her cheeks. What option did she have? She couldn't allow him to sue. The publicity would garner more attention than the photo shoot. She'd hope and pray that the fashion world didn't hit Hickory Falls. Most of the young families were eking out a living, trying to get by while the aging folks were worlds away from Dalton Designs.

~~*~~

For the second time in a month, Annie had a new look. The blonde roots disappeared with the application of a root touch-up. An adorable sassy haircut feathered layers framing her face, flipping up at the edges. The lack of jewelry drew attention to her endless neck.

Close-fitted sheath dresses were assigned to other models, those who would be in line for consideration of the title, *The Face of Dalton*. Annie modeled casual attire. Beach wear, short shorts, swimsuits, and flowing beach cover-ups. The photos included one with a deep-cut V that met midway between her breasts and her navel. Lifts had been fitted to enhance her cleavage. The off-shoulder photos were suggestive, giving the appearance that she had deliberated the fall of the clothing, her shoulder raised, her head turned, lips pursed.

Annie did what she needed to do, then disappeared to her suite, interacting with no one. It wasn't unique. Miriam had kept to herself as well. Except for Lacey. But now, Lacey only surfaced when summoned. She made no proactive steps to see if Annie had any needs.

The ten-day session ended early for Annie. On day eight, she received a notice stating they had completed all they needed, and she was free to go. She forwarded the message to Lacey and asked her to change her flight and arrange for a transport to the airport.

Details of the changes came with Lacey's resignation. She had accepted a position elsewhere. No personal touch. No visit before leaving. Only a cold e-mail notification.

~~*~~

Annie sat in the airport waiting to board. Ten and a half more months in her Dalton contract. It felt like forever. The next photo session would be in New York, followed by a red-carpet fashion show in Paris. How would she survive them? And what would Peter do to further humiliate her?

They called for first-class to board. She found her seat, laid her head back, and closed her eyes. The journal waited in her handbag. Charlotte, hidden away for years. The opposite of her own life. She'd been shoved into the limelight before she learned to read. Neither she nor Charlotte had a childhood. They had no friends. Both were denied the opportunity to sit in a classroom, to know what school felt like. Yet unlike her, Charlotte received an education. That defied the standards of an era when education wasn't for girls or blacks.

Annie tried to hide her lack of knowledge. She had a high school diploma, but she knew the hollowness of the calligraphed paper. She had learned the art of test-taking. Her only true areas of education were poetry and art, the self-taught topics she loved.

She had finally found peace. A place to belong. A chance to be herself, without pretense. Without a protective wall. Would it be swept away, stolen from her? Long ago she learned the love of poetry. The richness of verse. The depth of emotion. Memorized words came to her now. Words from a poet not always known for his tenderness. She silently spoke lines written by Edgar Allen Poe.

I stand amid the roar.
Of a surf-tormented shore,
And I hold within my hand
Grains of the golden sand—
How few! Yet how they creep
Through my fingers to the deep,
While I weep—while I weep!

14
Charlotte

Ma made a special dinner to celebrate Mr. Pearson's re-election as commissioner. She closed the blinds and locked the door so I could join them. Mr. Pearson ignored me, like I wasn't seated at the table, but that was okay. I was happy to be down on the main level.

"The good people of this county chose me to serve them because they see right through imposters like Walter Sullivan. He calls himself a southerner. What true southern gentleman would invite the union soldiers, who killed our men, to come and rebuild our towns—towns they destroyed? We don't need those carpetbaggers, and the voters agree. They stood with me."

Zachary shoveled a spoonful of collards in his mouth and spoke before he swallowed. "Even the blackies didn't support him. Right, Pa?"

A pointy finger aimed in Zachary's direction. "Do you want to know why? In the time since blacks were given the right to vote, hardly any come out. They're too illiterate to know the issues. I imagine most don't even know who's running. Besides, they can't read the ballots."

I ate my dinner surrounded by my own thoughts that would never be spoken. I read the City Gazette. Ma would bring it up when Mr. Pearson and Zachary were finished with it. The Klan was running wild through this part of South Carolina, killing and terrorizing Negros. Most were afraid to come out on election day. They stayed hidden behind locked doors so no one would think they tried to vote.

He pointed with his fork which still held a hunk of ham. "What I don't understand is how we ended up with a negro-loving Jew in the governor's mansion. Franklin Moses is giving blacks spots in the universities that belong to the white folks who made this state what it is today. We need to keep them in their place. Give blacks a little knowledge and they're going to be dangerous."

Ma kept stealing glances my way, probably wondering what I was thinking about all this talk. "James, I heard that they're almost finished rebuilding the Methodist church. Have you seen it?"

"They can take their good old time on it as far as I'm concerned. Folks around here are Southern Baptist."

"Some folks, James. The Methodist church always had a healthy congregation."

Zachary perked up and joined the conversation again. "Reconstruction codes say blacks can't go to our churches. Ain't that right, Pa?"

I watched Ma's defeated slouch. It could be because Zachary used the word *ain't,* but I think the real reason is that he brought the conversation back to the racial discussion.

"That's right, son. Southern states had to pass their own guidelines to protect our white heritage. People like Franklin Moses want to blend us all into one. They're messing with God's creation. God made different races for a reason."

When dinner ended, Ma brought out her real surprise, one I knew about because I helped make it. She carried her special recipe cake and set it before Mr. Pearson.

"Congratulations, dear."

My mouth watered thinking of that creamy custard, layered with pecans and coconut. Her secret ingredient was bourbon. I had watched her measure it out and soak the raisins, but then she took a little sip of it herself.

When dinner ended, I began to help Ma clean the dishes. The doors remained locked and the blinds were closed. The sound of horse hoofs out back sent us all into action.

"Scoot! Hurry!" Ma gave me a gentle push toward the stairs. Zachary hid the extra plate that hadn't yet been washed.

A loud rap sounded on the door the same moment as I pulled the attic door closed. I sat on the bottom step, not wanting my footfalls to be heard once the visitor had stepped inside.

Mr. Pearson's big voice thundered. "Otis, did you come smelling my wife's bourbon cake?"

"I recollect that from the last pot luck. It's a mighty fine cake."

Ma's softer voice could barely be heard, but I listened hard. "Would you like a slice, Otis?"

"Don't think I could refuse that, ma'am." A scraping noise came from the kitchen chair. "James, you heard the news around town?"

"What news? I've been home all day."

"With your blinds all drawn? You hiding out or something?"

Mr. Pearson's reply held some anger. "Keeping the heat from the sun out. Is that against the law, sheriff?"

"No, but lynching innocent Negros is. I arrested my own deputy last night. Jake and two others. Caught them in white robes fleeing from the Watkins' place. Leroy Watkins was killed along with two other Negros. Want to know what they all had in common?"

"I suspect you're going to tell me whether I want to know or not."

"They all voted."

Mr. Pearson laughed. "Lots of folks voted. That's a stretch, Otis. You're making a connection that doesn't mean anything."

"I don't think I am. You read the papers. This is a big deal. Federal government gave them the right to vote. We can't keep intimidating them from going to the polling places."

"Otis, they don't know how to read. That's what's keeping them away. What's going to happen to Jake?"

"He'll stand trial. If he's found guilty, he'll go to prison."

A loud thump hit the wooden table. "That's ridiculous. He's been a public servant in this town for years. You've got to let him go."

"Can't do it. He was caught red handed. He's not getting out of this, James. You know anything more about this?"

"What's that supposed to mean? I came home as soon as the election results were final."

"I wasn't suggesting otherwise. But did you know anything about it? Know what was going down after dark?"

"Are you accusing me of aiding and abetting?"

"Just asking, James."

"If you're finished with that cake, I'll see you out."

~~*~~

I changed into my night shirt in the upper room. We called it a night shirt, but it came clear down to my ankles. At least it used to. My legs must be growing taller because it now stopped mid-calf. I didn't want Zachary to see so I hurried into my sleeping room and pushed the door closed.

Ma came in to say goodnight. I stood to show her.

"Yes, you're growing into a young lady, tall and beautiful. I think it's time I make you a new one. And I better start talking to you about changes that young ladies go through. We'll chat about that tomorrow."

She tucked me in and read me the story about King David, how God chose him over his brothers, even though he

114

was the youngest and the smallest. She said he was chosen because his heart was pure.

"But didn't he sin with a woman and kill her husband?"

"Yes, sweetie. He wasn't perfect and made mistakes, but in his heart, he loved God. He was truly sorry for the things he did wrong."

"Do you think Governor Moses has a pure heart? God didn't choose him. The voters did."

"Yes, but God uses voters, like he used Samuel to choose David."

"So did God choose Mr. Pearson to be our commissioner?"

I waited through the quiet while Ma thought. Her response didn't come quickly. "These are big questions for a little girl. Why don't you think sweet thoughts and try to sleep?"

"Ma, can I ask one more question?"

"Of course."

"Do I have to wait until I'm twelve to stop hiding? Can it be earlier? I'll be turning ten real soon."

The swinging pendulum on the wall clock and the singing cicadas outside seemed to join forces as Ma pondered.

"Let me think about this, precious."

Zachary left for school and Mr. Pearson wasn't home. Ma sat in one of the little chairs as we were studying the science of plants. When we finished, she pushed the book aside.

"We need to talk about the science of little girls growing up. You've been fearfully and wonderfully made, and your body's going to go through some changes."

115

For the next hour, she talked about what would be happening. "These changes are normal. Every young lady goes through them. I don't want you to be afraid."

I looked at her rounded breasts and touched the spot where mine would someday develop. "Do you think they're starting to grow?"

"I think they're ready to. It may be soon, or it may take another few years. You'll be ten next month."

It was a strange feeling, looking at Ma, rounded and curved, and knowing my skinny body would do that someday.

"Charlotte, I spoke with Mr. Pearson about your question. You're quickly growing tall, and we think perhaps in one more year, when you are eleven, we can move you out of hiding. We would tell people you're an orphan that we took on as domestic help. How do you feel about that?"

One more year. I had hoped it would be sooner, but it's still better than hiding for two or three more years. I knew better than to argue with Mr. Pearson's decision. "Thank you, Ma."

"We have a lot of work to do before then. Our lesson time will be different. You've never been outside on your own, and there are some important things for you to learn. Things that will keep you safe."

I thought of the lynchings, but I only heard about the killing of black men, not women. Ma was probably being cautious, worrying too much about me.

15

My lessons began the next day. Ma said we'd start by getting me ready for my duties in the house.

"This is what we'll tell people. You are an unfortunate orphan and Mr. Pearson brought you home from his trip to Atlanta. He offered room and board in exchange for domestic duties. Cooking, cleaning, shopping, and help with gardening.

"Your parents disappeared during the conflicts and are presumed dead. We're not saying where or how because that leads to questions. Your name is Charlotte, but we don't know a last name or your true age."

I listened without answering. It was too hard to imagine a background that wasn't real. I feared I'd forget.

"I'm afraid Mr. Pearson was correct in his concern about calling me Ma. It's become too familiar and likely to slip out when a guest is present. I need you to begin calling me ma'am. If I'm not present and you speak about me, like asking someone where I am, you must say *Mrs. Pearson*. I'm sorry, sweetie, but we need to start this now, so it will be habit when people meet you."

I didn't like not calling her Ma. She's the only person I really belonged to. The person who would wrap her arms around me and say she loved me. The only one I could really talk to. I already felt the loss, even though nothing had changed yet.

"When you are our domestic help, you question nothing. If I ask you to do a task, your answer is always, *yes ma'am*, or if it's Mr. Pearson, you answer *yes, sir*. Even Zachary should be addressed as *sir*. You never question why or ask to do something later. When guests are present, you'll be asked to serve them, whether it's dinner or coffee. You don't speak unless spoken to. After you serve, you do not sit with guests. You remove yourself to another room, but one where you can hear if you are called."

Ma showed me how to make coffee and tea. I already knew how to set a proper table. I had helped with that before. The good thing about my training is that Mr. Pearson was more agreeable to my downstairs time. We still closed blinds and locked the door, but I spent more time with Ma.

The next week, Ma let me make a whole meal. We had meatloaf. She told me what to do and watched me. After mixing it and shaping it into a loaf, I shelled the peas and peeled parsnips. Ma cut the first one into matchsticks to show me how, then left me to cut the rest. I tossed them in melted lard and sprinkled them with salt, ready to bake. Ma showed me how to light the gas stove which scared me. I jumped backward when the fire caught.

Pie crusts fascinated me. I had watched Ma roll them, fit them in the dish, and use her fingers to make little scalloped designs on the edges. I wanted to try.

"Ma, could I ..."

"Ma'am or Mrs. Pearson."

"Sorry." That had happened before and she corrected me every time. "Ma'am, may I try a pie for dessert?"

"Yes, you may. What kind of pie would you like? I have fresh apples or blueberries. Canned peaches and pumpkin."

"Apple, please."

One day Mr. Pearson was sitting at the kitchen table reading the City Gazette while I was helping with dinner. I asked a question and forgot to say ma'am. When the word *Ma* left my mouth, he hopped to his feet and backhanded me

118

right across my cheek. My neck sprang hard to the side and a rainbow of colors flashed in my head.

Ma gasped. "James, that wasn't necessary."

"Next time she'll remember. You want her calling you Ma when Reverend Curtis is here?" Then he went right back to reading the newspaper.

He was right about one thing. It helped me remember. I never made that mistake with Mr. Pearson around.

~~*~~

After months of working with Ma, she turned most of the cooking over to me. She'd plan meals, check to see if I remembered, then she'd let me cook under the privacy of closed blinds. With a sense of pride, I set my first meal on the table. The chickpea ragout pie was Ma's recipe but this time, I made it all by myself. The crust had baked to a beautiful golden brown and the edges were crimped perfectly. I had broken a piece while crimping, but used a little water to force the fallen crust back into place. Once it baked, there were no signs of where it had broken.

We all sat at the table and Ma asked me to cut and serve the pie. I used the sharp knife to slice a wedge, slid a pie-shaped lifter under it, and lifted it to Mr. Pearson's waiting plate. I watched in horror as the filling drained out the sides and the top crust collapsed. Mr. Pearson's face turned red as a beetroot. He swatted the pie lifter sending crust and stew-like filling flying.

"James!"

Ma rarely raised her voice to him.

"It's your job to watch her." He pointed his finger right in her face. "What if we have dinner company and she serves this garbage?"

Ma looked at my crest-fallen expression. "It's happened to me, Charlotte. You needed a little more thickener. Instead of ragout pie, we'll have ragout stew.

119

Zachary, get the bowls while I help Charlotte clean this mess."

Zachary started to stand, but Mr. Pearson's words stopped him. "No! Stay where you are, Zachary. My son doesn't do kitchen work. The wench will clean it up herself."

Ma knew not to argue. I began to clean the splattered food while she got bowls for the stew. Zachary watched me with sad eyes, a silent message that he was sorry. Ma served each with a hunk of beautiful golden-brown crust over the top. When I finished cleaning the mess from Mr. Pearson's fit of anger, he told me to take my stew and eat in the upper room. For once, I was happy to retreat to the attic.

Ma came up later to take my dirty dish. She brought me a slice of the pound cake I had made that morning. She set it, along with yesterday's newspaper, on the table where neither of us fit.

"I'm sorry, sweetie. It wasn't firmed up, but it was delicious."

"But what if I make a mistake when guests are here?"

"Charlotte, when's the last time you knew of someone coming to dinner? We don't have dinner guests. And if we ever do, I'll be cooking right alongside of you."

"Should I come down and do the dishes?"

"Not tonight. We've opened the blinds. You can stay up here and relax."

When she left, I shifted to the cot. The child size chairs had grown increasingly uncomfortable. I took the City Gazette with me and read about the trial. Deputy Jake Mahoney was found guilty and sentenced to $100 fine and six months in jail. The other two Klan members had the same punishment, but the newspaper spent more time talking about Jake Mahoney because he was an officer of the law. A photograph, in its stark shades of black and white, showed two officers taking him from the courthouse to the jail. People formed a circular path carrying signs calling for his release. As the handcuffed deputy walked past them, escorted by police, someone in the crowd lifted a cross. A caption told readers that their voices joined together singing *Onward Christian Soldiers*. I closed the paper trying to envision the scene. How could it be Christian to hang a man? And why couldn't they catch Mr. Pearson some night?

~~*~~

When my eleventh birthday approached, Ma drew me a map of the town. It was a simple sketch, but she wanted me to learn the parts so when the time came, I wouldn't get lost. The good thing is we were right on the corner of the main street. Our backyard had a barn with horses.

She set the map on the table and showed me places where I'd be going to do her errands. The apothecary was directly across the street. The general store where I'd be fetching some groceries was down a block. A farmers' market had fresh produce for folks who didn't grow their own. Right beside that was a fish market. They had seafood brought in from Charleston on ice.

"When you step outside, keep your eyes down. When you meet up with white folks, never look them in the eye. Some will think you're challenging them. Best to behave subserviently. And Charlotte, you're an educated young lady. I've taught you well, and you've studied hard. Some white people won't like that. Never get into a conversation where your education shows. If the store owner makes a math mistake, don't correct him. Pay the difference."

"Yes, ma'am."

"Good girl. If a white person is waiting to buy something, step back and let them go first, even if you were there before them. Never ever use a public bathroom. Don't attempt to buy a soda when you're in the apothecary."

Freedom was beginning to sound like it wasn't free at all. I know Ma worried for my safety. She pointed back to the map, motioning way to the left.

"This section of town is where the blacks live. You should have no reason to go there."

"Do some Negros live in town?" I would like to have the chance to meet other folks who looked like me, especially young girls.

"Only domestic help, and only a few of those are live-ins." She sucked in a deep breath like she did when she had some news I wouldn't like. "Charlotte, sweetie, there's another big change that has to come. Live-in blacks are never permitted to use the same bathroom as the people they work for."

I knew that. I had read about it in the City Gazette, but fear of contamination seemed silly when I'd already been using it all my life. "But ma'am, I've already used it."

"I know, but when other people know you're here, they'll expect you'll have different facilities. We don't want any questions. We'll be moving your bedroom down in what's now the pantry. We're going to take out the shelves and make it a bedroom. Your shower and bathroom will be in the barn."

The barn sat right behind the house and was home to two horses. It was small with two stalls, yard tools, and a root cellar. I only knew it from Zachary's description.

"Zachary never said it had a bathroom."

"It doesn't. We'll be putting one in. It won't be … won't be exactly like ours. It's called an outhouse. I promise we'll fix it as nice as an outhouse can be."

I heard the sadness in Ma's voice so I tried to sound happy. "It's okay, ma'am. I'm looking forward to going outside. And I really want to see the horses." I'd only ever seen the huge animals from my window.

"Mr. Pearson's going to begin work on the pantry and the outhouse. Then we think you're ready. You've grown so tall you look older than you are. Since our story is that we don't really know your age, we can all say we figure you to be around thirteen."

"Do you think I might make some friends? Zachary told me about girls skipping rope and playing dolls at recess. He told me the name of one of the girls. Bess Martindale."

"No, my love, you will not be making friends with Bess Martindale or any other white children."

That was the first time I really realized I'd be stepping right into an adult's world. I'd never have childhood friends or play childish games. Time passed me by and I could never go backwards. I'd be free from hiding, but I wouldn't be free. Were any black people free? I knew the answer to that. I'd been taught well, and I read. A black student named John Henry Conyers had been accepted to Annapolis. It was all through the paper. Louisiana had a black governor. Frederick Douglas ran for Vice President. It could happen, but how? And when? Surely all of my hours spent studying and learning weren't so I could lower my eyes and move to the back of the line. Or pretend I was a nameless orphan so I wouldn't embarrass my family.

"Ma, I mean ma'am, is it okay to lie sometimes?"

Her eyes became watery. "Only when you're protecting someone you love."

~~*~~

I laid on the cot in the upper room and heard the rhythm of Mr. Pearson's hammer in my new bedroom. I was the one who asked to come out of hiding, but now it frightened me. What if I made a mistake and looked at someone the wrong way? Beatings didn't scare me anymore. I'd had my share. But could I be arrested? I couldn't stop thinking of those blacks who were free. The ones who did something important with their lives. I scoured the newspaper looking for more people. More good things blacks had done. I decided right then that I would be one of them. Someday.

I had a few more weeks to sleep in my upstairs room. I changed into my new sleep shirt that now flowed to my ankles. But as I changed, I saw the beginning of curves. Most folks would still call me skinny, but I suddenly had hips. And the first emergence of breasts. Time keeps on moving. My childhood was over.

16

Mr. Pearson never spoke with me except to holler or before he'd whip me. It took me by surprise when he called me to the kitchen. He sat me at the table and asked Zachary to join us so he'd know the whole plan.

"I'm leaving for a trip to Atlanta tomorrow morning. When I return, I'll make sure it's after dark so no one will be out talking to me, seeing me alone. The next day, you become our domestic help."

I knew Ma was sewing two new frocks for me. She measured my changing body and showed me the stiff gray cotton.

"I found you in Atlanta, in the care of a Christian family who had pity on you and allowed you to stay in their barn. You were a hardship on them, so I agreed to employ you in exchange for room and board and a small stipend, which you will not really receive." He pointed his finger for emphasis. "Slavery's been banned so I have to give you something in exchange for your work. If anyone ever asks, you receive your room, food, and a small sum to see to your personal needs. Understand?"

"Yes, sir."

"Should anyone ever inquire, you are free to leave anytime you wish. Understand?"

"Yes, sir."

"Don't embarrass me, girl."

"Yes, sir."

The following morning came with a soft drizzle of rain, but Mr. Pearson prepared his wagon anyway. He'd be gone two nights, and would return late on the third night.

~~*~~

I was still in my sleeping room in the early morning of the third day, the last day with Mr. Pearson gone. He would be home late in the evening. I heard a rap on the door but it allowed no time to scurry upstairs. Ma would be more understanding of that than Mr. Pearson would have been.

"Good morning, Otis."

"Morning, ma'am. James home?"

"I'm afraid not."

"Where's he off to this early?"

"He's away. He had business in Atlanta."

The sheriff left a long pause before he answered. "That so? When you expecting him back?"

"Sometime later tonight. Can I help you?"

"No, but you be sure to tell him I stopped."

Later that night, when darkness came snuffing out the light, Ma paced the floor and I could see worry all over her. Soon people would know I existed. It filled me with excitement and fear, all wrapped up together.

I laid on the bed in my sleeping room for the last time and listened for the wagon to return. Ma was awake. I could hear her walking her nervousness away. With the clop of horse hooves, I hopped from the bed and looked out the window through a sliver of an opening in the blind, not enough that Mr. Pearson would see. Jagged stars filled the sky, cutting through the darkness. I ran to my door to listen when I saw him walk to the house.

"James, did anyone see you?" Ma's voice told of her fearfulness. I guess if anyone saw him and knew he was alone, I'd be back up in the attic, waiting for another opportunity.

"No one I knew, and not round these parts."

"So, everything is set for tomorrow?"

"Yes, woman. I'm hungry and tired. Fix something for me to eat."

~~*~~

I woke to the silence of a sleeping house. No light crept in through the slice of space beside the window blind. I laid awake while my stomach jumbled into a big knot thinking of what the day would hold. I hadn't spoken to one human being in all my life except the three living inside these walls. Ma said I spent the first years of my life with family in Valdosta, but I had no recollection of those years. I knew Ma was the first one up because she moved softly. When Mr. Pearson woke, he always slammed doors and clomped down the stairs, not caring who he might wake.

I slid from my bed and used the bathroom for what might be the last time. Then I crept upstairs and dressed for the day. By the time I finished, I heard Mr. Pearson up and hollering in for Zachary. I waited on the bottom step behind the closed attic door, unsure if I should go down or wait. Before too long, Ma called me.

"Charlotte, will you join us in the kitchen?"

When I opened the attic door, I saw light streaming in from the windows. It burned my eyes and I had to blink a few times to erase the sting. I stepped slowly, looking out for any signs of people. There were folks walking on the street and a few horses pulling carts. But no one was paying attention to our house. I turned toward the kitchen with its big window looking out over the back. The barn, formed from roughhewn black wooden boards, looked larger than it had from the bedroom window.

Mr. Pearson walked from window to window. I didn't figure he'd be nervous about this day. I thought only Ma and me would be worrying.

He pointed a large gnarled finger at me. "Mrs. Pearson made coffee this morning. From now on, that's your job. It's to be made and ready by the time we come downstairs."

I turned my eyes downward. "Yes, sir."

"I'd like scrambled eggs, bacon, and biscuits so you'd best get busy."

"Yes, sir."

Zachary wore a satisfied smirk. "I'll have blueberry waffles."

I began to answer. "Yes, ..."

"No!" Ma's sharp word cut into my reply.

"She will make one breakfast for the whole family. Your father has requested eggs. That's what we will eat."

When I finished cleaning from the family's breakfast, I sat down and ate my own eggs. They were cold because I made them at the same time as all the rest. A mistake I wouldn't make again. After I ate, I peeked into the old pantry which was now my bedroom, stark and sparsely furnished. It held a cot and an old trunk that I had seen in the attic.

Ma walked up behind me while I stared inside. "The trunk's for your clothing. I'll move an oil lamp in here. You can bring whatever you'd like from the upper room."

I nodded my head. I don't know what I expected. Maybe something closer to the upstairs bedrooms. Maybe flowers on a bedspread or even color. But the coverlet had been fashioned from the same gray cotton as my new frocks.

"Yes, ma'am."

"Mr. Pearson's waiting to take you to the barn now."

"Yes, ma'am."

I turned and saw him waiting at the back door. He trekked to the barn assuming I was behind him. I hurried to keep up. Outside air felt different on my skin, a fresh tingly feeling. I breathed in something sweet. I had studied plants so I tried to identify the ones I passed while still keeping up with Mr. Pearson. I tried to find snapdragons but couldn't see any. The only one I knew for certain was the tiger lily. I remembered it because once Ma brought me a real one to see.

"Mrs. Pearson's informed you about your private facilities?"

"Yes, sir."

The barn door opened with his tug. New scents met me when we stepped inside. I couldn't decide if they were good or bad. The horses made an unfamiliar sound, tossing their heads back from the partial door that held them, their eyes pleading to break away from their captivity. I understood that look and wanted to touch them even though they frightened me.

A partial wall provided some privacy to the outhouse, but anyone entering could opt to look around that wall. When I followed him, I saw not a toilet like the one in the house, but a hole in the ground covered by a square wooden block with a cut out seat. A hinged wooden plank served as a lid.

"Close this lid every time you use it. I don't want to come in here and find a rank smell."

He moved too fast to hear my *yes, sir,* as I followed him. "You can wash up here." A metal tub had been set on a level board, but there was no access to water. "Well's over there. Carry your water in this." His foot poked a bucket that sat beside the tub. "See that you bathe every week."

The set-up offered no privacy whatsoever. Zachary could walk in. Or Mr. Pearson.

Ma waited in the kitchen. "I want to take you out today and introduce you to a few people so they'll know who you are. I'd rather do it that way than to wait until they see you and ask questions. We'll leave in thirty minutes."

It was a day of firsts. With my first step around to the front of the house, I saw the large size of the porch. Only the porch roof had been visible from the upper room.

"Don't talk while we walk, don't stand close enough that you'll brush against me. If I stop to say hello to anyone, fall back a few steps until we finish talking. If I introduce you, keep your eyes down and drop to a slight curtsy like I showed you. Ready?"

"Yes ma'am."

I stepped down to the road, formed of sandy dirt packed hard. I did as Ma said, staying with her but not too close, eyes down but not so much that I'd trip.

A few people craned their heads, but no one spoke to Ma until we opened the door of the general store.

"Good morning, Mrs. Pearson." An older man stood behind a counter.

"Good morning to you, Mr. Callahan." She motioned for me to step forward. "James has finally secured some help for me at home. I wanted to bring Charlotte by so you would know who she is when she runs my errands."

He peered at me over his glasses. I lowered my gaze and dipped slightly, then stepped back.

He looked back to Ma. "Good to hear it. That's a big house you've got. Glad you're getting some help." He never acknowledged me, like Ma had shown him a new kitchen trinket or something.

"You know, we had house help before the war. It's taking everyone time to return to normal."

"Yes ma'am. It surely is. What can I get for you today?"

She slipped him her list. When he filled her order of flour, sugar, and a few other necessities, he carried them over and handed them to me. "Good day to you, Mrs. Pearson." He hadn't uttered one word to me.

"Thank you, Mr. Callahan."

She turned and stepped outside before speaking. "Good girl. You were perfect."

It was a good thing that I followed Ma or I might have turned the wrong way. I tried to picture the map, but everything was new and confusing. We walked toward home, but were delayed when a lady recognized Ma. She looked me up and down, then turned her attention back to Ma.

"Is she yours?"

"She's an orphan. James found her in Atlanta and thought I could use the help. This is Charlotte. You'll be seeing her around town when she is out on errands."

The lady shook her head. "I wish I could have my housemaid back. We lost her with the emancipation. My husband says we aren't paying, so I'm left to take care of that big house on my own."

"Times have changed."

"Did you hear about the governors' mansion?"

I knew she hadn't heard anything because Mr. Pearson hadn't been out to fetch a newspaper. An uneasy look passed over Ma's face. Standing still made my package feel heavier and my arms began to ache.

"No, what happened?"

"Night before last, the Klan had a revolt. Paper called it an insurgency. About 50 Klan members stormed the governors' mansion attempting to kill Franklin Moses."

I watched as Ma's face turned shades lighter right there. "That's terrible. Is Governor Moses all right?"

"Yes, they didn't reach him. Gunfire broke out. Most got away, but a guard and two Klan members were killed."

As we approached the house, Ma's steps slowed. Sheriff Beltzhoover was walking toward our front door.

Mr. Pearson opened it as the sheriff reached the door. Ma and I were steps behind.

"Otis, glad you're here." He pointed and the sheriff turned around. "This here's an abandoned orphan I've employed for domestic help. We think her parents are dead."

The sheriff looked me over and tipped his hat. "Morning, Miss."

He was the first person to actually acknowledge me. I'd seen his photograph in the City Gazette, but he looked kinder in person. Maybe it was because he called me *miss*. Or maybe it was because he wore a big white hat.

"Where'd she come from, James?"

131

"A family in Atlanta tried to help her but didn't have the means. I relieved their hardship while employing some help for my wife."

Mr. Pearson motioned him into the house and motioned me to the back door. I wouldn't be using the front entrance.

"What were you doing in Atlanta?"

"I don't know that it's any business of yours, but I was visiting family."

Sheriff Beltzhoover removed his hat and scratched the side of his head. "Thought your family was in Valdosta."

Mr. Pearson motioned toward a kitchen chair and the sheriff sat. "Valdosta's not far from Atlanta. Some have trickled up that way. What's this about, Otis?"

I had removed myself as instructed, but still had a good view from my pantry bedroom. A gun hung from the side holster strapped on the belt of the sheriff's gray uniform. Black stripes lined the shoulders and a shiny gold badge was pinned above the right pocket. Otis sat staring, holding his hat in one hand. His other elbow rested on the table and he held his chin in the hand propped above it. I had heard his voice many times, but it was different seeing the man. I felt the heaviness of his job.

"Guessing you heard about the failed attempt to take down the governor."

"I heard. A real shame that they failed."

The sheriff's eyes were saying he knew. Knew what I knew and probably Ma as well. Mr. Pearson hadn't gone to Atlanta.

17

Annie

By the time Annie traveled from LAX to Greenville, she had relaxed about the effects of the latest photo shoot. Peter hadn't said where he planned to have Miriam's named splashed on a cover promising a new look on the inside pages. The only place he truly had control of was the Dalton Catalog. No one in Hickory Falls would receive that. He may sweet talk an editor from Vogue or Glamour, but even then, a reader would have to open it to see the pictures. If it sat on a newsstand where shoppers walked by, they'd never connect it to Annie when they saw the name Miriam. How many Hickory Falls people actually bought those titles? The release wouldn't be for three more months. No sense fretting about it now.

Dusk was covering the town as Annie drove down Main Street, passing Sweet Simone's, Generally Speaking, and finally Hickory Falls Hardware. A new excitement filled her. She was home. And Nana was waiting. She turned onto Larkspur and into her driveway, recalling the first time she entered the drive to find her garage door open. The first time she met Seth Walker. The culture shock of a small-town lifestyle. How quickly it had become home.

Charlie, Seth and the evening nurse sat in the living room with Lillian. Seth and Charlie both stood when Annie entered with her luggage. Seth waved Charlie off and reached for it.

Annie smiled at the gathering. "Thanks, but I'm good. What's this? A party?"

Seth ignored her and took the rolling suitcase, closed the handle, and picked it up. Then he reached for the carry-on dangling from her shoulder. "Let me drop these upstairs for you." He swiftly made the transfer from her shoulder and took both bags.

Annie went to her grandmother and leaned down to kiss her cheek.

Charlie settled back in his chair. "No party. We saw Lillian on the front porch when we were closing shop. Sat for a few minutes till we got tired of swatting at the skeeters. They were biting like an angry dog. We didn't aim to stay this long."

Seth was down the stairs in a flash. "I set those in the doorway of the first bedroom."

"Thank you. That's perfect."

"Did you have a nice visit?"

Annie blanked for a moment. Visit? Then she remembered—she was visiting friends. She had categorized Lacey as a friend. Obviously, a mistake.

"Let's just say I'm glad to be home. Long flight."

Seth looked in Charlie's direction. "Dark's settling in. Guess we best leave these ladies to catch up."

"Yep. I'm plum tuckered out. Think I'll head on home and hit the hay." He stood and reached for Lillian's hand, giving it a little squeeze. "I'll tell Patty you'll be stopping in to see her. She'll like that—if she's having a good day."

Annie walked to the front door. "Goodnight fellows. Thanks for keeping her company."

Charlie tipped an imaginary hat. "My pleasure."

Seth gave his lopsided smile. "Goodnight, Annie. Glad you're home."

~~*~~

With the trip behind her, Annie's Dalton e-mail remained silent, and she managed to put the fashion industry out of her mind. She turned her focus back to painting. If she and Darlene were going to have a showing, she'd need some quality pieces. She looked at the canvas in her studio. The waterfall seemed to frown at her. The cascade of water looked artificial. Shades of white, gray, and blue sounded right, but somehow, she had missed any resemblance to realism. Maybe it was the sunrays. Did they illuminate the waterfall or distort it?

Annie opened her computer and looked up Crown Peak Falls. The photos were lovely. Yet she had used a different waterfall photograph as an example and still missed something crucial. She entered the address into her GPS app. The falls were about 40 minutes away and the directions looked easy, but Seth said they could be tricky.

She walked to the window to see if he might be out back. Her studio offered a view of her back yard as well as the hardware store's. Behind that was some undeveloped land. Is that where Seth hoped to build a house? That might be a pipe dream considering the wage of a hardware store clerk. Annie scanned the yards but there was no sign of Seth. She decided to go to the hardware store to ask him about the waterfall. She needed some solvent anyway.

The bells jingled when she opened the door. Today it was Seth behind the counter. She saw no sign of Charlie.

"Morning, Annie."

"Hi. No Charlie today?"

"Nope. Patty's doctor was stopping in to see her. Charlie wanted to be there. What do you need today?"

"I usually buy my supplies from an art distributor, but I figure it won't matter what solvent I use to clean brushes."

He stepped around Useless sleeping in his usual spot, and motioned for her to follow. "Depends on your paint. You using oils?"

"Yes. The acrylics clean with water."

Seth picked up one choice in a can and another in a bottle. "Either of these will work. If you're using any kind of varnish or shellac, you'd want a different product."

"No, only the oils. I'm trying to repair my waterfall." She paused for a breath. "I looked up Crown Peak Falls. It looks beautiful. I think I'd like to see it."

Seth's crooked smile was becoming familiar. "Just say when."

"Well, I hate to put you out. I think I can find it if you tell me what the tricky part is."

He nodded. "I can do that if you want to be alone. But you need to know you'd be denying me a trip to one of my favorite spots."

She had figured it to be a polite offer, but maybe he really did want to go. "Well, I don't want that on my conscience." They both chuckled. "My time is more flexible than yours. What's the best day for you?"

"How about Wednesday morning?"

"Perfect. Thank you."

She glanced at a collection can on the counter. A picture of a young boy in a wheelchair had been taped to the cylinder. *Help Mikey Walk Again.*

"What's this about?"

"Mikey McCann. Goes to Charlie's church. He needs surgery to correct hip dysplasia, and the parents have no insurance. It's grown too painful for him to walk."

Annie shook her head in dismay before retrieving a five-dollar bill from her wallet. She slid it into the container.

When she left the store, Annie sat on her front steps and called Darlene. They set up a painting date for the end of the week when Darlene's mother could watch Selah.

~~*~~

Nadine helped Lillian to the sofa and set her cup of tea on the end table. She sat there sipping the herbal tea. Annie curled up on the chair across from her. "Nana, before I moved here, you said something about this house, about it holding secrets. What did you mean?"

Her grandmother had been looking healthier. She talked more and tired less. But the reminder of that conversation brought a sigh. "I guess all houses have history that people aren't proud of if you look deep enough. I suspect you've been looking."

"I have. But I can't fill in all of the gaps."

"And you're hoping I can?"

"You said you knew some of the history."

"I guess I did say that." She patted the sofa seat beside her. "Come here, and tell me what you know."

Annie moved to the sofa, tucking her legs beneath her. "The painting in the kitchen—the setting is the attic. I saw child's furniture, the dolls, and the tea set."

Lillian nodded. "What else did you find?"

"The journals. I've been reading them. I'm only on the second one."

"So, you know about Charlotte."

It wasn't a question. Her grandmother had obviously read them. "But who is she? I suppose she's an ancestor, but how? Do you know she never mentions her mother's first name?"

Lillian sat quietly while Annie waited. When she finally spoke, it was a single word. "Davina." She exhaled a ragged breath. "You haven't seen the name because Charlotte's the writer. She only refers to her as ma or ma'am."

Annie wanted more, but sensed her grandmother's mood rapidly shifting. She wouldn't push her. Lillian closed the conversation. "Keep reading, child. When you're finished, we can try to fill in the gaps. There's much more shame to come."

It was almost more than Annie could stand, but she didn't want to push her grandmother. There were four more journals ready to tell their part of the story.

~~*~~

On Wednesday morning, Annie walked to the grassy area behind the hardware store. Seth's truck was parked in the driveway. He bounded down the outside staircase that led to his apartment. One look at her and he shook his head. "Those shoes will never do. We have some trails to hike."

She glanced down at her feet. The slip-on shoes were open-toed and had no backstrap.

He eyed her legs. "And you might want to consider long pants."

She frowned. "And you might've told me that before now! Give me five minutes."

Seth laughed and called after her. "Don't get snarky. It only leads to apologies later."

Annie returned wearing jeans and sneakers, carrying a lightweight hoodie in case there was something else he'd forgotten to tell her. She held her arms out to the sides. "Will this do?"

"Trust me, you'll be glad you changed. Ready?" He held the truck door open for her.

The truck left Hickory Falls and headed for the interstate. They traveled the winding I-40 west for about fifteen minutes, then exchanged it for a smaller ascending highway. Hickory Falls sat at a high elevation, but nothing like the mountain passes they climbed. Annie looked out her window nervously. "Why don't they have guard rails on this road?"

His brows lifted. "And obstruct the beauty?"

"Humph! It wouldn't be too beautiful if a car misjudged the curve."

Seth gave no answer other than a miniscule smile.

They continued to climb, puzzling Annie. Shouldn't they be going down? Somewhere near the base of the falls. "Are we going to the top of the waterfall or the bottom? I'd like to see a little splash."

"Almost there."

Seth pulled the car off of the mountain road onto an unpaved passage leading to a small parking area. "Now we walk. This is the tricky part. Problem is, your GPS takes you down instead of up. You'd stand off to the side on an overlook."

"And that's a bad thing?"

"No, but not necessarily the best thing. You'll see."

The hike took them up and down some rugged terrain.

"How far are we walking?" They had to have walked close to a half mile of trails.

"Almost there." A gentle rumbling sound intensified with each step that drew them nearer to water, finally becoming a roar. A turn in the path instantly opened the view of the falls. Her gasp was audible. She hadn't expected to see it so suddenly. "That's breathtaking."

Annie stole a glance in Seth's direction. He gazed at the falls with a look that matched his face when he had examined *Stormy Sea*. An ethereal look. "It is a thing of beauty."

They both stood mesmerized, drinking in the grandeur of the rushing water. "So, does that hold the power you want to capture in paint?"

Huge stones offered a place to sit. She lowered herself to one stone and kept her eyes riveted toward the falls. Water crested over the stony precipice and dropped to a powerful stream below where rocks created a spray of whitewater constantly changing direction. Rays of sunbeam broke through the mist and painted the waterfall in various hues of blue, gray, purple and red. A shimmering opal constantly changing. The water didn't land in a whisper. The thundering sound amplified in the watery chasm. At the base

139

of the rocks, the backsplash created a wall of spray the width of the falls.

In the quietest voice, Seth whispered. "Power dwells apart in its tranquility; remote, serene, and inaccessible."

Percy Shelley! Seth quoted the words of the famous poet. He had found the perfect quote, and the words slid through his lips as smooth as honey.

Power in the constant movement, set in the midst of this remote spot, tranquil, serene. Annie looked up at the height of the crest and down at the turbulent stream. Inaccessible. They sat in silence while she took in every nuance, wishing for her easel and paints right here in this remote spot. Before leaving, her camera would capture what it could, but no picture would match details that could only be seen in person.

Seth had dropped to the rock that sat inches in front of Annie, allowing her to see the profile of his face. It showed a depth of emotion she was unaccustomed to seeing in a man. Seth Walker had an eye that saw beauty, a heart that showed kindness, an honesty not often seen. He knew poets enough to recall their words; saw beauty in nature and beauty in art. He worked hard, yet showed no desire for more than he had. Did he have goals and dreams beyond working in a hardware store? Or was he truly as contented as he appeared?

Annie touched his shoulder and he turned to face her. "Thank you for bringing me here."

The grin returned, always slight, bringing flecks of light to his eyes. "You're welcome."

She lifted a camera from the tote bag. Seth saw and moved out of the way. After snapping multiple pictures, she paused to view them.

Seth lifted one eyebrow in question. "Bet none of them caught it."

Annie shifted her eye away from the viewer. "Caught what?"

"The majesty. I don't think a picture can hold it."
"You're right. It can only be held in the heart."

18

Darlene opened her tote bag and removed two canvases, an 8x10 and a 5x7. She also pulled out a library book of paintings.

"I have to see something while I'm painting. My mind sees images but I can't quite get the details without a picture to look at."

Annie pondered that, thinking about the upcoming art show. "I know people replicate other artists when they're learning to paint, but if we want to sell pictures, I think we need more originality." She glanced at Darlene's supplies. "And perhaps larger canvases."

Her friend's expression turned to dismay. "I have a limited budget. I squeeze pennies left from food money so I can get art supplies."

Annie stole a glance at her own stock. "If you're buying one panel at a time, you're probably paying more. I'll bet my larger ones cost the same since I buy in quantity. Here." She pulled out two larger canvases and handed them to Darlene.

"I can't take yours."

"Then trade me for your 5x7. Sometimes I need a small one and I don't have any that size. Let's look through your library book."

They sat in front of the easel and propped the book open. Leafing through the pages, they stopped to examine a few, then stayed on a painting titled The Gardener, by C.P Arthur. It featured an old man, bent over a row of strawberry plants, sweat beading his wrinkled forehead, but his eyes held a sparkle as he looked at the red berries filling the basket beside him. His mocha skin may have been sun-darkened or ethnic.

Darlene ran her finger over the one-dimensional page like she could feel the pastoral realism. "I like it, but I'm not sure I could catch an expression like this artist did."

"Why don't you borrow some elements of the picture, painting to your strength, changing it to make it your own?"

They brainstormed some elements, settling on a picture that focused on a gardener's hands. He would be kneeling, one hand holding a spade and the other holding a cluster of berries. His work-worn face would be in profile, enough to show the brown, sweaty skin, eyes partially shielded as he looked down at the berries in his hand. The lift of his mouth would wear the pleasure of accomplishment.

Annie looked again at the artist's name. C.P. Arthur, Contemporary American Artist. There was a world of little-known artists out there. Could she and Darlene join them? Could they paint scenes that people would want to own? Pictures that might one day be displayed in a book for others to copy? That accomplishment held much greater appeal than displaying someone else's fashion designs.

After four hours of painting, they cleaned their supplies. "I enjoyed this. Would every Friday work for you?"

"I can try. It depends on whether my mother's free to watch Selah."

"Let's try. If not, we can each paint on our own. I'm thinking early October would be a good month for an art show. Right in time for the holidays."

"Three months. Do you think we'll be ready?"

"I do. And I think the deadline will keep us motivated."

When they chose a date, a new excitement filled Annie. An excitement that modeling never carried.

~~*~~

Iris rang the doorbell holding a homemade apple pie. Annie took the pie from her outstretched hands. "Iris, you're going to make me chubby."

"I'm happy as a tick on a wet dog when I'm baking. I'm fixin' to enter the bake-off at the church fall festival. I need someone to practice on. Besides, you can use a few pounds. You're skinny as a toothpick."

"It smells delicious. You'll surely win." She motioned her inside. "Nana's with Nadine. She'll be out in a few minutes."

As Annie began to close the door, she saw Seth and Simone leaving the coffee shop. Simone's heel caused a slight stumble and she hooked her arm through Seth's. Annie closed the door, but continued to watch through the sidelight. They crossed the street and moseyed up the sidewalk toward the hardware store, her arm still snuggly cocooned in his. Annie almost laughed at Simone's obviousness while hoping Seth wasn't gullible.

She turned from the front door, still holding Iris's apple pie, warm and aromatic. "I better put this away before I eat every bite." She strolled to the kitchen and found a spot in the refrigerator. When she returned to the living room, Nana had joined Iris.

An hour's visit had become their morning routine. Iris always came with the latest Hickory Falls gossip itching to spill from her mouth. "Myrna Mayfield, you remember her, from the Baptist church? She's having a hissy fit about giving money for Mikey McCann's surgery. She stuck two one-dollar bills in the jar, then heard that the surgery's been paid in full. She's wondering if she can get her two dollars back."

Lillian chuckled. "Oh, dear. Charlie told me about the boy. Who paid for the surgery?"

144

Iris sat at the edge of her chair, bubbling over since she had a tale to tell. Her eyes shone with delight. "That's the strangest thing. They don't rightly know. Hospital called to schedule the surgery and said all expenses have been taken care of. Buck McCann said he ain't questioning anything for fear it's some big mistake. He really wants this surgery for his boy. You know he's so poor he couldn't jump over a nickel to save a dime."

"Then I'm sure they can use the money that's been collected for other expenses."

"I reckon they can. I hear tell it's upwards of $200."

Lillian nodded, but didn't share Iris's excitement. "That's not a lot of money when you consider gas for hospital trips, parking, prescriptions. They'll go through $200 pretty quickly. I hope they keep the jars in stores."

"Oh, Lord have mercy. Myrna Mayfield will be on her high horse."

"I'll talk to Charlie. All they have to do is change the wording. Say they're collecting for medical expenses, not for the surgery."

Annie had listened long enough. She excused herself to go upstairs. The third journal waited with a tale of its own.

~~*~~

The following morning, Annie laid awake as dawn broke through the darkness. Muted light began to creep in despite the window blind. Charlotte's journal sat on the claw-footed nightstand beside her, a ribbon bookmark dangling from her last page. What must it feel like to live indoors in isolation, then feel the air on her skin, with every sight and smell new? What new experiences waited in the pages to come?

Annie dressed and made a run to The Coffee Grinder before her grandmother woke. Margie gave her a wave as she walked through the door. "Skinny vanilla latte?"

"Yes, please."

Seth sat alone and pointed to the chair beside him. "Time to sit?"

Annie nodded, paid for her drink, and carried it to the table. "No Simone today?"

"Guess not. Some days she's here. Not always."

"I saw you helping her across the street yesterday. Is she that frail?" Sarcasm dripped from the question.

Seth chuckled. "Selective fragility."

Good. Seth wasn't that gullible. He saw through her actions.

"How's the waterfall coming?"

"I worked on it but it's not finished. Darlene and I spent time on some other things. Did I tell you we're planning an art show in October? She's really very talented."

"That makes two of you. Let me know how I can help."

Annie was ready to say goodbye so she'd be home when Lillian woke, but the door jingled, announcing a customer. They both glanced to see Simone enter. When she saw Annie, her smile faded and her piercing eyes shot a look of contempt. Annie decided she wasn't leaving after all. She'd stick around a little while longer.

"Good morning, Simone." Annie's voice dripped as sweet as a warm glazed donut. Seth's greeting was polite, but his expression said he enjoyed the interchange. Annie suddenly realized what she had done. She had played Simone's game. Seth was a friend. She didn't want him thinking that she, like Simone, had ulterior motives. She had no desire of anything beyond friendship. Simone went to the counter for her coffee. Annie turned toward Seth, her voice hushed. "Maybe I should go." She began to push her chair back when he caught her arm.

"Don't." His eyes held a plea.

At the moment that his hand covered her arm, Simone turned toward them, her mass of red hair swaying with the

146

movement. She stopped short, and turned abruptly toward the door. Her heels clicked every decisive step. The door swung closed with a thud. They stared at the large window and watched her cross Main Street and head down the sidewalk toward her restaurant.

Annie frowned. "Uh oh. Did I just make an enemy?"

"Not just." He sipped his coffee. "You made one the day we ate at Sweet Simone's. Shake it off, Annie. She has some misguided idea that she and I are more than friends. We aren't. I'm happy to be friendly with her. I'd welcome her to sit and have coffee, like I would with anyone in this town. But that's all. She'll get over it."

Annie exhaled a breath of relief. *Like I would with anyone in this town.* That included her. Simply friends.

"Okay. I really don't like having enemies. Maybe I'll take Nana there for dinner. See if I can get on her good side. Speaking of my grandmother, I really better go. The night nurse will be leaving and I need to make sure Nadine arrives. I don't like her to be alone."

Seth pushed his chair back as well. "And I need to open the store. Let me know when the waterfall's done."

~~*~~

Three days later, Annie finished her landscape. She stepped back and turned around, facing away from the painting. This had become a habit when she completed a piece. An artist created a painting stroke by stroke, blending colors, deciding how to contrast light and dark. Turning away allowed her to take a breath, erase the close-up image her mind held, and then see it with fresh eyes.

When she turned back to face the painting from a distance, her breath caught in her throat. It may not hold the majesty of the real Crown Peak Falls, but it was close. The water cascading from the rocks appeared to jump off the page. She could envision the sound and the spray. The sunbeams illuminated the water and the rocks, clothing them in a surreal light.

"Power dwells apart in its tranquility; remote, serene, and inaccessible." She would borrow a word from Shelley's poem. She named the painting Tranquility.

Annie recovered from the surreal moment, anxious to show Seth. She pulled out her phone and sent a text. *WHEN YOU'RE FREE, STOP OVER TO SEE MY WATERFALL.*

A return text came immediately. *ABOUT FIFTEEN MINUTES.*

Annie looked at her messy workspace. It was too soon to move the painting downstairs. Oils need time to dry and cure. Instead, she scrambled to clean up paints and brushes. She cleared the path from the doorway to the easel. She wanted nothing to distract his attention.

The doorbell rang and Nadine answered. Then Seth's footsteps sounded on the stairs. Annie met him in the hallway. When he neared the door, she reached for his shoulders and turned him around. "Don't look yet." He faced the bare hallway wall, opposite from the painting as she had done. "Take a few steps backward."

When he stood in the doorway, she gave him the okay. "Turn around."

She saw his face in profile, but it was enough to know that he shared her amazement. "Annie." It was little more than a whisper. He gazed at the picture for a few moments before stepping nearer.

Annie caught his shoulder. "Closer is not usually better."

"I know, but I can't believe how you accomplished this. Are you planning to sell it?"

"I hope so."

"How much?"

Annie hadn't thought that far. Her New York instructor would have recommended over $1,000, but this wasn't New York. It felt boastful to price it that high. "I don't know. Maybe $400 or $500. What do you think?"

A time of silence followed before he spoke. "I think it's priceless."

19

Two months had passed since Annie's trip to Los Angeles. She'd heard nothing about the new catalog which would launch in approximately four weeks. She had at least that long before she had to worry about periodicals that might hit Hickory Falls newsstands. Peter would never allow a magazine to feature his designs before his own launch.

Information on the employee website indicated that the New York photo session would begin in three weeks, followed by the red-carpet fashion show in Paris. She'd arrive home in time for the art show. Lacey had always kept Annie on track, but now she had to seek information on her own. Her e-mail had remained empty since LA.

Annie needed to book her flight to New York. Hopefully, the Dalton private jet would take them all to Paris. Unlike her last trip, Annie had no apprehension about her appearance. They all knew how she'd changed. She exercised, but not to extreme. No HIIT, no heavy bags. Only some core exercises and the elliptical. And daily walks on Main Street, sometimes with Lillian and sometimes alone.

Taking a deep breath, Annie opened a blank e-mail to compose. She hit the letter P and Peter's address populated.

Hello, Peter. I'm sure you're aware that Lacey no longer works for me. I have not received information about the upcoming events. I plan to arrive in New York two days prior to shooting. Will the Dalton jet be taking us from New York to Paris?

I have not received my portfolio photos from the LA shoot. They are typically downloaded to my digital portfolio. I'm not sure if Lacey had done that or someone from the corporation. Can you please advise how I am to view those photos?

Thank you for your assistance. Miriam

She re-read the e-mail. Cordial. Professional. Nothing in her tone should set him off. She hit send.

It was six days before a reply came from Dalton Designs. It came via registered mail. The correspondence was from the solicitor in the form of a termination letter. The document stated that Dalton Designs was terminating their contract with Ann Gentry aka Miriam Gentry for her failure to meet industry standards. It cited numerous contractual obligations that Annie had failed to fulfill. She scanned the sited infractions, her chin trembling as the list went on. She'd had a verbal amendment from Peter, but foolishly had nothing in writing.

Annie felt silly for the tears that threatened. She wanted out of the contract and now she was free. But it stung that they terminated her rather than accepting her resignation. It hurt that they stated the cause as her failure to live up to her commitments. At least the termination came without the threatened law suit. Peter knew her well enough to know she wouldn't fight his accusations.

Peter didn't answer her questions about the portfolio photos. She hadn't looked at that site since sending him the e-mail. Annie opened her laptop and logged on, pulling up her portal. A new file titled *Los Angeles* waited to be opened.

A click of the file brought the photos to life on her monitor. Annie watched, feeling the blood drain from her face. The photos looked like Annie Gentry—short, brown hair, some with glasses, some without. Less make-up created a wholesome appearance. Pictures that anyone would recognize as her. But as she scrolled through the photos, the clean, wholesome look ended. Long legs suggestively positioned to be noticed. Cleavage that she didn't possess accentuated through clothing implants. Wind blowing her short hair along with her blouse, causing it to fall suggestively. A beach cover-up over a tan suit perfectly matching her skin tones, giving the appearance of nothing beneath it. Another wind picture blowing a skirt high enough to see bikini-cut panties beneath.

How had she done this for three years, thinking it was right? The clothing she modeled for various ads before landing Dalton's exclusive contract had been generic. Dalton was a whole new level. She had been a loner. No close neighbors or friends. It didn't seem to matter how people saw her or what they thought. Until now. What would Hickory Falls residents think if they saw these photos? Darlene. Seth. Charlie. Annie couldn't bear the thought. Seth had viewed Stormy Sea and Tranquility with amazement. But these pictures, he'd see as sleazy. Sordid. He'd never be able to look at her the same way again.

But it was done. Legal and with her consent. Annie closed her laptop and laid on her bed. She stared at the ceiling, tears trickling to dampen her sheets. She was thirteen again. Sleezy. Sordid. Soiled. Was that with her consent? She honestly didn't know.

The photos would be published. The exploitation would come. The question was—where? Where would they appear? And when?

20

CHARLOTTE

My fear lessened each day. A sense of freedom surged through me each time I walked down the main street. Ma went with me the first few times, but I liked it best when I strolled alone. Sometimes I'd quicken my pace and swing my arms. One time I tried to skip but my steps were awkward.

The first time I saw another black face, it startled me. I stopped cold in my steps for a moment. He sat in the driver's seat of a two-horse carriage, waiting in front of the apothecary. The man was aged and I imagined he had spent his life in slavery. I suddenly felt shy and lowered my gaze to the ground as I walked. But I wondered about the old man. What had his life been like? Had he been born into slavery or captured and taken to a slave slip? Was he ripped away from a family? Was he beaten or treated kindly? I suppose he was too old to flee to freedom when emancipation opened those doors.

Emancipation. The word was enough to bring a shiver prickling my arms. It made me think of Ma on her terrible day, and the man who had been my pa. I felt sure that he ran to wherever freedom waited, perhaps fleeing the south altogether. One thing was certain—I'd never know my real pa. And he'd never know he had a daughter.

With a brief glance up, I caught the carriage driver looking directly at me. He flashed a smile showing a missing tooth on the top. It was to the left of his two front teeth which had a wide gap between them. The smile caused deep creases to appear on his forehead, like it had forced his leathered brown skin upward. Still, it was nice. I ventured a return smile, but mine was more cautious. A slight rise at the ends of my closed mouth. He surprised me once again when he spoke.

"You that orphan girl staying with the Pearsons?"

I could feel my eyes widen into two saucers. I touched my chest as if to ask if I was the one he had spoken to. But of course, I was.

I stuttered a reply, lowering my eyes, even though he wasn't a white man. "Yes, sir."

"Well come on over here and say hi." His hand scooped the air, beckoning me to step closer.

With a few tentative steps, I approached the carriage.

The man thrust his hand toward me causing me to take a startled step backward. Then I realized he had extended his arm to offer a handshake. I never had anyone want to shake my hand. My arm tremored when I lifted it to meet his. A calloused hand grasped mine. It puzzled me how the handshake managed to be firm and gentle at the same time. He threw his head back and laughed. "Times they are a'changing, little miss. My name's Hiram. I work for the Danville family."

I nodded, though I had no idea who the Danville family could be.

"And your name?"

His question made me realize that I'd allowed too much silence to follow his introduction. "I'm Charlotte."

His wide smile returned. "A right pretty name. Pleased to meet you, Charlotte."

The door to the apothecary opened and a man in a business suit and a homburg hat strode toward the carriage. Hiram's demeanor shifted abruptly. The smile disappeared and his gaze lowered. I took two steps back, pivoted, and began to put space between us. The man barked out an order, and Hiram replied. "Yes sir." The clomp of horse hoofs announced their departure.

Later that evening, I climbed the stairs to the attic. My easel held a blank painting board with a textured canvas surface. I searched my mind to remember details of the carriage, the fine Morgan horses, the studded reins, the leather tack. I sketched them before beginning the first faint lines that would become Hiram. That would be the hard part. I wanted every detail. The missing tooth. How his eyes shone with the wide smile. The creases on his cheeks and forehead. Wrinkles that told a story of hardship, but deepened with the pleasure of a smile. This would be a picture of the first black person I'd ever met.

~~*~~

As much as I loved the freedom of going outside, walking on the packed dirt street, and living on the first floor of the house, I detested the bathroom. When Mr. Pearson and Zachary weren't home, sometimes I'd sneak into the house bathroom. If Zachary knew, he'd tell on me, and Mr. Pearson would beat me.

My first two baths in the barn carried a panic that someone would walk in and find me buck naked, sitting in a tub with a few inches of water. I never filled the tub high since I had so far to carry the bucket. After those two hurried baths, I moved the task to the early morning hours when the house slept. At five in the morning, I'd carry enough water to clean myself and wash my hair. I'd be back in the house by five-thirty to begin breakfast.

~~*~~

Ma planned a dinner of fresh collard greens and catfish. I made a list of a few things we'd need from the farmer's market. The fish market beside it usually carried catfish from the Saluda River. A few times Zachary would go fishing and return with perch or catfish. But today, I'd need to purchase it.

Since meeting Hiram a few weeks ago, I began seeing other black faces. Hiram told me that townsfolk were starting to hire more help. An abundance of blacks needed to find jobs and would work for next to nothing.

I was at the fish market when I first saw the girl. She stood in front of the counter and waited while the vendor retrieved three large slabs of fish. She nodded and he wrapped them in brown paper. I stared because I'd never seen a black girl my age. I still hoped to find a friend.

When she paid the vendor and turned, stepping free of the crowd, I followed her. My sprinted steps caught up quickly. I suddenly felt awkward standing in front of her. I remembered Hiram's smile and how it helped me to relax. I attempted a grin, which I knew wasn't Hiram's wide, easy smile, but it was the best I could do.

"Hi. I'm Charlotte."

She wore a guarded look, but then answered. "I'm Deborah."

"I've never seen you here before. But I've only been coming for a few months."

Deborah appeared to relax. "That's longer than me. This here's my second week. I lived up in Pickens till my ma found work for us here."

I pointed to our house a block and a half away. "I live there, in the white house on that far corner. I work for the Pearsons. Where do you live?" I hoped it was somewhere close. Somewhere right in town where maybe we could see each other sometimes.

Deborah stared wistfully at the large corner house, then pointed over her right shoulder. "I'm in the village."

I knew *the village* referred to Coltrane Village where most of the blacks lived. I'd seen pictures of it in the City Gazette. The dwellings were crudely built shanties and lean-

156

tos. There was no running water and the well often went dry when rain was scarce.

My curiosity brimmed. "Are there many girls there our age?"

"A few."

I guess I had a pensive look because Deborah said, "You can come out there sometime."

Ma had told me never to go there. "I don't know if I can. Cause, you know, I'm working for the Pearsons. But I really wish I had a friend." Perhaps that admission would spur Deborah to want to come to town more often.

Instead, her face held defiance. "Well, you're not their slave. You can do what you want when you're not working."

Could I? When wasn't I working? We never talked about me having time to myself. I lived in a world somewhere between daughter and employee. The lines were blurred.

21

I took care to never take the City Gazette until Mr. Pearson had finished it. Then I'd sneak it into my room to read, returning it in the morning. He probably had no idea I'd been reading it since my early days in the attic. He knew Ma taught me but probably thought I'd be too simple-minded to learn. I wondered if Deborah could read. Or Hiram. Probably not. It had been illegal to teach blacks to read. That held a little irony. If we were too stupid to learn, why would they need a law?

The cover story in today's issue talked about the heated election between Wade Hampton and Daniel Henry Chamberlain. Southern democrats rallied for Hampton, certain he would restore the old south. Chamberlain had already been in office since Franklin Moses left in disgrace. The City Gazette predicted Chamberlain would have the vote of blacks, giving him the numbers to win. Blacks were rallying together to gain support. Harlan Jackson and Oscar Williams, two rebellious activists, traveled the state speaking out on Chamberlain's behalf.

I served meals to the family every evening. When they finished eating, I ate alone before cleaning up. Ma tried to convince Mr. Pearson to allow me to take my meals with them, but he wouldn't budge.

"You can't break routines when it suits you. We'll not be closing our blinds and having neighbors wonder what's going on over here." He waggled his finger at her, making little jabs with a dirt-crusted fingernail, and bellowed in his naturally loud voice. "You knew this when I agreed to keep her all those years ago. She's our hired help. Black housekeepers don't eat with the family." He looked up at me and barked an order for more coffee.

I turned and lifted the metal coffee pot from the stovetop. Anger surged through me. A new and frequent emotion. When I lived in hiding, I lived with fear. Fear of being discovered. Fear of beatings. Fear of the unknown. A taste of freedom changed that.

A few weeks back, I sassed Ma when she wanted to know why my errands took so long. Ma said it was my coming of age making me rebellious. She said that happens on the road to becoming an adult. She also said I better never use that tone of voice with her again.

Or what? I bit back the question. If Zachary sassed or disobeyed, he wasn't allowed to fish or go for a swim, or visit his friend's house. What if I sassed? What could she take from me? I had nothing. Would she beat me? She never had, but it didn't matter. Beatings didn't scare me anymore. Would she make me stay in my room or send me back to the attic? No, that wouldn't happen. Even Ma enjoyed the new freedom of having someone to clean and do laundry.

I clenched my teeth and turned back to the table. The acrid aroma of coffee floated up as I refilled Mr. Pearson's cup. His hand was propped on the table near the coffee cup, and I had a strong urge to swivel the pot and pour the steaming brew on his hand. Instead, I stood tall, pushed my shoulders back, and stomped back to the stove. After replacing the coffee pot, I slipped away to my pantry bedroom. Mr. Pearson didn't want me cleaning the pans while they ate, and he didn't want me standing around looking at them. Yet he wanted me close enough in case he had to holler for more of something, like he couldn't stand up and get it himself.

~~*~~

I saw Deborah occasionally. She picked up and returned laundry to the homes that hired her mother. We always found a few minutes to talk. I learned that she was fourteen. I figured it was okay to say I was thirteen. I was already taller than Deborah. Then I remembered, I wasn't supposed to actually know my birthday.

"When are you coming out to the village? I told Dora about you. She wants to meet you, but can't come to town cause she's a house maid over on the east end."

"I don't know. I work every day for the Pearsons."

"So, come on Sunday. We have church together right in the village."

Church. Ma, Mr. Pearson, and Zachary always went to church. Ma used to teach me the stories from Zachary's Sunday School lesson. That was before I became their orphaned maid. I hadn't heard a bible story since then. Could I do it? Would Ma allow me to go to the village? Or should I sneak away while the Pearsons attended Hickory Falls Baptist? That wouldn't work because they'd be expecting lunch when they returned.

"Maybe. I have to prepare Sunday lunch, but maybe I can work something out. Will I see you before then?"

"I'll be in town on Friday."

What would it be like to go to the village for church? Even if it wasn't a big building like the town churches. I had read articles about how black people worship. Singing spirituals, shouting and praising and long teachings. I imagined myself in the middle of a crowd. Would I even know the songs? It was doubtful there'd be any hymnbooks since most blacks couldn't read. They would have memorized the spirituals.

160

Ma was in the kitchen when I got home with my fresh produce. A greased cake pan waited while she stirred ingredients. "Ma'am, would you like me to do that?"

"No thank you, Charlotte. I feel like I'm losing my touch since you do all of the cooking." She flashed me a smile. "I thought I should practice my baking skills from time to time."

Ma seemed happy today. Almost carefree. Then I remembered Mr. Pearson was away. He'd be gone until tomorrow. He told her it was town commissioner business. This may be the best time to ask.

"Ma'am, I have a friend I see sometimes when I'm at the market. She and her ma do laundry for some town folks, so she's in town each week picking up and delivering."

Ma's face became guarded for a moment, then relaxed. "That's nice, Charlotte. What's her name?"

"Deborah."

"And I assume Deborah is a young lady of your age and color?"

"Yes, ma'am."

"Remember the town rules. A little conversation but don't dilly dally. It wouldn't be good for either of you. Oh, and Charlotte, do not go the apothecary soda counter."

"I'm aware that it's for whites only." My annoyance surfaced and my tone was bumping up next to sass. I choked it back. "Deborah invited me to visit Sunday for church. I'd like to go."

Ma stopped stirring the batter and rested the spoon on a plate. "Where? Where does her family worship?"

"It's only her and her ma. That's all the family she lives with."

"Where?"

I knew I hadn't answered her real question. "I don't know. All I know is that it's in the village."

Ma's shoulder's slumped. "Oh, Charlotte. I really don't want you to go there."

"Why?" I couldn't help it. My shoulders thrust back and I knew I would argue. "Why can't I go to church? Would you rather I go with you and Mr. Pearson?"

It was an impotent threat. We both knew that wouldn't happen. All sound was swallowed up by her thinking. I waited, but my face told her I wouldn't give up easily.

"Okay, Charlotte. But church only. Go and then return immediately when it's over."

I threw myself forward and hugged her, then realized the windows were open. "Sorry. Ma. I mean, ma'am. Thank you. I'll have lunch ready before I go."

"No need, Charlotte. I can make Sunday lunch this week."

~~*~~

Ma drew me a map to show me how to get to Coltrane Village. It was only two turns off the main road, but she said it was a good distance after the last turn. Deborah agreed to meet me at the bend.

I broke my own rule about bathing in the early morning hours. Saturday evening when everything seemed quiet in the house, I sneaked out to the barn to bathe. I didn't want anything to hold me back in the morning. I retrieved the pail and went to the pump. I had to prime it a few times before the water would flow. When I carried the fourth bucket in and emptied it into the tub, I slid out of my clothes and quickly began to wash. Using the pail, I scooped water to pour over my hair, lathered the soap, and massaged the foam into my hair.

Then I heard the sound of horse hoofs. They stopped outside the barn. I grabbed my towel and hopped from the tub, running to the outhouse with the partial wall. Then I remembered my clothes, draped over a hook on a stall door. I dashed back, scooped them up, and made it in time to take cover.

The footsteps were cushioned by the hay scattered on the barn floor. Mr. Pearson's voice, usually so loud, was muted. "We need Wade Hampton in the governor's seat, no matter what it takes. Jackson and Williams will be in Columbia next week. We can't afford to let them have their rally."

Another voice sounded, not quite as hushed as Mr. Pearson's. "What are you suggesting? Where would we head them off?"

"They're coming from the south. I have sources saying they're staying in Swansea the night before the rally. The home of a friend. Problem is, it's a populated area. We'll have to sneak in during the night and take them out quietly. I hear they're armed."

I held my towel and clothing close to my bare, wet skin. Soap from my lathered hair dripped down my face, stinging my eyes. Goosebumps formed on the flesh of my arms and legs causing them to shake. Muscles in my legs burned from my crouched position, and I wished I'd have had time to sit before the men entered.

A third voice joined the conversation. "Might be best to make it the early morning hours. A time when they're sound asleep."

"There will be no time for the noose. We'll have to use firearms, then get away fast."

"What about the family they're staying with?"

Mr. Pearson's voice replied. "May have to take them out as well."

"Hey, James. I don't do women and children."

"They're black, Lucas. Ain't like taking out white women. Besides, we may not have to. They'll most likely hide in fear while we get away. Just don't go getting yourself shot."

"Hey, why do you have a tub of soapy water in here?"

163

Panic gripped me, almost causing me to gasp. Would they search the barn? Not only would they find me, but they'd find me naked.

Mr. Pearson's voice had gained some volume from the hushed tones of earlier. "That girl! My orphan wench bathes out here. I'll have to whip her for forgetting to empty it."

The tightness in my chest eased slightly.

"Okay, men. Thursday night. There'll be five of us. Be armed and ready to leave early morning. We'll handle this problem. A victory for Hampton is a victory for the south."

Footsteps sounded, followed by the closing of the barn door. I allowed myself a slight shift in my rigid position, but otherwise didn't move. Mr. Pearson had to be upstairs in bed before I could enter the house. After a good fifteen minutes, I covered myself with the towel and went back to the tub to rinse the soap from my hair. Then I slid into my clothing and watched until the house went dark. I left the tub full with my bath water since he thought I'd forgotten to empty it. I'd be gone in the morning for my trip to the village, then I'd brace myself for the beating.

22

Ma always dressed in her finest frock when she went to Sunday services. Always a hat and gloves. Mr. Pearson wore a vest under his suit coat and shoes that I had shined until they glowed. I looked at my meager supply of clothing. Nothing came close. The gray coarse cotton repeated itself in each dress. The only hat I owned was a mop hat.

What would my wardrobe look like if I were a real daughter? A white one? If, all those years ago, they had found out I was Mr. Pearson's daughter? I'd have a chifforobe filled with baby blue crinoline and pink satin with ruffled sleeves and a petticoat. My shoes would be worsted wool or leather with fine, shiny buckles.

I lifted the drab gray dress and slid it over my head, consoling myself with the knowledge that people in the village would not be wearing crinoline.

Ma told me that the trek should take me about 30 minutes. She allowed me to leave 40 minutes before services would start and reminded me that I was to be there for church only. Then come directly home. I had hoped to stay for lunch, and started to argue. Ma put on her sternest face and held her hand up, palm out. "No. If you want to go back next week, you must obey me."

Next week? I hadn't thought past today. Was Ma actually expecting that this would be a weekly occurrence? That this would be my church? The thought made me giddy. Another new freedom. They were slow coming, but little by little, my world was growing.

When I was far enough from the house, I began sprinting. If I could make the trip in less than 30 minutes, I'd have more time to visit and meet other girls. When I made the second turn off of the main street, I saw Deborah up ahead. She walked toward me, filled with smiles.

"I wasn't sure you'd really come." She hooked her arm with mine and we walked like we were best friends. A satisfied warmth overflowed in me.

My first glimpse of Coltrane Village shocked me, even though I'd seen pictures of it in the City Gazette. The buildings were not much more than sheds. Some had no solid front wall, but were draped with a sheet of burlap to block the wind and rain. People were moving about, tending fires, carrying water, trying to corral children who were running and playing. A scent of burning wood mingled with something close to the odor from the barn outhouse. I scanned the grounds and saw two outhouse buildings off in the distance.

Deborah tugged my arm. "Come on. Let's go to the hill."

I had no idea what that meant, but followed her anyway. We circled to the right and up a slight grade. People were gathering and sitting on the grass. I saw a cluster of young people and realized that's where Deborah was taking me. One girl hopped up.

"Are you Charlotte?"

I nodded, but Deborah took over. "This is Charlotte, my friend from in town." She pointed to each one as her arm spanned the circle. "Dora, Cassie, Ezra, Jem, and Tyrone."

Dora and Cassie were close to Deborah's age. Ezra looked older. Jem and Tyrone were younger, possibly ten or eleven. The girls pumped out questions in rapid fire fashion, like I was someone important. I couldn't answer them fast enough. I had to make sure that my story didn't change and that it made sense.

166

"I don't know when my parents died. I don't remember them."

"I stayed with some people in Atlanta before I came to work for the Pearsons."

"It's a big house but I have a little room off of the kitchen.

"No, I bathe in the barn."

Even with my meager space, I had more than anyone in Coltrane Village.

While the girls buzzed with questions, the younger boys ignored us and talked among themselves. Ezra, however, watched the girls and me with interest.

When there was a break in the conversation, he asked, "How long you been here."

Here? Did he mean in the village or in Hickory Falls? I opted to answer the first. "I got here like ten minutes ago."

"No. How long have you lived in town?"

"I reckon it's been almost a year." It was a teeny bit of a lie, but before that, I had lived in my attic.

"Your daddy white?"

I suppose my expression looked as panicked as I felt. I stuttered my reply. "I … I said, I don't remember my Ma and Pa."

"You look part white."

Ezra's skin was dark as a coffee bean. But there were others around us who had my creamy brown complexion. It made more sense that the pa would be white. Slaveowners were known for using their women slaves. I never heard of anyone besides me having a white ma and black pa.

I shrugged his question off. "Said I don't know."

I was glad for the booming voice that called attention to the gathering. The area had filled with people. This hill must be their church. The man with the booming voice prayed loud and long. Ma and I had prayed together when I was younger, but never like this. Never praising a God who brought freedom from captivity and food to the hungry.

167

People were calling *Amen* and *Yes, Lord,* raising their hands high like they might reach right up to heaven.

Then the singing started. Drums, rattles, and a harmonica joined the voices singing *Swing Low, Sweet Chariot* and *Steal Away.* I'd heard of them but didn't know all of the words. I closed my eyes and soaked in the sound. When they sang, *Nobody Knows the Trouble I've Seen,* I thought of the attic, the beatings, hiding away for years. I opened my eyes and gazed around the crowd. Everyone had different troubles, different memories. Many would be much worse than mine. I turned toward the young people and watched Deborah, Dora, and Cassie sing. The younger boys looked indifferent, but Ezra's eyes were closed, his hands stretched toward heaven.

One song ended and another seamlessly began. Hands clapped during the faster, spirited songs while people swayed and turned, as if consumed by the music. When it finally ended, my energy was sapped. People sat on the grass and the man who prayed stood in front of the crowd again. Deborah leaned over and whispered. "That's Reverend Platt. He don't live here but he comes every Sunday to bring us the Word."

Suddenly his voice filled the hillside. It wasn't like Mr. Pearson's bellowing, filled with anger and hate. The Reverend's voice was loud with excitement, like he couldn't wait for everyone to hear. It must have worked because people were calling out *Amen* and *Yes* and *Praise Jesus.*

"The devil wants to tell you that you're worthless, that you're less important. Oh, he might use a white man's mouth but don't be fooled. It's the devil sending you that message. God doesn't think you're worthless. He created you with His own hands. He has work for you to do. Kingdom work. His holy word tells us we're valuable, precious in His sight. The devil can speak his lies but here's God's answer."

He reached behind him and picked up a cross formed from two pieces of rough wood, and held it high for everyone to see. *Amen* sounded in unison.

"The blood of Jesus spilled to the ground beneath the cross. That's how much God treasures you. That's how important you are to Him. Don't let no white man tell you different. But I said God has work for you to do. Kingdom work. Every person here has lived with pain. You've lived with beatings. With the slave ships and the auction block. With families torn apart. Some of you never knew slavery, but you've known hunger. You've known prejudice. You've known hatred. God's calling you to forgive your enemies. Forgive those who stole you from your native land. Forgive those who used the whip to get more work out of you. He's calling our nation to heal, and it has to start here, on this hillside of hurting people."

The crowd grew quiet. No more praises or amen.

Reverend Platt's tone softened, yet his voice still projected through the crowd. "Now some of you don't want to hear that. Your hearts ain't ready for forgiving. But you aren't the only one who was beaten. Jesus was scourged with a whip. But it wasn't only a leather strap. The Romans were known for using a cat o' nine tails. You're probably wondering what that is. Well, I'm here to tell you. It's a strap embedded with metal balls on each end. How many lashes did Jesus receive? The bible doesn't tell us, but in the book of Corinthians, Paul speaks of the Romans giving 40 lashes minus one. Jesus most likely had 39 lashes with the metal-studded strap. Yet what did he say from the cross? 'Father, forgive them.' Don't say you're not ready to forgive. The blood of Jesus was spilled for you, and He forgave. Go and do likewise. I know it's hard, but it's time for healing."

Every word he spoke went straight to my heart, till it was so full up I thought it would burst open. I never heard anyone talk about Jesus that way. Mr. Pearson talked about God wanting segregation, making Him sound like an angry, vengeful God. Ma taught me water-colored stories about bible heroes like David slaying Goliath and Noah saving his family by building an ark, but not much about Jesus except to say He loved me. I couldn't understand that since Mr. Pearson's God clearly didn't love me.

Reverend Platt didn't tell stories. He showed what Jesus did for me. I thought of the time I got five lashes instead of three. My legs could barely carry me up the steps. Thirty-nine lashes! Tears stung my eyes when I thought about it.

A touch on my shoulder jarred me from my thoughts. Deborah had stood and towered over me. "You okay?"

I couldn't answer and she slid back to the grass and sat. People were talking, moving, heading back down to where the shacks were located. I saw Ezra seated a few feet away. He must not have heard the message with his heart as I did because a fierce anger had settled in his eyes. The Reverend came right on over and knelt beside Ezra. They locked eyes for a moment. Then he placed a hand on Ezra's shoulder.

"How old are you, son?"

"Eighteen."

"So, you saw, what, maybe five years of slavery before we were set free? I can't imagine you remember much of those years."

Ezra glared at him. "You'd be surprised what a five-year old remembers. Pa falling over dead in the field when it was over 100 degrees. No break. Not enough water. You never forget when you're ripped from your ma's arms so she can be sent to auction."

"No, son, I don't expect you ever forget that. Here's the problem. Until you learn to forgive, you're still living in slavery. You just have a different master." He stared hard, like he wanted that thought to sink in. "I want more for you than that. I suspect your ma and pa would want to see you step into the arms of freedom."

170

The anger switched into sadness. "It's hard."

"Sure is, son. It sure enough is. The first hundred years are the hardest." They clasped hands, then the Reverend stood. He turned toward me. "Now who's this young lady?"

My eyes still felt moist from his message. "My name's Charlotte."

Deborah draped her arm on my shoulder. "I invited her. She lives in town."

"Well, Charlotte. It's a pleasure to meet you. You are welcome any time."

I obeyed Ma. The service had been long so I said my goodbyes and started the trek home, where a beating awaited me.

23

Sure enough, I got my beating. Ma pleaded. "James, it's only a tub of bath water. Everyone forgets things."

"And I aim to help her remember. It's bad enough I had to give up half my barn for her."

I leaned over my bed, ready to count the lashes. One. Two. Three. He stopped at three. Did Mr. Pearson notice that I didn't cry out with each whack? Instead I thought of that metal-studded whip that dug into Jesus' flesh possibly up to thirty-nine times. I thought of Jesus asking God to forgive them. I knew I should say those words. I should say, 'Please forgive Mr. Pearson,' but I couldn't. Was I a slave to bitterness, like the Reverend told Ezra?

That night, when the others went to bed, I opened the family Bible. I looked inside the front cover where names had been entered in a flowing script. I knew what I'd see. James Wendell Pearson. Davina Ruth Pearson. Zachary James Pearson. My name was not among them. I hadn't expected it, yet the omission hurt. *The devil wants to tell you that you're worthless. Less important.* I spoke aloud, needing to hear the words. "I'm not worthless. I'm not worthless."

~~*~~

The City Gazette ran another article about the upcoming election, calling Chamberlain the front-runner. They expected Wade Hampton to lose. I couldn't stop thinking about it. In the house where I lived, everyone wanted Hampton to win. To restore the south to its old glory. That's what Mr. Pearson called it. But in the village, all the talk was about Chamberlain. How we had to keep him in office so the south would heal from its wounds. I had a foot in both worlds and wasn't sure where I belonged.

I was sure of one thing. I couldn't let two men die when I knew what was about to happen. For two years I had suspected Mr. Pearson of being in the Klan. I heard about lynchings and hanging innocent people but it was like reading the news. People I didn't know. Nameless. Faceless. Being in the village changed things. I still didn't know the two men who rallied support for Chamberlain, but I felt like they were a part of me. Like I was part of something bigger.

I couldn't go to the sheriff. There were people working in his office who might be part of the Klan. They'd tell Mr. Pearson. My skin prickled with fear when I thought about it. Who could I tell? I thought of Reverend Platt, Somehow, that didn't seem right. And besides, how would I arrange to see him again? Next Sunday would be too late.

On Monday evening, I laid in my bed fretting about it when the solution became clear as a morning sunshine. I got out of my bed while everyone slept and tore a page from my journal. I printed in boxy block letters in case anyone would think to check handwriting. But even so, they wouldn't think of me. No one expected an orphaned black girl could read or write. I wrote that Jackson and Williams would be staying with friends in Swansea on Thursday night, and that the Klan planned a night attack on the house.

I kept it short, saying only what was necessary. Then I put it in an envelope, sealed it, and wrote Sheriff Beltzhoover's name on front. I slid the envelope under my pillow and went back to bed. Sleep didn't want to come. Instead I kept wondering about the best way to deliver my note.

When morning came, I tied the corset that Ma got for me when my body began changing. Before I gave it a final tug, I slid the envelope securely inside. Then I tightened the laces. The envelope wouldn't fall. The only problem would be getting it out when I wanted it. I'd have to worry about that later.

I made breakfast for the family, keenly aware of the envelope secured against my body. After I cleaned the kitchen and had eaten my own breakfast, I asked Ma what she'd like for dinner. My hopes dropped when she said she'd like to use the leftover roast beef and potatoes, so I should make stew. I needed to get out to the market so I could find a way to deliver my note.

"Last time I was at the farmers' market, I saw some nice plump peaches. How about if I get some of them and make a cobbler?"

"We have plenty of apples. Why don't you make an apple cobbler?"

"I keep thinking of those fresh peaches. They looked big and juicy. Can I at least get some of those to eat fresh?"

Ma laughed. "Peaches do sound good. It's a beautiful day. Maybe I'll go with you. I'd love to meet your friend, Deborah."

My heart plummeted. I needed this time alone. "Deborah doesn't come every day."

"That's okay. Let me change my shoes and I'll be ready."

I went back in my room and retrieved my dimity pocket. I always tied it to my waist when I went into town. I had no intention of sliding the envelope in there. I needed it to be safer than the carry-all bag. I unlaced my right shoe and slipped my foot free. Then I reached to my corset lace, loosened it, and found the note. After tightening the corset, I folded the envelope and placed it in the bottom of my shoe. When I put my foot back into the high-top and retied it, I felt the uncomfortable bulge, but it made the note more retrievable than in my corset. I had to get free from Ma. How

174

would I accomplish that? Why did she insist on coming today?

When we stepped to the street, I saw Hiram's carriage parked in front of the apothecary. He flashed a big smile and waved.

"You know him?" That seemed to surprise Ma.

"We talk sometimes. His name's Hiram."

We went to the end of the walk and turned left. The farmers' market was a block away in that direction. I had to walk slightly behind Ma and keep my eyes down when she stopped to talk with a friend. Anger burned inside my belly. I wanted to lift defiant eyes and look directly at her friend. *I'm not worthless.*

The farmers' market came into view and we found the peaches. Ma picked one up and examined it, turning it from side to side. "My goodness. They do look delicious." She ordered a dozen. The vender placed them in a basket and handed it to me to carry, then turned back and thanked Ma.

We turned toward home. I stayed a few steps back and carried the basket of peaches. Panic rose up from my knees to my belly, then began to grip my chest. How would I get the note to Sheriff Beltzhoover? If I can't deliver it, two men will die. When we reached the house, Ma turned. "Let me take those. Would you mind making a trip to the general store? I think we're low on sugar. Oh, and pick up a pound of coffee beans also."

I wanted to hug her, but managed to keep my face even. "Yes, ma'am." I handed her the peaches and continued up the street. When I reached the general store, I kept walking. The sheriff's office was up ahead another block. Before I reached the office, I crouched low and loosened my right shoe. A sweeping gaze showed no one close enough to worry. I tugged the envelope free and dropped it in my dimity pocket. When I approached the sheriff's office, I hung back as two men stood in the doorway talking. They finally departed and I took one more glance behind me. Then I lifted the envelope from my pocket, smoothed its creases, and slid it under the door. I resisted the urge to run from there, but kept my feet to a fast walk. When I reached the general store, I glanced backward. The road remained empty.

~~*~~

Thursday morning, I was inside the barn with the doors closed. Even though it was only a little after five a.m., I heard the oversized door swing open and Mr. Pearson walked in. I began to scurry from the outhouse but his words stopped me.

"Mrs. Pearson's still sleeping. Tell her I had county business. I'll be gone all day. She should not to wait up for me. I'll be late."

"Yes, sir."

Did Sheriff Beltzhoover get the note? Would they be able to stop the Klan? Two men's lives depended on it.

24
Annie

The Hasselblad camera, a gold standard in the industry, had been a splurge. Annie made the purchase so they'd have the ability to photograph their own prints. Plans for the art show opened a whole new world for Darlene. She wrinkled her forehead in confusion. "Why are we making prints? Aren't we selling our originals?"

"Yes, for those who want an original work of art and are willing to pay for it. But some people can't pay that higher price."

"Well, that I understand all too well."

"If we have prints made, they sell for less, increasing our sales without increasing our painting time. We sell those in addition to the original. We'll retain the digital copy of the artwork if we want prints in the future."

Darlene's brow furrowed. "Won't people see the lower cost and buy the print instead?"

Annie shrugged. "Some people will. But real art connoisseurs will settle for nothing less than an original."

"Humph! I guess I'm not that hoity toity. I'd go for the cheaper one."

Annie suppressed a chuckle. "I suggest we get an art appraiser to help us price our originals."

Darlene began biting her bottom lip, "How much do they charge?"

"Don't worry about that, Darlene. I'll cover it."

Darlene's skepticism turned to determination. "No, if we're partners in this, I need to do my share. I know we have expenses for advertising and refreshments."

Annie didn't care about the cost, but had no desire to undermine Darlene's dignity. "Okay. How about if I front the money for expenses, and we split it after the show?"

She went back to lip biting. "That's good. How much was that fancy schmancy camera?"

You don't want to know, Darlene. "That fancy camera is mine. We're not splitting that cost."

"Okay. Let's hope I sell something. If I don't, I'll be paying you in monthly installments.

Annie turned to scan the paintings lined against the studio wall. Her eyes rested on *A Mother's Love.* "Yours will sell. Trust me."

~~*~~

"Nana, would you like to try a local restaurant for lunch today?"

Lillian glanced up from the book in her lap. "Oh, Annie. You know I don't eat that much."

"I know, but I think you'll enjoy a change of scenery. Sweet Simone's. It's not far. It's down on the corner of Main and Verbena."

"Simone. Is she Estelle Boyle's daughter?"

"I have no idea. Who's Estelle Boyle?"

"She went to school with your daddy. Married right out of high school and had a baby way before nine months passed. Had tongues wagging all over Hickory Falls. She named the baby Simone."

"I know she's originally from here. Seth said Simone fancies herself French even though she grew up in Hickory Falls."

Lillian laughed. "That's her. Estelle was born in the south of France. Montpellier, if I remember correctly. She

178

came here with her parents when she was a baby. Probably had no recollection of her birthplace, but talked about it all the time. Yes, Annie. I'll go to Sweet Simone's with you."

Annie had no intention of telling her grandmother that Simone disliked her. She planned to win her over with some French flattery. She'd choose the most ethnic meal on the menu and gush over Simone's expertise.

They invited Nadine to join them, but she declined, leaving Lillian with a reminder about her dietary restrictions. Annie pulled a sweater over her grandmother's shoulders before pushing the wheelchair down Main Street.

As they passed Generally Speaking, Lillian craned her neck to see inside. "That was the General Store all the years I lived here. When I was a child, I loved going in there for penny candy. They had little brown paper bags, no bigger than a 3x5 photo. All of the candy was behind glass, and I'd tell him which pieces I wanted and how many. For a dime, I could have a nice little treat bag."

The General Store. That was the same simple name Charlotte called it. Was it here, in this same location? She had spoken of the dirt road. Annie tried to envision it. Tried to remove the paved surface and traffic. The parking meters, sidewalks, and ornamental trees. She tried to see Charlotte's Hickory Falls of a hundred and fifty years ago. How different it must have been.

They reached Sweet Simone's and were ushered to a table. Annie wheeled Lillian's chair to the empty spot the hostess created by removing a chair. After a brief look at the menu, Lillian ordered a simple cup of chicken consommé and *salade verte* which was basically a bowl of greens with a Dijon honey vinaigrette dressing. Annie ordered coq au vin, chicken braised with wine, mushrooms, bacon, and onions.

They ate their meal with no sign of Simone. When the server came back to check on them, Annie asked. "Is Simone in today?"

"Yes, I believe she's in her office."

"Would you ask her to stop by if she has a moment?"

"Sure. Who should I say is asking?"

Annie hesitated, cutting a glance at her grandmother. "Tell her an old friend of her mother's."

A few moments later, Simone swayed out through the doors of the kitchen, shoulders back, all smiles. When she looked to their table and saw Annie, she stopped short. The smile stayed, but tension pulled at her lips in her attempt to maintain the look. It more closely resembled a sneer. She resumed motion and stopped near their table, but not as close as she'd been when Seth sat there.

"Hello, Annie. What's this I hear about you knowing my mother?"

Annie put on her brightest smile, hoping she looked sincere. "Not me, Simone. I'd like you to meet my grandmother, Lillian Gentry."

Simone was all too happy to shift her attention toward Lillian. She pivoted and her back was to Annie, as it had been the first time they met. Fortunately, she gushed over Lillian. Annie would have been furious if Simone had given her grandmother the cold shoulder.

They chatted about Estelle going to school with Annie's father. Lillian appeared oblivious to the snub. When she was able to jump into the conversation, Annie complimented the food.

"Simone, the coq au vin was delicious. I've never had chicken so tender. I'm thinking of trying the Tarte tatin for dessert. Would you recommend it?"

Simone stood tall, shoulders back, and gave a snide response. "Well of course. If I couldn't recommend it, I'd never allow it to be on my menu."

"Good. I think I'll try some. I love pineapple upside down cake, and it sounds like this is similar with apples."

Simone crossed her arms over a rigid torso, both eyes squinted. "It's nothing like that. My tarte tatin has apples caramelized to perfection, a flaky crust on top, drizzled with a sweet apple cinnamon glaze."

So much for winning her with compliments. "Nana, would you like to try some?"

"It sounds delicious, but I'd never be able to eat it. Perhaps I'll have a taste of yours."

Simone held a demure hand towards Lillian, fingers drooped in front showing her horrid nail color. "Charmed to meet you. I hope you'll come back again." She motioned to the server. "One tarte tatin for this table."

The attempt to win Simone over had been a dismal failure.

When they returned home, Annie set about the task of photographing prints of the artwork. She would order one trial copy to compare the color resolution of the print against the original, but had full confidence in the Hasselblad. Once she was satisfied with the color resolution, she'd order all of the prints of her artwork and Darlene's, and would have them matted. She ordered a trial print of Tranquility, the Crown Peak Falls scene.

Three days later, Annie drove to the printer in Asheville to pick up the finished copy. He showed her the print before wrapping it in brown paper. At a glance, it looked great, but she needed to examine it side by side with the original.

Annie took advantage of her trip to Asheville to visit an art gallery comparing prints on canvas and polar matte cardstock. Her viewing also gave her some ideas about reasonable pricing. The art appraiser had been hired, but Annie wanted an idea of costs in this region. Works similar to Tranquility held price tags around $750. She pictured Seth's expression as he stood in the doorway looking at the newly completed waterfall. He called it priceless.

When Annie made the trip back to Hickory Falls, she turned her Camry into her driveway. Seth road the lawn tractor behind the hardware store. Annie knew he'd scoot over and mow her small grassy space as well. She had been unsuccessful in her attempt to pay him. She waved and he cut the motor.

"Another painting?" He motioned toward the brown paper wrapping.

Annie stepped closer to the tractor. "No. Actually, it's Tranquility. I tried a print with my new camera. It looks pretty good, but I need to see it beside the original."

"You decide on a price? I mean for the original?"

"I have an appraiser coming to help us price everything. That's hard for me. I'd probably go too low. Hey, I wanted to tell you, I took my grandmother to Sweet Simone's a few days ago."

His eyebrows arched but didn't hide the look of amusement in his hazel eyes. "How'd that go? Did you get the burr out of her saddle?"

"Afraid not. She gushed all over Nana and ignored me. I even complimented her food. Then I offended her by comparing the torte tatin to the apple equivalent of pineapple upside down cake."

Seth laughed out loud. "You're done for. I doubt she'll ever get over that."

"I'm through worrying about it. I better take this picture inside and get busy. I'll see you later."

A moment's hesitation passed before he responded. "Yeah, tomorrow at noon. I'm taking you to lunch."

Annie stopped in her tracks, her free hand going to her hip. "Are you asking me or telling me?"

He grinned. "I guess I'm asking, but I want to show you something."

She relaxed her hands. "Okay, but we need to work on your social skills. You need some serious practice asking a girl out." As soon as the words left Annie's mouth, she felt the heat climb up her neck to her face. "I mean, I know it's not like asking me out, but still, you're going to need…"

He interrupted, saving her from tripping over any more words. "Well, by dictionary definition of the word *out*, I think this fits that category." The smirk on his face said he was enjoying her faux pas.

Her hand went back to her hip. "You know what I mean, and if you don't stop smirking, I may decline your tactless invitation."

"My apologies." He gave a slight bow from the seat of his tractor. "But methinks the lady doth protest too much. I'll see you at noon tomorrow."

Really? Shakespeare? He started the tractor, turned, and drove off with a backward wave of his hand. Sometimes Seth could be sweet and sometimes he could be downright infuriating.

25

Annie had no idea how to dress for lunch. Seth made it sound like no big deal, so she dressed in jeans and a casual blouse. She didn't want him coming to the door to pick her up. That had the feel of a real date, which this wasn't. Instead, she walked out the back door, hoping to catch him coming down the stairs from his second-floor apartment. A door stood opened to the shed behind the hardware store. Was he inside the shed? Annie waited, then saw him driving out on a golf cart. He hopped off and closed the shed door.

By then, Annie had walked over to join him. The golf cart still idled. "This is our transportation?"

"Yep. You ready?"

She answered with a skeptical look that held questions.

The cart had two front seats and a rear-facing bench seat in the back. A cooler was attached to the bench seat with a Velcro strap. Seth made a mock gesture of opening an imaginary door on the side. Annie slid onto the passenger seat. He jaunted to the driver's seat and kicked the golf cart into gear. They turned toward the open field behind the hardware store and began up the slight grade.

"Where are we going?"

He'd become an expert at ignoring her questions. A little further up the grade, Annie saw a table and chairs in the middle of nowhere.

A grin formed as he stopped the cart and cut the motor. "I told you this technically fit the definition of the word *out*."

Annie hopped off before he could go through his act of pretending to open her door. He reached in the back of the golf cart and loosened the cooler.

"Our lunch," he announced as he held it for her to see.

A card table had been set up with two folding chairs. Seth unzipped the cooler and retrieved a tablecloth, flipping it in the breeze and laying it on the card table. Then he pulled out a chair and held it for her. That's when she noticed the stakes on the ground. The table had been set up inside the staked-off area.

She sat, perplexed. "Why are we here?"

"We're in the exact spot of my new kitchen. Think of it as the first meal in my home."

"Seth! Are you kidding me?"

"Nope. I've been talking with a contractor and finally picked a plan."

His face beamed with pleasure and Annie's annoyance of the unanswered questions dissipated. She had dismissed his talk of building a house to be a pipe dream.

He laid two paper plates on the table and retrieved sandwiches, fruit salad, and cookies from his pack. Last, he pulled out two bottles of water.

"I hope the menu suits you."

Annie opened her bottle of water. "So, tell me about the house."

He pointed toward the fruit salad from the grocery's deli. She scooped a spoonful onto her plate and passed it across the table.

He talked while Annie ate. "It's a cape cod. Four bedrooms. Three up and the master down. Brick. Two car-garage."

185

This didn't sound like a home for a single man. This would be a family-sized house, not a bachelor pad.

"I confess I do have an ulterior motive for bringing you here today."

Annie forked a sliced strawberry and held it up. "I guess it's true that *there's no such thing as a free lunch*." Her response held the amusement she felt.

Seth's answer was the slightest lift of a smile, but his eyes sparkled.

Annie laid her fork down. "So, what's the cost of my lunch?"

"You're an artist. I figure you have the creative brain. I need some help planning the kitchen."

"Oh, goodness. Everybody has different taste. I'm not sure how much help I can be."

"Like I said, you have this creative ability to see what others can't. I want to know what you see in this kitchen."

She looked around again, seeing nothing but weedy grass and stakes waving pink strips of plastic. She needed more information before she envisioned a kitchen. "What are the dimensions?"

"The plans are for a 12' X 14', but I might have a little wiggle room if I want to change that."

She bit into her sandwich, seeing kitchens in her mind. Seth would one day bring a wife here, raise a family on these grounds. "I can tell you some things I might like, but everyone's taste differs."

"Annie, I'm not the decorator type. I need help. Close your eyes and see your ideal kitchen, then tell me what you see."

She inhaled a deep breath of the fresh air. Her ideal kitchen? The only kitchen that brought fond memories sprang to her mind—her grandmother's kitchen from the home she had before moving to assisted living. Any semblance of warmth during her childhood came from that room. "Well, I'm not seeing a modern, state-of-the-art kitchen."

186

"Really. What are you seeing?" He leaned forward, riveted on her words.

"I'm seeing something rustic and cozy. An oblong table with a bench on one side, chairs on the other. Placemats adding a splash of color to the wood surface. It sits in an alcove with a big triple window beside it. No curtains. Maybe a gingham valance. The cabinets are white with a black or maybe a gray countertop. Perhaps a little speckle. There's a double porcelain sink with a white brick backsplash. Color is added through basket liners and linens, something pastel. A mint green or baby blue."

Seth listened intently. "What's on the floor?"

"I see something warm, like hardwoods."

"Not ceramic?"

She scrunched her nose. "If you like that look, it works. I think it looks cold."

"How about an island?"

Annie's skill in the kitchen had come a long way in the last few months. "Islands are good if you have the space, but everything in a kitchen should be functional. Maybe a butcher block island, and one with drawers for storage. Above all, lots and lots of natural light, as much as space will afford."

Seth sat and nodded, his elbow on the table supporting the chin resting in his hand.

With the exception of the island, Annie had described her grandmother's old kitchen. "Seth, you've got to get what *you* want. I'm different. Survey a dozen ladies and something modern and flashy would probably win."

He wore his usual grin, bright all the way to his hazel eyes. "Do I look modern and flashy to you?"

Annie smiled, but didn't respond. They both knew the answer to that.

They finished their lunch and began to bag the trash. "Anything else I can help with?" She actually enjoyed the lunch and a chance to help Seth make plans.

187

"Yep. One other thing."

"What's that?" She expected him to say the bathrooms.

He leaned back with his arms locked behind his neck. "Well, yesterday, you so kindly pointed out that I may need some pointers on the proper way to ask a girl out."

Annie groaned inwardly. She didn't want reminders of that conversation. "Well, you don't *tell* a girl you're taking her out, you *ask* her. Give her the opportunity to say no."

"How would I do that?"

Seth had no difficulty talking to people. A walk down Main Street with him was enough proof. Most mornings he sat in The Coffee Grinder chatting with whomever happened by. Did he really need pointers to ask a girl out? "Don't say, 'What night are you free to go to dinner?' That leaves her no options. When you ask, 'If you're free Saturday evening, I'd like to invite you to dinner,' she has an excuse if she doesn't really want to go."

He leaned forward. "And if I don't want to give her an opportunity to decline?"

Annie shook her head, all amusement gone. "Don't do that. If she isn't interested, it's lots easier on both of you if she can tactfully say she's busy."

"You mean, she can lie?"

Did he see everything black or white? "Not lie. Maybe she's busy reading a book or washing her hair." Did he really need this help? It was common sense, something Seth had plenty of.

"Okay. What would be the most convincing way to ask? What might make her want to say yes?"

Annie's curiosity burned to know who he planned to ask. Please let it be anyone but Simone. "Be yourself. Say, I enjoy your company and if you're free on Saturday, I'd love to take you to dinner."

He was leaning back now, his chair perched on the two back legs. "And you think that'll do it?" He wore his half smile.

"If you want her to go out with you, it's worth a try."

"Okay." He leaned forward and reached for her hand. "Annie, I enjoy your company and would love to take you to dinner on Saturday if you're free."

Seth's large hand enclosed Annie's completely, making small circular motions with his thumb. His eyes were glued to hers.

Annie's pulse began to throb. Was he practicing? Or was he asking? "I, uh, that's good, except ..." She attempted to pull her hand free, but he held it, his eyes still fastened on hers. "Except maybe you shouldn't hold her hand." Her voice faltered, barely able to get the words out.

He scooped her other hand in his and sat there, leaning forward, holding both hands. "Annie, would you have dinner with me Saturday evening?"

The warmth of his hands and the intensity of his eyes left no mistake about his intent. Annie found it hard to breathe, muddling her thoughts. "Seth, I ..."

"Please don't tell me you'll be busy washing your hair."

The endearing half grin made her smile. But she needed to free her hands so she could think. She gently turned them and loosed herself. "Seth, I'm not sure that's a good idea."

"I think it's a great idea." He still leaned forward, as close as the card table would allow.

"You're my friend. A valued friend. I don't want to mess that up."

He lost the grin but still held her eyes. "Annie, valued friendship is the best basis for a relationship. I'd like to give it a try."

She sat back in the chair, scanning the mountains, trying to escape his gaze. There was no question that his hand

189

holding hers had her heart skittering. Firm but gentle. Seth would make such a good husband. A good father. He deserved someone equal. Annie had no idea how to be a good wife or mother. She'd had no example in her life. "You can do so much better than me."

"I don't think so. I think you're as good as it gets."

Thoughts of the Dalton photos flashed before her. The years of talent shows, strutting around stage with a phony smile. Memories of her dad, climbing into her bed when she was thirteen. Telling her it was okay while she was too naïve to know what was and wasn't normal. Her eyes pooled. "You don't really know me."

"I know you, Annie."

How much should she say? She couldn't tell him about Dalton. A multi-million-dollar supermodel could never have a normal life in Hickory Falls. "No, you know nothing of my background. I come with baggage."

"Doesn't everybody? Sometimes our baggage makes us stronger. We can learn from it, then leave it behind. It shouldn't define us."

Quiet surrounded them, the peaceful, grassy field a contrast to the turmoil Annie felt.

Seth broke the silence. "Dinner?"

"I don't know, Seth."

"Don't say no, Annie. Just friends. We'll be friends spending a little more time together."

Would that carry a false hope? Lead to other expectations? Annie had come to terms with remaining single. She couldn't imagine wanting a man to touch her. Yet how many times had she longed for a love like her grandmother's? One that would be fresh and true over the span of a lifetime.

"Annie?" He took her hand again.

She ignored the inclination to pull it back. He was such a good man. She couldn't do it, couldn't give him false hope. But *no* sounded so harsh. "I can't, Seth. I have some things to work through first."

His eyes held hers, impossible for her to read. Was it hurt, anger, embarrassment? Maybe a little of each. But then that sweet smile formed. "Well, that wasn't exactly a *no*. I'll take that as a *not yet*."

26

Annie stood in her studio gazing out the window. The field behind her house would soon buzz with the activity of new home construction. Melancholy washed over her. Someday Seth would live there with a wife and probably children. It wouldn't be her. That was Annie's choice, so why did it carry such sadness? She'd never, in all her life, felt as comfortable with a man as she was with Seth Walker. The men in her life were like Peter and Rocco and male models puffed up with self-importance.

With Seth, people saw exactly who he was. Real. Sincere. Humble. His contentment still puzzled her. Even her rejection didn't bring him down. He managed to find a glimmer of hope. Did he always look for the positive?

For days Annie battled with the memory of his hand enclosing hers, making it hard to think. She expected any touch from a man would be repulsive. But instead, it felt comforting. Safe. Should she have said *yes*?

Annie shook off the thoughts. She had too much work to do. Darlene was on her way and the art appraiser would be here within the hour. The color resolution of the Tranquility print matched the original with perfection. The rest of the prints had been ordered and would be ready by the week's end. Twenty-four originals and five prints of each. Almost 150 pieces of art for sale.

The canvases had been moved to a second bedroom. Annie heard the doorbell, knowing Nadine would answer.

She called downstairs. "Come on up, Darlene." When Darlene reached the top, Annie saw Selah with her.

"I'm sorry. Bobby had to work overtime so I had to bring her."

"That's fine. We won't be painting." Annie reached for the child. "Hey, Selah. Can I hold you?" The child came easily, wrapping her arms around Annie's neck. She had the sweet scent of baby.

"What can I do?" Darlene asked.

"Nothing. We're waiting for the appraiser. Let's sit."

Selah began to squiggle, trying to get down. "I don't think she's happy with me."

"You can put her down. As long as we close this door."

They closed her in the bedroom, away from the stairs. She crawled around until she reached her mother's chair. Then pulled herself to her feet.

"She's been taking steps and is pretty proud of herself. I think she wants to show off."

Darlene was right. Selah took about four steps before plopping to her bottom, smiling all the way down to the floor. Bright eyes looked between the two ladies to make sure they'd seen. Annie scooted to the floor to play with her. With no siblings and no close friends, she'd never had occasion to interact with a child. This was new territory for her. Darlene tossed out a few toys from her bag and the baby laughed out loud as Annie played with her.

A deep longing like she'd never experienced filled her to overflowing. Without warning, Annie's eyes pooled with tears. Darlene gasped. "What's wrong?"

"Nothing. She's so precious it overwhelmed me."

Darlene smiled. "I know. I'm with her every day and sometimes it still happens to me."

But no one found me precious. One mother gave me away. The other used me for her purposes. Annie would never allow anyone to take her child. She'd be like Darlene, succumbing to tears of joy.

~~*~~

The art appraiser professionally examined each painting. She masked any signs of enthusiasm, but her pricing showed her respect for the collection. Darlene's mouth gaped open but she didn't speak.

"When is your showing? I know some collectors who would be interested."

Annie provided the details, then walked her downstairs to see her out. When she went back upstairs, Darlene could no longer restrain herself. She let out a whoop of excitement.

"$700 for The Gardener's Hands." Then her practical side took over. "No one will pay that. Maybe we should make it less."

"Absolutely not. It's worth it." But what if she talked Darlene into keeping it high and no one bought it? That happens, even with quality art. You can't always match the painting and the buyer at the first show. If it was still available on the final day of the show, Annie would make sure it sold.

Press releases had gone out. Social media shouted out the details. Local businesses posted flyers, although Annie knew that locals were not their target audience. Still, she expected many townsfolks would stop in out of curiosity and boredom. Two more weeks. The art show would occur during the same week Dalton's catalog was due to launch.

~~*~~

Sleep was elusive. Annie's mind was far too active to shut down. Dalton's catalog held no concern. She'd view it online, but no one from Hickory Falls would think to visit the

194

website. The real danger came in the following weeks when periodicals might print features for Peter. He paid plenty to advertise with them. She laid in bed thinking of the dreaded photos. Of her lunch date with Seth. Of the way her hand felt wrapped in his. Of Selah, laughing out loud. Of the art show. Of Charlotte. One thought bumped against another until they all jumbled together.

She eased herself out of bed, glancing at the clock. Five o'clock. Earlier than she wanted to rise, but no sense laying here with her colliding thoughts. She tugged on yesterday's jeans and a fresh T-shirt before tiptoeing downstairs, not wanting to wake her grandmother. The night nurse sat on the sofa, reading a book. Annie whispered, "I couldn't sleep. I'm going to make a cup of chamomile. Would you like something?"

"No, thank you."

Annie made her tea and took it out to the front porch. She carried a fleece throw to wrap around herself. The sleepy town had an eerie look in the pre-dawn hour. She peered at the descending moon thinking of the journals. Charlotte rose at five to bathe in the barn before the household woke, the same spot where her garage now sat. Charlotte probably carried a lantern. The moon might have lit the path, but she'd have met pitch black when she reached the barn. Where was Charlotte's art? She wrote about painting, but all Annie had seen was the one picture. A doll's tea party. *Where are the other paintings, Charlotte?*

27
Charlotte

Wade Hampton was victorious in winning the governor's seat for South Carolina, but not before the United States Supreme Court intervened. Chamberlain thought he had won, but Hampton contested the race and it threw the state into chaos. In 1877, the year I turned 14, we had a new governor, Wade Hampton and a new president, Rutherford B. Hayes.

The two men who traveled the state rallying for Chamberlain still lived. It was my secret accomplishment. I could never tell anyone what I did, but it swelled my heart with pride. The Klan's attempt to ambush the house in the still of night was thwarted. They were met by officers of the law hiding in the brushwood. Two were captured and tried, including the one Mr. Pearson called Lucas. Three escaped. Mr. Pearson paced the house for days. He couldn't say anything to Ma, but I knew he was wondering how everything went wrong.

Reconstruction of the south officially ended and the federal troops left to return to their home states. Everyone called it a new era, but I don't know why. Blacks weren't permitted to use public restrooms, attend white schools, or live in white neighborhoods. Poverty was a way of life, much like slavery had once been. Rebel supporters grumbled because slaves were free, upsetting their way of life. People who supported the northern cause to abolish slavery were boastful about their victory. But blacks still lived in the village in lean-tos or shanties, no running water, eking out a living. It didn't feel like a new era in Coltrane Village.

Reverend Platt's voice thundered his message letting it fill the hillside. Deborah sat on one side of me and Ezra on the other. He sat close enough that our arms brushed against each other. My friendship with Ezra had grown over the past year. We always had our lunch together and would sometimes go for a walk away from all the others.

"The prophet Isaiah said, 'Learn to do right. See that justice is done; help those who are oppressed, give orphans their rights, and defend widows.'

"In the book of 1 John, we're cautioned. 'Rich people who see a brother or sister in need, yet close their hearts against them, cannot claim they love God.' Church buildings in town are filled with people who claim to love God. But are they do-ers of the Word? Are they helping out folks in need?

"Every day I see people in this village community serving other people. Folks with barely enough to set a dinner table sharing their food, caring for youn'uns who aren't their own, doing extra for older folks. I see God at work in Coltrane Village."

Reverend Platt's words always resonated with me. Since I lived in two worlds, I heard different kinds of preaching. Mr. Pearson preached about how God made white men superior, created in His own image. Ma preached about Jesus love, but wasn't bold enough to stop Mr. Pearson from beating me. She had to know he wore the white hood of a Klan member, but she didn't confront him. The only preaching that made any sense was Reverend Platt's.

"Staying for lunch today?" Ezra leaned over and asked me, his lips so close to my ear it gave me an odd, prickly feeling. I wanted to turn my head in his direction, but his closeness meant our lips would be inches apart. I looked straight forward while folks stood and began moving off the hill. "Yes, I'm planning to stay." With one big leap, he stood and held his hand out to help me up. My fingers had grown long, more proportioned with my tall torso. When he took my hand, my fingers naturally gripped his, and he held it for a moment longer than necessary. We skirted around our interest in each other, but never spoke it. It never went beyond friendship. He was five years older than I was, but it didn't feel that way. We'd both grown up fast.

I'd been staying for the Sunday lunches for the past six months. Ma had relaxed about my time here at the village. The lunches consisted of whatever they had the opportunity to secure in quantity. Sometimes catfish from the Saluda, sometimes gumbo with more okra and greens than meat. Today the meal was mostly chitterlings. I'd never eaten them in the Pearson house, but found them to be quite good. I'd developed a taste since we had them often. One of the village folks worked for a butcher who gave the intestines in abundance. Flavored up with garlic and onions, the aroma filled the air.

Ezra and I carried our plates to a shaded patch of grass where we could lean against his aunt's shack. Aunt Imani wasn't blood kin, but she raised him when his Ma was sold at auction. Ezra set his plate of chitterlings down in the grass so they wouldn't spill while he settled himself against the building. I lowered myself beside him, knowing I'd be scrubbing grass stains from the gray cotton frock later today.

"What are you painting now?"

I swallowed the hunk of corn bread I'd taken. "I finished one this week. It's the trio of men who played the instruments at service a few weeks back. It's not really them since I didn't get a close-up look. Besides, it's easier to paint people who aren't real."

"When do I get to see some of your paintings? I've been past that big, white house where you're living."

He had mentioned a few times that he knew where the Pearsons lived. The thought of him coming there, meeting Mr. Pearson, well, it filled me with terror. As far as I knew, no black person had ever entered the house. Except me, of course. "I told you, you can't come there. Maybe I'll bring a small painting some Sunday if you promise not to show it all over camp."

He grinned showing white teeth against his dark skin. "You bring it sometime."

I noticed he didn't promise not to show it around. But his smile always melted me. "I'll try. What are you reading?" Ezra could read. He learned in the Negro elementary school about five miles to the north. Seven kids attended from the ages of five to fifteen. He didn't have much access to books, but Reverend Platt tried to leave some each week. Since blacks couldn't use the public library, some folks in Greenville arranged an in-home library where they collected used copies to lend them to literate negros. I managed to bring Ezra my library book once, Walt Whitman's Leaves of Grass, but when Ma wanted to return it, I had to tell her I couldn't find it. The following week, I gave it to her, claiming it had been in the barn. I didn't fancy lying to Ma.

"Reverend managed to get a copy of Harriot Beecher Stowe's new book, The Key to Uncle Tom's Cabin. Seems that southerners all over were outraged by the depiction of her characters in the original Uncle Tom's Cabin, so she wrote this one to give real examples. Things that actually happened to people."

"Mrs. Pearson wouldn't get me a copy." I always had to talk about Ma without saying ma. "I wanted to read it. Someday I will."

"You want me to ask Reverend Platt?"

"No. Best if he gets books for folks here. At least I have access to reading material."

Our lunch spot against the side of Aunt Imani's house also offered a tiny bit of privacy. No one really poked their heads around the corner. Deborah was eating with her ma and Dora. When we both finished our lunch, Ezra reached for my empty plate and set it on the grass. I figured he'd stand and reach for my hand like he usually did. But instead, he turned toward me and clasped my hand while sitting.

"I have something to tell you." His face held a somber expression that worried me.

"What's that?" I asked nervously because I knew he had searched for his ma. I figured after the 13th amendment was signed, nothing stopped her from coming back. It should be the mother who does the searching since Ezra would have still been a child. I reckoned she was dead, but I never said so to Ezra.

"I've been talking with Reverend Platt. He says the only answer for our people to escape poverty is education. He's been helping me get into college. Reverend Platt told me this morning that Payne Institute will take me. He found a family who will sponsor me for a two-year program."

Emotions crashed together inside me. Happiness for Ezra. Sadness that I'd miss him, especially since I'd been hoping for something more between us. Envy that I wouldn't have the same opportunity. Few blacks had the chance to attend college, and certainly not female blacks. But I managed to answer with the happiness part of me. "Ezra, that's wonderful. I'm so happy for you."

"There's something else, Charlotte. I don't know quite how to say it." His eyes were locked on mine, and I knew there was something deep he wanted to say.

"You can tell me anything, Ezra."

Instead of answering, he stood, still grasping my hand. I rose as well and he gave my hand a little tug. Without saying anything more, I followed him, leaving our plates behind. We walked to the back of the house, away from the main area of camp where people gathered. Stepping behind the house, he turned to face me, placing both hands around my waist. He leaned in and kissed me. The kiss was gentle and full of questions. My legs felt like they couldn't hold me, so I hooked my arms around his neck. When I got over my surprise, I answered his question by returning his kiss. My head swirled with a new sensation, unlike anything I imagined.

When it ended, he smiled, a sight I had grown to love seeing. "I guess that was my way of saying it." His voice sounded deep and raspy.

I suddenly felt shy, not sure how to respond. I was fourteen and he seemed so grown. A man, not a boy. What did this mean now that he'd be going away? Could this last?

"When do you leave?" His arms were still around my waist, and mine were looped loosely over his shoulders.

"In two weeks. I'll leave with Reverend Platt after services."

Two weeks. That meant I'd have two more Sundays to see him. And Reverend Platt always left right after preaching. He had another community waiting for him to speak to their folks. My face must have given away my disappointment because Ezra gave me another quick kiss. A brief touch of his lips to mine.

"I'll come back as often as I can. The school's in Hodge. If I can make it up to Greenville Sunday mornings, I can catch a ride with Reverend Platt."

"Every week?"

"No, Charlotte. It's about 50 miles to Greenville, too far to walk. It'll have to be when I can catch a ride with someone. I promise I'll try."

We stood like that, hooked together looking at each other. He moved his hand from my waist to my cheek, stroking it with his work-rough fingers, yet it felt like the softest velvet. "I love you, Charlotte."

My eyes instantly filled with tears that trickled down the side, right onto his hand. He closed his hand, making it look like he'd captured the free-falling drop. "If you'll have me, I'll catch all of your tears."

I didn't know what he meant by *if you'll have me*. I only knew I wanted to be with him always. I didn't belong in the Pearson house. I belonged with Ezra.

"I'll have you, Ezra. Only I'm not sure what that means. Can I come with you?"

His head moved slowly. "No, Charlotte. I wish I could take you, but it's impossible. Besides, I want our love to honor God. If you can be patient, I'll come as often as I can. When I finish college, you'll be sixteen and we can marry."

My head spun with all that had happened in the last ten minutes. Words swirled around all bumping into each other. *I love you. Marry. Our love. Honor God.* I realized I had said little. Despite all that happened, I still felt shy. I placed my cheek against his so I wouldn't have to look at him when I said it. Then I whispered the words. "I love you too, Ezra." As I spoke, my boldness grew. It was true. I loved him. And he loved me. Joy as I'd never imagined soared through me, filling me to overflowing like I'd burst open.

He held me tight and I understood a little about the feelings that happened between a man and a woman. He must have felt it too because he stepped back, loosening his hold. "Honor God, Charlotte. That's the only way."

28

Keeping my news to myself was the hardest secret of my life, except maybe the note I wrote to Sheriff Beltzhoover. It hurt that I was planning to be married in two years and couldn't tell my own mother. It was bursting to come out of me, but I feared she'd be upset and wouldn't let me go to the village anymore. If that happened, I'd be forced to leave home and move there. Ezra said I could move in with Aunt Imani if I ever needed to. I kept one foot in each of my worlds, but something had changed in the past year. I needed the village more than I needed Ma.

I could barely sleep for thinking about Ezra. What really happened between a man and a woman? Ma told me about changes in my body, but nothing beyond that. I couldn't ask her for a library book to explain those things. That would bring too many questions. I imagined him lying beside me, touching me in places no one ever had. My hand caressed my own body, thinking of it. Then I remembered my scars. I had no looking glass in my bedroom, but the few times I sneaked and used the Pearson's bathroom, I could turn and see scars lacing my back and my buttocks. Maybe Ezra had scars too.

Ezra. He'd be my husband. He'd be educated. Our marriage would honor God. We'd have children and no one would ever beat them. They'd never know the sting of a whip on bare skin. I slid from the bed to my knees to give thanks. Reverend Platt said the Bible tells us every knee will bow. He said to make sure we bow on this side of eternity.

~~*~~

A box remained in the attic with treasures that I kept over the years. My two favorite dolls, their toy tea set, beloved books, and numerous paintings. I couldn't exactly say why I stashed them in the box, except somewhere over the course of years, in the back of my mind I knew I'd eventually leave this house. I wanted to protect a few treasured items. My mind began to think about setting up my own home, mine and Ezra's. It would never be as fancy as this, and may in fact, be in Coltrane Village, but it would be ours.

Going back downstairs, I stopped at the quilt thrown over the back of a wing chair. My fingers traced the mosaic pattern, examining each fine stitch. Tiny hexagons provided the fill inside a larger hexagon. The repeated pattern gave it the mosaic name. I recognized some of the fabric from old dresses and shirts the family wore. I searched for something that had been mine, but almost gave up the search. Then I found one. A patterned dress I wore when I was about six or seven years old. But that fabric had been extra, left over from Ma's new dress. The quilt fabric wasn't mine after all.

"Charlotte, you look like you're lost in dreamland."

I hadn't heard Ma enter the room. "Sorry ma'am. I was wondering, do you think I could try making a quilt?"

Ma picked up a corner and admired it with me. "Well, I made that block quilt a while back, so I'm not sure we have fabric saved up for another one yet. People aren't sharing scraps like they used to."

"I thought I'd like to try one."

"Next one I make, we'll do it together. Okay?"

"Okay." But that wasn't what I wanted. The quilt would still belong to the Pearsons.

A slamming door startled us both. "Davina?" Mr. Pearson hollered.

Ma scurried to the kitchen. "I'm here, James. What's wrong?"

"Have you heard anything about the Negro school over by the textile mill?"

"No, dear. But that school's been there a long time. It started up right after the ..."

His booming voice interrupted her. "I know when it started. I don't have to be reminded of that blasted amendment. It started with a barely literate black trying to teach what they didn't know. Now they've gone and hired a white woman to teach. I want to know who's behind it. And who's paying her. No one in that shanty town has money to pay. If I find out the church is helping, there's gonna be trouble."

Ezra. He was the one teaching it. Now that he's leaving, they had to replace him. But a white woman? How did that happen? Ezra took no money for teaching, as long as he could fit it in around his hours at the textile mill.

Ma tried to calm Mr. Pearson down. "I'm certain the church is not involved in this. And what does it matter who the teacher is?"

His fist slammed the table. "Are you daft, woman? Blacks teaching blacks ain't going nowhere. They were fooling themselves. A white woman could change everything. The last thing we need is blacks who can read, thinking they're qualified to vote."

A boldness filled me, even if it meant the whip. I lifted a defiant chin. "We already have the vote. You don't have to know how to read to know what's going on out there."

It would have been better if he'd slammed a fist or hollered. Instead, his eyes became thin slits and he walked toward me, his shoulders hunched up with fists readied at the end of his flexed arms. I stood steady although my insides were shaking like a wet dog.

Ma jumped between us. "No, James." She called over her shoulder. "Charlotte, go to your room." I stayed as they stared each other down. Ma called again, in her hollering voice. "I said go."

I scurried to my room, but it offered no safety. It was a mere few feet away with no lock, not that a lock could stop an angry Mr. Pearson. I closed the door as I heard the crack, and Ma's cry. It was the first time I knew of him hitting her.

"Don't you ever defy me again, woman. I'll not have that piece of black trash challenge me in my own home."

"That piece of black trash, as you call her, is my daughter."

Another crack sounded. "You think I don't know that? I look at her every day and remember what that that black man did to you. You're soiled goods. And that white teacher, she may find herself hanging at the end of a noose."

The kitchen door slammed and then I heard him taking a horse from the barn. When the clopping sounded its distance, I opened my door a crack. Ma was on the floor where she must have fallen. I went to her as she had done for me so many times over the years after my beatings. I held her head against my chest and stroked her silky hair. "I'm sorry, Ma. I'm sorry for everything." My tears landed on her hair. I knew what I had to do.

In less than twenty-four hours, I had experienced my greatest joy and my deepest sorrow. There would be no quilt. No treasure box. No telling Ma about my Ezra. I couldn't wait until night. Mr. Pearson might return to give me the beating that Ma took for me. Only I'd get far worse. I helped Ma off the floor and upstairs to her bedroom. I kissed her cheek and told her to rest. Then I went to Zachary's room and took his haversack. I hated stealing it, but had nothing of my own. I stuffed my few garments into it and looked around at what had been my home. Yet it never truly was. I would have liked to trek upstairs and say goodbye to my attic, but I was afraid to tarry. I hoped Ma would forgive me, but I took

206

the bowl of apples on the table and dumped them into the haversack. I wouldn't take their belongings, but I knew people in the village had too little to eat. I'd be an added burden until I could get a job.

Sliding the haversack over my shoulder, I made the familiar trip to Coltrane Village, my new home.

29

When I turned the bend that brought the main area of camp into view, I saw clothes drying on a clotheslines and children playing in the street. Otherwise, it was strangely quiet. I'd never been to the village on a weekday. I wouldn't find Ezra at home. He'd be at the textile mill working for a fraction of what white men were paid.

The children knew me and ran down the road, surrounding me as I walked. I scooped up two-year-old Jaycee while older children skipped around me, asking why I was here when it wasn't a Sunday.

Aunt Imani stood outside her home, hands on hips. Would she really take me in? One thing was certain; I couldn't go back. Her typically jolly face looked stern. I lowered Jaycee to the ground and scooted her in the direction of the others. When I drew closer, Aunt Imani's face softened. What I thought had been sternness, had really been concern. She extended an open arm. "You needing help, child?" Her voice made me think of Ezra's hand stroking my cheek—like velvet. I'd only ever felt velvet once, but it's a feel you never forget.

Tears welled up and I nodded. She wrapped an arm around me. "You come to the right place." She led me inside the rough little building. We stood in one room with a partition separating a sleeping area. Ladder steps led to a loft suspended by vertical wood planks thick enough to hold the weight of the floorboards above. No railing protected a person from falling. A table and two chairs were the only furniture. Boxes were scattered here and there. Two in the loft, two near the table, and one visible in the partitioned-off sleeping area.

"Sit down, child." Aunt Imani led me to a chair. "Do you want to tell me about it?"

I could never betray Ma. Her secret must never be spoken. Mr. Pearson had called her *soiled goods.* Many white people would think that. They'd never look at her with respect again. I shouldn't have come. There was no room for another person. This community had enough troubles of their own. I could have handled the beating. "I'm sorry. I didn't know where to go."

"I told you, you come to the right place."

"You don't have space for me to stay here. I can't add to your burden."

"There's always space for one more. And you couldn't never be a burden. My Ezra's mighty smitten with you."

"Ma'am, who's taking over teaching when Ezra leaves?"

"You remember Ezra told you the good Reverend found him a sponsor? Mr. and Mrs. Tomlinson. They's some Christian white folk who don't like what their kind done to our kind. They think highly of education. They's helping Ezra go to college, and the wife's gonna take over teaching. The children go two days a week, and some grownups go one evening."

"I have reason to believe that she's in danger if she does that. Some whites don't like it and they're going to try to stop her."

Aunt Imani kept nodding her head. The slow, repetitive movement indicated she was thinking things through. "I reckon she thought of that possibility before she offered. Tonight's the first time she'll be there, but Ezra will be with her. He wants to be there when she meets the grown-up men. Make sure they trust her. Trusting don't come easy for some folks."

Ezra's aunt didn't sound worried. But she didn't know Mr. Pearson. He'd stop at nothing short of murder to keep blacks subservient. I couldn't slip another note to the sheriff since I had no details. No plan with a time and a place. If the teacher wasn't a white woman, the town's men wouldn't be up in arms. What if I were the teacher? I could teach children and their parents to read and to do their sums. I wanted a place where I could make a difference in this world. I poured over newspapers, reading accomplishments of blacks, promising myself I'd be one of them. Teaching was a profession that touched generations to come. I'd talk with Ezra tonight.

A bed of sorts had been crafted from two worn but fluffy blankets. "These here are a blessing right from the Lord. A white woman I used to clean house for was tossing them out. I told her I'd be right happy to have them. Been holding on to them knowing the day would come when I had a need."

A second sleeping area was fashioned in a corner of the main room, directly under the loft. Aunt Imani finished spreading the blankets and managed to find a pillow made from an old canvas bag. It wasn't like the feather pillows at the Pearson's home, but it was better than nothing. "When Ezra leaves, the loft will be yours."

"Thank you, …" My hesitation let her know that I wasn't sure what to call her.

She finished my words for me. "Aunt Imani."

A bright spot in a brutal day. *Aunt* gave me a feeling of belonging. "Thank you, Aunt Imani." The aunts I had in Valdosta weren't really my aunts, like Mr. Pearson wasn't really my Pa.

A few hours later, Ezra opened the door. He stopped dead in his steps when he saw me. When he got over the shock, he ran toward me. "Charlotte, is something wrong?"

I told him what I'd told his aunt. It was the truth, but not the whole truth.

"Mr. Pearson was in an uproar about a white woman teaching at the Negro school. I know I shouldn't have talked back, but he made me so mad I couldn't hold my tongue. He came after me and Mrs. Pearson stepped between us. She must've thought she'd calm him, but he was too enraged. His fists were showing and I know he'd have beat me good. I've had the whip before, but I've never had his fists. He slammed the door and left. Mrs. Pearson saved me from that beating, but I knew I'd have it when he came home. I figured it was time to leave."

I wished he'd put his arms around me again, but I knew he wouldn't with Aunt Imani sitting there. "Charlotte, you never told me he used a whip on you. You should have come here sooner."

"Ezra, I'm frightened for that teacher. Mr. Pearson's got friends from town who think like him. He said she may find herself hanging at the end of a noose."

He lowered himself to sit on a wood crate since both of the chairs were being used. His deep brown eyes staring at nothing. I saw creases form into folds on his forehead as he looked for an answer. "I'll tell her tonight. It might be best if we close the school until we can find a black teacher."

"How about me? I can teach them."

"No." His answer came quickly and laced with anger. "I don't want him knowing where you are."

"But he would only know that we found a black teacher. And that would be alright with him. He wouldn't bother to ask who it was."

"I'm not taking that chance with you. Besides, you're fourteen."

I squared my shoulders and gave him the same defiant chin that got me in trouble. "I may be a child to you, but I've read the works of William Shakespeare and selections from Paradise Lost. I think I can teach folks to read."

He reached for my hand and wrapped it inside of his larger one. "I'm sorry, Charlotte. I know you're able. I just … I can't let anything happen to you."

Aunt Imani laid her hand on my shoulder. "He's right, Charlotte. You need to let the situation with your old employer calm down. Right now, we don't know how he'll act when he figures out you're gone. Besides, there's plenty to do around here."

I knew my leaving would be welcome news to Mr. Pearson. Only Ma would grieve. I had to listen to their advice. I needed shelter and wanted to please Ezra. "Okay, for now. But it's something I'd like to do someday. I want to make a difference."

Ezra squeezed my hand. "You will, Charlotte. I know you will."

Aunt Imani had a dinner of cornbread and collard greens. The Pearsons never ate a meatless meal but I suspected it was common throughout the village. I pulled out my apples and watched the delight on Aunt Imani's face. "I've been doing the cooking and cleaning for a few years now. I'll help in any way I can till I get a job. I'm thinking I can get a housemaid position somewhere else."

Ezra answered between bites of the juicy apple. "Might be hard if word gets around that you left the Pearsons. You don't know what stories he might have spread around."

There was truth in those words, but I had to find work. Ezra had already told me he worried how his aunt would manage when he left. He knew the community would help, but it was still a concern. After we cleaned up, Ezra motioned for me to meet him outside. Once out the door, he said, "Let's go for a walk."

He claimed my hand and we walked side-by-side down the road leading toward town. "Where are we going?"

"Nowhere. We'll turn in a few minutes. I have to leave for the school but I wanted a few minutes to talk first."

"Are you upset that I came?"

He freed my hand and wrapped his arm around my shoulder, drawing me closer. "No, Charlotte. I'm upset that you didn't come sooner. I didn't know you were being mistreated."

"It wasn't really like that. It's been a while since Mr. Pearson used the whip on me."

"I want you to think about something. Instead of looking for work in town, how about the textile mill? That way, you wouldn't have to worry about what the Pearsons are saying, and you wouldn't run into them."

"You really think the mill would hire me?" I knew I'd miss town. Miss shopping at the market and talking with Hiram. I'd miss Ma something terrible, but I couldn't say that.

"I do. And other folks work there, so you'd have safety getting there and home together. Why don't I take you tomorrow and you can talk with my boss? I know they need help."

"Okay, Ezra, but I want to go into town sometimes. Maybe when I get some wages, I can go to the market."

We had turned a bend and the village was out of view. Ezra pulled me into his arms and kissed me. "I can't stand to think of anything happening to you. All I can think about is our life together when you'll be my wife. I love you, Charlotte." He buried his head against my neck, his breath pulsing against my skin. My heart beat strong against his, swelling with love. We stood like that until we both knew it was time for him to leave.

"Ezra, does Aunt Imani know? Does she know we've talked about marriage?"

"No, but she knows I'm crazy about you. We'll tell her soon. There's no rush since it's two years away. Will you promise me something?"

I had already promised I'd wait faithfully for him. "What's that?"

"Promise me you'll take care of her. She has no one but me. And now she has you."

"I promise. I love you, so she's my family now too."

~~*~~

I laid on my make-shift bed with a lantern lit beside me, reading the story of Ruth and Naomi. Ruth took care of her mother-in-law, like I planned to take care of Aunt Imani. *Your people will be my people, and your God will be my God.* It kept me from missing Ma too much. Yet I did wonder what she thought when she found me gone. When she realized I wasn't coming back.

I heard the door open and saw Ezra in the dimly lit room. Aunt Imani called from behind her partition. "That you, Ezra?"

I came to a sitting position on my blankets, and he leaned down and kissed my forehead. "It's me, Aunt Imani."

She stepped around the divider. "Did you tell Mrs. Tomlinson about the threat?"

He dropped into a chair at the table and reached in his pocket. "I didn't have to. Some trouble-makers told her with this." He held a paper that was crumbled into a wad. "It was taped to a rock and came flying through the window, shattering glass everywhere."

"Read it," his aunt said.

Ezra smoothed it against the table as I carried the lantern closer. The flicker of the flame cast an eerie shadow on the wrinkled page. *If you know what's good for you, you'll leave that school to the blackies. No respectable white lady should be there. If you stay, someone's going to get hurt.*

Aunt Imani shook her head. "Well, at least they warned her without anyone getting hurt. So, do we have to close the school?"

214

Ezra looked older than when he left a few hours ago. "No. Mrs. Tomlinson said she won't be bullied. She said she's here to stay."

I gasped. "Oh Ezra, she can't do that. I know these men mean business. You must convince her to stop."

"She's determined, Charlotte. Who am I to tell her what she can and cannot do?"

Dread filled me up until my chest hurt and pulling in a breath was hard. "I know Mr. Pearson. Someone's going to get hurt."

30
Annie

Annie swallowed the last of her chamomile tea before she heard the commotion from inside the house. The night nurse yelling for her to come in. To call 911. She bolted into the house to find the nurse in motion at Lillian's bedside checking her pulse. Her grandmother's pallor was pasty gray.

Annie's adrenaline soared, propelling her into action. Her phone! Where was it? She saw the nurse's cell and grabbed it, thankful it had no password protection. She reached the dispatcher and shouted for them to hurry.

The ambulance siren screamed its way up Main Street, stopping in front. Two EMT's sprinted up the sidewalk, pushing a gurney. Annie held the door open and motioned toward Lillian's bedroom. She watched from the doorway with hands pressed against her mouth. They didn't hurry to transfer Lillian to the gurney. Instead, they checked vitals, calling out medical terms in their staccato voices. One called 'Ventricular fib'. The other spat out 'Defib. Set at 120.' The machine emitted a low-pitch hum before a sharp signal sounded. They placed the electrodes on her bared skin and one held the paddles. One EMT yelled, "Clear the space." The night nurse scurried back away from the bed. They activated the shock and Lillian's body jolted in response. After checking vitals, they transferred her to the gurney.

Annie ran to find the shoes she'd left by the kitchen door. She held the front door for them and watched as they loaded the gurney into the ambulance. Annie didn't ask about riding with them. She simply climbed into the passenger seat of the ambulance. They sped off, the siren announcing their departure to all of Hickory Falls. The driver pushed a few buttons and connected with dispatch. "On our way to Greenville. Female. In her 80's. Myocardial infarction."

The EMT's wheeled Lillian through double doors that denied Annie entrance. She was relegated to providing information at the nurse's station. After that, her job was to wait. The ER had few patients at 6:30 in the morning. She intermittently sat and paced. She couldn't bear to lose her grandmother. She's all Annie had. Lillian was the one who loved her through childhood. The one who saw the person beyond behind the pageants, behind the model. She knew who Annie really was way back when Annie didn't. And her grandmother helped her find a way out. *Please, God. Don't take her from me.* After about thirty minutes, she went to the desk to ask for any updates, only to be met with a sympathetic smile and platitudes about calling her as soon as they had any information.

As Annie turned from the desk, she saw Seth hurrying toward her.

"Annie." He lifted his arms and she stepped into the comfort of them, feeling some of her tension melt away. "What are they telling you?"

Annie stepped back, as Seth loosened the circle of his arms, capturing her hands instead. "I think she had another heart attack. They had to shock her at the house." Tears streamed freely as she recalled the frightening scene, and Seth drew her close once again.

"Let's sit down. Can I get anything for you? Coffee? Something to eat?"

The thought of food made Annie queasy. "No, thank you."

217

They sat on a vinyl sofa. Seth kept his arm resting on her shoulder.

"Thanks for coming, but don't you have to open the store?"

"It can wait until Charlie comes in."

Annie attempted a stab of humor to lighten the moment. "I hope he doesn't fire you."

He chuckled. "I think my job's secure."

"I hope so. That's a pretty big house you're building."

"I sent Charlie a text, although texting still baffles him. If he doesn't open it, he'll hear the news and know where I am. That ambulance let most of Hickory Falls know they need to be on their knees. You can take comfort in knowing lots of folks are praying."

"Thank you. That reminds me, I should touch base with Nadine. The night nurse will have told her, but I'm sure she's wondering what's going on. I left in a hurry and don't have my phone."

Seth pulled his from its holder and handed it to her.

Nadine answered on the first ring. Annie recounted what had happened. "I don't have any further information, but wanted to touch base. My phone is at home, so when Seth leaves, I won't have one with me."

When they finished talking, she handed the phone back to Seth.

"Annie." His voice was soft, his eyes riveted on hers. "I'm not leaving you."

His eyes unarmed her, and she found herself wanting to be held in the cocoon of those strong arms, her cheek resting against his chest. Her pulse hammered as she inched toward him. He apparently read that slight movement on her part and wrapped her in an embrace.

He held her for a moment then loosened his hold.

"Thank you, Seth. For everything."

Another hour passed before a doctor came through the swinging doors. The nurse motioned him in their

218

direction. A blue surgical mask dangled from its elastic band, blending with his scrubs.

"You're Lillian Gentry's granddaughter?"

"Yes, how is she?" Tension returned, despite Seth's calming presence.

"She had a mild heart attack. While I say *mild,* that's significant with an already weakened heart. She was compromised before this attack. We were able to successfully place two stents which provided immediate relief to her collapsed arteries. I want to keep her here overnight. Then we'll make an assessment. She may need more care than home can provide."

A nursing home? She finally made it back to her beloved home in Hickory Falls. Annie didn't want that taken from her. But at least her grandmother was stable. "When can we see her?"

"Right now, if you're ready."

"Yes." Annie stood.

Seth remained seated. "I don't want to intrude. I can wait here, if you'd like."

She shook her head. "I'd rather have you with me."

They were escorted upstairs to cardiac ICU. Lillian's eyes were opened but her voice was barely above a whisper. "Annie. Seth."

Annie kissed her pale cheek. "Don't try to talk, Nana. Save your energy."

Seth reached for her hand, giving it a gentle squeeze. "Doctor said you did well, Miss Lillian."

Her weakened voice came out in a whisper. "Thank you for taking care of my Annie."

His eyes traveled from Lillian to Annie and back again. "I'll always take care of Annie."

Annie's eyes pooled. At this moment, despite the circumstances, in spite of the ICU, she felt loved. Loved and blessed.

"Go home, Annie. I need to rest."

"No, Nana. I'm staying here. I'll be in the waiting room and come back in a while."

"No, child. Go home."

Annie looked between Lillian and Seth, wanting to do the right thing.

He shrugged. "Your call, Annie."

Lillian moved her head slightly. "Please. I'll rest better knowing you're not sitting out there worrying."

"Okay, Nana. Only because I want you to get better. Gain some strength so you can come home." She kissed the aged cheek again. "I'll come back later today."

Seth offered to get the truck from its parking space and pick her up, but she needed the walk. "How were you planning to get home if I hadn't come?"

"Ha, I gave no thought to that. I guess I'd have called an Uber."

"I hope you'd call me or Charlie first. I told you, neighbors help neighbors."

When she climbed up into the truck, Seth closed her door and walked around to the driver's side. He climbed in and reached to turn the key, but Annie's hand on his arm halted him.

"Seth, if it's not too late, I'd like to change my mind?"

He stopped his motion. "About going home?"

"No. About the dinner invitation." She watched his expression. "Saturday night?"

A slight smile played on his lips. "I think that can be arranged."

~~*~~

The hospital released Lillian to a rehab facility. The temporary move offered resources to build her strength and provide occupational therapy. Annie wanted to hire someone to do in-home therapy, but the doctor convinced her the facility couldn't be matched by in-home care. Lillian agreed. "I'll be home, child. Give me a few weeks to build myself up. And Annie, don't visit me every day. You have an art show coming up. Give it all you've got. I'm not bashful about making new friends. I'll be fine."

"Okay, Nana. I'm almost finished with the journals. Perhaps we can talk about them when you come home. I still have many questions."

She exhaled deeply. "Yes. It's long past time. We'll talk when I get home."

Annie picked up her handbag and started for the door when her grandmother called after her. "And Annie, about Seth—he's a good man. You know that, right?"

"Yes, Nana. I know that." *And I have a date with him on Saturday night. Twenty-four years old, and going on my first real date.*

~~*~~

Either Seth or Charlie checked in daily to ask about Lillian. Iris wanted to visit and Annie promised to take her one day the following week. Annie was reminded of her first week in Hickory Falls when everyone stopped to welcome her. Now, it seemed like everyone dropped by or called to ask about Lillian. Churches kept her on prayer lists, regardless of the denomination. *Neighbors help neighbors.* Annie didn't mind the interruptions.

Annie answered the ringing doorbell to find Charlie waiting. "Hi Charlie. Come on in."

"Oh, no thank you. I'm dropping something off for Miss Lillian. Thought she might get a kick out of seeing these pictures. I was doing a little reminiscing, and dug 'em up last night. Some of her and Patty. Some with her and your granddaddy along with me and Patty. Don't know how we ended up with so many copies, but she can keep 'em."

"Thanks, Charlie. Remember, this is temporary. We plan to bring her home in a few weeks, as soon as she gains a little strength."

"Oh, Lillian's got gumption. She'll be back."

"Thank you. She's blessed to have such good friends."

He gave a mock tip of a pretend hat. "Have a good evening." He limped a few steps and turned back, like he planned to share an afterthought. "Just bears saying, I ain't never seen Seth smitten like he is. I always knew it'd take one special girl."

With that, he clutched the railing, went down the few steps, and headed back to the hardware store. Annie closed the door and leaned against it. One special girl? And without her silver blonde hair and designer clothes.

Curling up on the sofa, she opened the envelope and leafed through each photo. She'd seen pictures of the time her dad was young, but these were earlier. Her grandparents had been teenagers. Charlie and his girlfriend, who was now his wife, were so young. He had hair and no limp. She looked at the teens, laughing and carefree, and realized the pictures were taken 60 to 70 years ago. Love that lasted a lifetime. It could happen. It happened for these four people. They made her believe.

Charlotte and Ezra were teenagers when they found love. Did theirs last a lifetime? Charlotte certainly deserved a little happiness.

A text message swooshed on her phone. Seth. I'LL PICK YOU UP AT 6:00 TOMORROW. WE HAVE 6:30 RESERVATIONS AT NANTUCKETS IN GREENVILLE. THANKS FOR SAYING YES.

31

All of her Dalton designer dresses remained in New York, a reminder that she needed to empty the penthouse apartment and put it on the market. She'd never live there again. Pictures from Nantucket's website gave Annie an idea what to expect. Nantucket's specialized in seafood, upscale yet she could wear dressy casual. In Manhattan, a dinner date may have required evening wear. Annie had grown comfortable in jeans and sneakers. Formal attire no longer held any appeal.

She chose a casual pencil skirt and a V-neck cashmere sweater in a pale green. It was a Dalton design but didn't have the appearance of extravagance. She loved its cloud-soft lightness. Annie slipped on a pair of heels and stepped before the mirror. She quickly kicked them off. The last thing she wanted was to look like she went out of her way to impress. She tried flats, but they were too mundane. Finally, Annie selected a low wedge heel. Comfortable. Understated.

It was crazy to feel nervous. This was Seth, the most down-to-earth man she'd ever known. The easiest to talk with. The kindest spirit. A man unimpressed with things like sweaters and shoes. Waterfalls impressed him. Waterfalls and works of art.

The doorbell announced Seth's arrival. Annie grabbed her handbag, a small cross-body beaded bag with a gold chain. She opened the door while slipping the chain over her shoulder. For once, Seth didn't wear his royal blue hardware store shirt. Instead, he sported an open collar hunter green dress shirt. Casual but dressy and a compliment to Annie's pale green sweater. She looked for his truck, but didn't see it.

"Where's your truck?"

He gave no answer except his slight smile as he led her down the steps. They approached a vintage antique thunderbird. Pale blue with a white convertible top. Annie stopped in her tracks. "What! This is yours?"

He dangled the keys before her. "Did you think I stole it?"

"Of course not. I … I never saw it."

"I like the truck for day-to-day travel." He opened the passenger door and held it for her.

"Where do you keep this?" Annie slid onto the white leather seat, running her hand over its softness.

"Bucky's Garage. I rent a stall from him."

And to think she worried about impressing. Seth had pulled out all the stops. He looked pretty pleased with himself, much like Selah looked when she showed off those four steps. Annie began to ease into the softness of the leather until she glanced across the street. Simone stared at them through the front window of The Coffee Grinder.

"Uh no. Did you see …"

"I saw." He reached and squeezed her hand. "Shake it off, Annie."

They parked downtown and walked to Nantucket's. Annie had only been to Greenville to an attorney's office when she moved here, and then to the hospital when her grandmother was sick.

"I haven't seen downtown Greenville. It's so quaint. Look at the statues." She began reading the historic placard at the base of a Joel Poinsett statue.

"We can walk around after dinner. Have you seen the Liberty Bridge?"

"No. Where's that?"

He pointed. "Almost directly across from us. That's Falls Park. The Liberty Bridge is a suspension foot bridge over the falls."

"A waterfall? Right here."

"Not like Crown Peak. You'll see." He opened the door to Nantucket's where their reservation waited. They were seated and given menus. Seth pushed his aside unopened. "I already know I'm getting the low country shrimp and grits, but I hear their sea bass is wonderful."

"I still haven't developed a taste for grits. I think I'll get the sea scallops."

"Okay, but you have to try my grits. I believe you'll change your mind."

Annie scrunched her nose. "Grits are so … so gritty."

"When I was in college, I learned to make every possible variety of grits. Cheesy grits, buttered grits, garlic grits. It stretched the food money to the end of the month."

All Annie heard was the word *college.* She was becoming aware of the many erroneous assumptions she'd made about Seth. "Where did you go to college?"

"Furman. Right here in Greenville. My grandfather paid for me to attend, but wanted me close to home. My choices were Furman, Anderson, or Clemson."

"What did you study?" And why was he working in a hardware store?

"Business. I always knew I wanted to be a small business owner. When my grandfather died, he left me a little money. I bought the hardware store and the property behind it. I had dreams of building a franchise." He stretched his hand like a banner. "Seth Walker Hardware spread all across the south. But once I bought Hickory Falls Hardware, I realized it was enough. I didn't need to be immortalized through accomplishments. Life's not a competition."

Annie's mouth still gaped open bringing Seth a chuckle. "I know you thought Charlie owned it and I worked for him."

"I'm sorry. Obviously, a false assumption. But you let me think that. You could have corrected me."

"I thought about it, but it sounded boastful. Besides, Charlie's been there longer than I have. He about runs that place."

"Charlie was there when you bought it? Charlie and Useless?"

"Yes to Charlie. Useless came with me."

"He's yours? I thought he belonged to Charlie. I could see him naming a dog Useless."

"He's mine. His name's Duke, but when he proved not to be a watchdog, my mother called him Useless. It kind'a stuck. He lived upstairs with me, but he can't make the steps anymore. I'll be glad to move him up to the new house. He always slept on the floor beside my bed."

"I need to stop making assumptions."

"I'm sorry I didn't tell you. Honesty matters, especially in relationships. I shouldn't have misled you."

"No, you shouldn't have." She thought about reminding him they were friends. They weren't truly in a relationship.

"Alright. Full disclosure. The painters at your house? They work for me. I run a painting crew and a landscaping crew. It's a good compliment to the hardware business. People come in wanting to know if we do the work as well as selling the product. About two years ago, I decided to add the crews. When I can't keep them busy, I sub them out to the competition in north Greenville."

Seth was full of surprises tonight.

They talked through dinner, mostly about Hickory Falls. When they finished eating, Seth moved his dish aside. "Enough about me. Tell me about Annie Gentry, the amazing artist."

Annie's eyes darted back and forth, looking for a restroom. She wanted no part of a conversation about her.

Instead she forced a laugh. "We'll see how amazing after the art show. It's a week away."

"Where are you displaying the art? Do you need any help?"

Maybe she had effectively dodged any personal questions. "Our space isn't ideal, but I'm hoping the grace of the vintage house will make up for that. It will all be displayed in the living room and dining room. We will minimize the furnishings by moving out anything small enough and eliminating any clutter. We'll use the wall space, floor easels, and table top easels."

"That sounds like something I can help with. When will you start moving things?"

"Wednesday, if not sooner. With Nana gone and no visiting nurse, it's only me. I won't mind the disruption."

"I'll set aside time Wednesday morning."

Annie leaned in playfully. "At least I won't have to worry about you being fired."

Seth twined his fingers through hers. "Sorry about misleading you. I really do value honesty. It's core to a person's character."

The playfulness fled and her chest tightened. She had to tell him. If Annie wanted what her grandparents had, it couldn't be based on deception. He'd have to know about Miriam. He'd have to know about two years of sexual abuse. But not yet. She needed to see if this budding relationship had roots.

After dinner, they stepped outside into the coolness of the October evening. "You up to walking?"

"Yes. I'd like to see the waterfall."

"Remember, it's not Crown Peak Falls."

Seth reached for her hand. They crossed Main Street and entered Falls Park. The Reedy River flowed through town. Nothing like the Hudson in New York, the Reedy was scenic, more like a stream. They walked hand-in-hand onto the pedestrian bridge and stopped in the center to view the waterfall. Water cascaded over a rocky precipice about twenty feet high. In places the flow was merely a trickle, while other rocks carried a sheet of flowing water.

Seth pointed to people climbing on the rocks below. "I've done that a time or two myself. The water's pretty gentle unless there's been a storm. The Reedy's really a tributary of the Saluda River."

"I love this, and the bridge. I want to paint it."

"I thought you might. It's a popular site for artists. We'll have to come back and snap some pictures when dusk's not settling in."

They left Falls Park and ambled through town looking in store windows.

"Now I'm going to show you something, but it's a little teaser for another day. Do you know about Mice on Main?"

"No, but I'm not a fan of mice."

"Tap into your artistic side. These are bronze mice, not furry ones. Look over there."

He pointed and Annie saw the little bronze mouse."

"Oh, a mouse with his own little statue."

"And he's not alone. You can go online and download the clues. There are nine of them hidden around town."

"How fun."

"Next time we come to Greenville I'll print out the clues. But before that, I'd like to take you to Chimney Rock. Do you enjoy a little hike?"

"I don't know. I've only ever hiked with you to Crown Peak Falls."

"That's okay. Hiking up can be strenuous. We can ride up and walk down. The elevator up is built right into the mountain. You'll want your camera. The view spans 75 miles. It steals your breath."

Annie couldn't remember having a nicer day. Seth had plans beyond this dinner date. That much was clear.

When they returned home, Seth walked Annie to the door. She braced herself, not sure if he would kiss her. The thought terrified her. What if his kiss repulsed her? If she'd squeeze her eyes closed waiting for it to end? Or would it be different with a man like Seth? He encircled her hand, gave it a squeeze, and said goodnight. She wouldn't find her answer.

32

Lillian's stay at the rehab facility helped with space for the art show. Darlene's husband, Bobby came to help. One look and Annie pegged him to be about eighteen. Long lanky legs and rail thin. Bobby and Seth moved all but the sofa from the living room. They squeezed excess furniture into Lillian's bedroom. The extra space accommodated the easels they'd rented along with the display cloths and lighting. Annie managed to achieve a perfect balance of the house's charm and a professional art display. Spacing allowed each original piece to be lighted and viewed.

When Iris heard they planned to serve refreshments, she wanted to bring a double fudge chocolate cake. It took effort for Annie to persuade her otherwise.

"Thank you, Iris, but we only want light refreshments. Finger foods. I've ordered a cheese and cracker plate and some petit fours."

She pouted a little before relenting. "Well I hope you ain't expecting some big strapping men. I seen those little cakes. Ain't nothing but one bite."

"We want them to focus on the art, not the food."

Everything was ready Thursday evening for the three-day event. Darlene stepped outside. Before her husband joined her, he called to Annie. "I'm fixing to leave, but I wanted to say thanks for all you've done for Darlene. She's pretty excited about this."

"You're very welcome. I enjoy our time together."

"Hope she calms down before tomorrow. She's nervous as a caged raccoon."

Annie laughed. "She'll be fine."

She closed the door behind him, leaving only Annie and Seth.

"Looks great, Annie. I'll plan on helping you move furniture back. Sunday night or Monday morning?"

"Monday if that doesn't interfere with work."

He looped his arms loosely around her waist. "Monday it is. Two questions and I'll leave you to get some rest. First, how about I take Tuesday off and we ride up to Chimney Rock?"

Annie wasn't sure what to do with her hands. The only logical solution was to place them on his shoulders. She did so but kept them loose. This wasn't like the hospital when she needed comfort from her distress. "I think that will work. It looks like my grandmother will be at least another week. Next question?"

"Will you consider a pre-sale?"

"What do you mean? Pre-sales are typically for a selective group of patrons. It's a little late for that."

He shook his head. "Not a group. Just me. I want to buy Tranquility."

The painting already wore its price tag on the signature card, attached to the lower right corner. She had listed it at $750. "Oh, Seth. I'd love to give you one of the prints. I have one printed on canvas."

"Thanks for the offer but I think I'll go for the real deal. I can picture it hanging over my new fireplace. If you don't want to do a pre-sale, I'll be here tomorrow when you open your doors."

She couldn't accept that much money from him. "If you're determined to have the original ..."

"I am," he interjected.

"I'll reduce the price."

"Nope. It's worth every cent."

"Seth, I can't take that from you. You're always over here helping with something, and you won't take my money."

"That's different."

"How?"

"Friendship doesn't have a price. Works of art do."

Annie had no response. She knew him well enough to know he'd win this argument. As they stood entwined, looking at each other, she again had the feeling he planned to kiss her. Instead, the corners of his mouth inched into the start of a smile. "Besides, helping with wallpaper and painting gave me a chance to spend time with you."

He dropped his hands and stepped back. "How about I leave it here until Monday with a sold sign on it? It's a good one for you to show off." He pulled a folded check from his pocket. He had already written it for $750.

~~*~~

The three-day event began at 4:00 on Friday afternoon and would end at 6:00 pm Sunday. Darlene's mother and sister-in-law volunteered to help. They provided extra hands to package final sales and keep refreshments filled, allowing Annie and Darlene to circulate and discuss the artworks. Name tags identified them as the artists.

Friday proved to be moderately successful, but mostly with prints. The first original, other than Tranquility, sold on Saturday—The Gardener's Hands. Darlene barely restrained herself from jumping up and down, but managed to handle the sale first. Annie could tell she was about to explode with excitement and motioned her to the kitchen, letting her mother wrap the painting in brown paper.

"I can't believe it! $700 for one painting. And the prints that sold last night. I have over a thousand dollars."

The money was inconsequential to Annie. Above all, she wanted Darlene to see some reward. A future of art sales would be life-changing for her little family.

Darlene's mother poked her head in the doorway. "Seth Walker's here, asking if y'all need anything, and there's a man out here asking for Annie."

Annie put on her brightest smile and walked through the dining room. Seth stood talking with a man whose back faced her. She immediately saw the wide stripes at the cuff of a dark sport coat, marking it as a uniform. A pilot's uniform.

Seth smiled at her approach, but quickly altered his expression. Annie's rigid body posture was unmistakable. She forced a calm demeanor for the sake of the setting, but her chest pounded with indignation. How dare he come to her art showing. He had to know he wasn't welcome.

Annie hadn't seen her father in over two years. His hair had grayed and his paunch had rounded. But the eyes were the same. Beady, sneaky eyes. They sent prickles down her spine.

"Why are you here?" She kept her voice to a whisper, but crossed her arms over chest.

Seth looked on, wide-eyed. She should temper her reaction. It would require too many explanations later. Yet her anger was too great.

"I had to hear from my mother that she had another heart attack. Did you not think to call me?"

"No, I didn't. And I told you not to come here."

"She called me and asked me to come. She wanted you to have family support for your showing."

"Alright. You came, and now you can go."

Annie turned and began to walk away. Her father clutched her shoulder. "Wait."

His touch brought a cold, white fury. She swung free from his hand, her eyes blazoned with rage. He held hands up, palms forward. "Okay. I'm going."

Kurt Gentry walked out the front door, but Seth stood statue still, staring at her. "Annie?" That one whispered word held a world of questions.

Her gaze ping-ponged between the door and Seth, then around the room where a few possible customers browsed. "Not now, Seth."

His dazed expression remained. "Are you okay?"

She forced a smile that may have appeared as more of a grimace. "I'm fine."

~~*~~

By the end of the art show on Sunday, Annie had sold three originals and Darlene had sold two. Many prints had been purchased. Most of Hickory Falls residents came, fueled by curiosity. A few bought prints, but most left empty-handed, except for the petit fours.

"Oh, Annie. You were right about the prints. I made as much in prints as I would have with one more original. I'm ecstatic. And exhausted."

"So am I. Overall, I'd say it was a success."

"Definitely. Bobby's already urging me to keep painting and plan the next show. He's so psyched he'll be hotter than a chili pepper tonight."

That was more information than Annie wanted. "I'm too tired to think about the next show. Let's keep painting and talk about that someday. We'll need to space them apart."

They both scanned the room, still filled with artwork and easels. "Tomorrow, Darlene. We're both too tired tonight. Seth's coming to help."

"Bobby won't be around. He'll be working. I'll come, but may have Selah with me."

"Really, don't worry about it. There's nothing that Seth and I can't handle."

Darlene left and Annie opened her laptop. She hated to lose the sense of euphoria, but needed to check Dalton's website. She'd been monitoring daily for the release of the new catalog.

The tab stared at her. Summer Catalog. She clicked it open and saw familiar faces of models with whom she had worked. Interspersed were photos of Miriam. And Annie. Photos from the London shoot showed off her blonde hair and sapphire blue eyes. Photos from the LA shoot showed Annie—a sexy, sultry Annie, a brunette with a short sassy cut and suggestive beach poses.

Now that the catalog launched, would Peter use a renowned magazine to advertise, sullying Annie's name? Of course, he would. It carried great advertising.

Annie's head jerked upward at the sound of a knock on her kitchen door. Seth. She clicked off the website, then pushed the laptop aside. "It's open."

Seth sat across from her. "So, are you pleased with the response?"

Annie shifted her thoughts from the Dalton website back to the art show. "Yes. I'm especially happy for Darlene. She needed to believe in herself."

"Yep. It's got to be tough having a baby at seventeen."

So Annie was right. "I suspected she was still in her teens. Was she able to finish high school?"

"She graduated five months pregnant. She and Bobby married weeks after graduation."

"She loves that baby."

"Yep. They both do."

Annie motioned to the plate of petit fours, but Seth shook his head. "No, thanks. Can I ask you what's going on with you and your dad?"

Annie sighed. How much should she tell him? Isn't Seth the one who said to leave the past behind? "We don't get along well."

"That much was pretty clear." He waited for more, the silence becoming uncomfortable.

"I'm leaving the past behind like you suggested."

He tilted his head with a puzzled look. "Are you sure about that? Seems to me you're holding tight." His tone was soft, not critical or accusatory.

"No, I'm not holding the past. I'm keeping it at arm's length."

"Might be better to deal with it."

Annie's jaw clenched. She didn't want to have this discussion. "You have no idea what you're talking about. Some wrongs can't be made right."

Seth scratched his head. "I don't know about that, Annie. I'd hate to see bitter steal the sweet. Give it a foothold, it'll grow."

This topic needed to change. "Bobby's working tomorrow and Darlene has Selah. Think you and I can move things ourselves?"

His slack-eyed expression said he wasn't satisfied with where they'd left the topic of her father. "I'm sure we can handle the furniture." He stood to go.

Annie followed him to the door. "Seth, I know you want to help, but I can't talk about my father."

He cradled her hand. "My questions aren't about your father. They're about you. Bitterness can eat away at a person. All the while, it doesn't hurt the one they're angry with. Seems like it's a pretty useless emotion. When things take root, they grow."

Annie thought of the journal—of Reverend Platt telling Ezra that without forgiveness, he was still enslaved. Encouraging him to run into the arms of freedom. She had seen the wisdom of those words when it involved someone else. It was much more difficult when they pointed at her.

Seth still clasped her hand. His hazel eyes held no judgment. Seth, slow-moving country boy, a little red-neck, lover of nature and art, contented with life. Now Annie had to add *full of wisdom* to her growing list. "I'll try, Seth."

He leaned forward and dropped a kiss on her cheek. "Stay sweet, Annie."

33
Charlotte

I had viewed the heavy black smoke from a distance, but as Ezra and I approached the mill, its source appeared. A tall, cylinder-shaped tower spewed exhaust that overpowered the sky. White, puffy, cumulous clouds were marbled with soot, the sun hidden behind the veil. A massive brick building had two rows of windows along the front and the one side within my view. More windows than I could count. Even from a distance, I heard the clanging and groaning noises of machinery.

Offices adjoined the main building. Ezra knocked, then turned the doorknob. "Mr. Collins?"

"Come on in, boy."

"This young lady's looking for work. I hear you're needing to hire."

He waved us closer and we approached his desk. He eyed me top to bottom. "How old are you?"

"Fourteen, sir."

"Hours are long and the work's hard."

"Yes, sir. I can do it."

"Can you read?"

"Yes, sir."

"Good. No fraternizing with other employees. I tolerate no breech of modesty. No part of your arms or legs can be seen. I need ten-hour days, six days a week. Your wage will be $3.25 weekly. You start next Monday, first shift, so be here at 6:00 am. I'm busy now." He swept his hand over the paperwork on his desk. "Stop in here first thing Monday so I can get your information."

I knew the wage was lower than Ezra's $4.70 each week, and lower than a white man's $9.92 a week. But I had no argument. After all, I'm female and fourteen. "Yes, sir. Thank you."

Mr. Collins turned toward Ezra. "She'll work at the industrial loom. Show her where to go."

We left the office and walked toward the mill entrance. When Ezra opened the door, deafening noise met us, along with stifling heat. The machinery continued to clang in disharmony, despite the airless room. Ezra led me toward the left and stopped at a row filled with giant looms.

"These are the power looms. You'll probably start at the smaller ones." He pointed toward the next row. Each loom had a worker in front guiding the mechanical rods as taut threads gathered to form a solid sheet. A supervisor walked up and down the row to make sure every machine and every person continued to work.

A sick feeling gathered in my belly. I'd rather be cleaning and cooking for a Hickory Falls family, but I would honor the wishes of my future husband. I'd work in this oppressive mill for two years until I became his wife.

We left the factory and began the forty-minute walk home. The air grew cleaner as we put distance between us and the textile mill. "What will you study at the Payne Institute?" I wanted to think beyond next Monday at the mill.

"I've been thinking about that and I have to make a decision soon. I think I'd like to become a solicitor. I talked with Reverend Platt about the requirements. If I do two years at Payne Institute, he feels sure I'll be able to obtain an apprentice position. With the new amendments, there's going to be a great need for civil rights lawyers."

"I can't see many blacks affording lawyers."

Ezra laughed. "That's going to change. I'm certain of it. Things are already changing in the northern states. We have blacks in congress and black attorneys working in firms with whites. Hickory Falls isn't the best example of what's ahead for us. I'm excited about the future."

I caught his excitement, like we were on hold, waiting for the floodgates to open up good things. I had an image of Reverend Platt, his hand on Ezra's shoulder, saying, "The first hundred years are the hardest." Maybe we didn't have to wait a hundred years. Maybe good things were coming before we met eternity.

"Ezra, I'm so proud of you. And I'll be proud to be your wife." I gave a dreamy look up into his eyes. "Mrs. Ezra Williams. I'll finally have a real last name."

"And my future wife, will you want children?"

"Of course. And they'll be smart. They'll study things like science and history. They'll go to college and become lawyers like their daddy, or maybe doctors."

Ezra, my love, gathered me in his arms. "They'll be anything they want to be. And they'll be beautiful like their mama."

The moment was so lighthearted. I wanted to hold on to it forever. "Where will we live?"

"It depends on where I can work. But we won't live in an outcast community. We'll be respected neighbors in a real house."

"And I'll plant a garden. Fresh vegetables and lots of snap dragons."

"Oh Charlotte." He pulled me closer. "I can almost taste it."

My lips were close to his ear. I whispered into it. "My cup runneth over."

He finished the thought. "Surely goodness and mercy shall follow me all the days of my life."

I kissed his cheek. "And we will dwell in the house of the Lord forever."

We returned to Coltrane Village, as happy as I'd ever been in my life. I wouldn't think of the oppressive textile mill. I wouldn't think of poor Mrs. Tomlinson who'd placed herself in danger. I wouldn't think of evil men who plotted to harm her. I'd think of the future, bright and brimming with hope. Then I saw Aunt Imani by her front door and I knew something was wrong. Very wrong. Ezra must have seen it too, because he let go of my hand and sprinted toward her. I hurried, steps behind him.

"What's wrong, Auntie?"

"I wanted to catch you before we go inside. We have a visitor." She looked directly at me. "Mrs. Davina Pearson would like to see you. The only reason I gave ear to her request is because she stepped between you and her man to help you. But if you don't wish to see her, you two walk away and I'll get rid of her."

Ma's here. Right here in Coltrane Village, where I'd never seen a white person enter. That took a monumental decision for her to come here. I couldn't picture Ma walking up the trail with every eye on her. And now she sat in the one room rugged house, seeing my sleeping area and sitting in one of the only two chairs.

"I'd like to see her. Would it be possible for me to have some privacy?"

Ezra's eyes glowered and I knew he wished I'd send her away.

"Please?"

"I'll be right out here. You holler if you need me."

I squeezed his hand. "She'd never hurt me." I took a deep breath and went inside, where my two worlds collided. The first thing I saw was the deep purple bruise on Ma's jaw. She stood and I ran to her, thankful the front of the house had no window. "Ma." I wrapped my arms around her and she gathered me close.

"Come home, my precious. He won't hurt you. He's mighty sorrowful about this." She pointed toward her bruise.

"He never hit me before. We've talked and he agreed you're too old for the whip. He promised not to use it, and I've taken both of them from the house."

I couldn't picture that conversation. I didn't think Ma would lie, but perhaps exaggerated. Maybe she heard what she wanted to hear. Mr. Pearson didn't apologize. Ever. Besides, I made Ezra a promise and I wouldn't break it. It was my job to take care of Aunt Imani. "Ma, I can't come home. This is my home now."

Her eyes clouded in dismay. "Charlotte, look around. This isn't what I want for you."

"Ma, there's some things I haven't told you. I'm betrothed. I'll be getting married in two years when my Ezra finishes school. He's going to be a lawyer. We'll have a good life together. I have to stay here. I've made a promise and I won't break it. Ma, I love him so much."

Her face went blank. She knew me enough to know I meant what I said. I wouldn't break my promise.

"I want you to meet him. He doesn't know you're my ma. But he knows you were kind to me."

"Oh, Charlotte." She dropped her head into her hand and cried. "I wish things could be different. I wish I could plan a beautiful wedding and watch you become a wife." She sobbed and I wrapped an arm around her.

"I love you, Ma. I know you did your best."

She wiped her eyes and tried to smile. "I guess it's time for me to meet your young man. But one more thing—I want you to come to me anytime you have a need. If you need food or clothing or money. Anything. Okay?"

"Okay." But I knew I wouldn't. I would work at the factory where Ezra thought I'd be safer.

We stepped outside where Aunt Imani and Ezra waited. He wore a stony expression and I sent him a pleading look. I wanted Ma to see the goodness in him. We walked toward each other and when he was close, he spoke. "Mrs. Pearson, I'm Ezra Williams. Thank you for intervening on

Charlotte's behalf. I'm grateful that you protected her." I heard his intentional diction, designed to ensure her that an educated man spoke the words. He motioned toward her bruise. "I'm sorry you were injured."

He still wore a guarded look. No easy smile lit up his brown eyes. I moved from Ma's side to Ezra's. It was a simple move, but symbolic. I no longer belonged with her. I belonged with Ezra. His arm draped around my shoulder, showing her that we were one.

Ma began to speak and I heard the crack in her voice. "I'm … I'm quite fond of Charlotte. She knows she can come to me if she needs anything."

Ezra stiffened. "Thank you, ma'am, but that won't be necessary. I plan to take care of her, and when I'm away, this community takes care of each other."

We stood in our little circle filled with love and tension. There was little else to be said.

"I should be going. Thank you for seeing me, Charlotte." She turned toward Ezra. "Thank you for taking care of her."

The words were polite but I heard the emotion she held in check, the cry that wanted to break through her words. I wished I could hug her again, maybe walk part way with her, but I didn't. This had to happen. She had to let me go. I stood cloaked beneath Ezra's arm and watched her slouched form walk the path until she was out of my sight.

34

Time moved too quickly. Living in the same house as Ezra provided a glimpse of life with him, our dream for the future. Like we'd done on our walk home from the mill, we made plans. They were our dreams. Our flights of fancy. When Aunt Imani went to her sleeping space, Ezra would sit beside my blanket-bed and read to me. He still had The Key to Uncle Tom's Cabin and shared excerpts. He'd read various passages from the Psalms, his voice deep but smooth as satin. We talked about characters from books we'd both read. Being with Ezra was nothing like I saw with Ma and Mr. Pearson. It made me sad for my ma.

Ezra wanted me to paint, suggesting I go to art school once we married. I promised I'd start painting again when I had some wages to buy supplies.

After Sunday services, we talked with Aunt Imani and Reverend Platt about our decision to marry when Ezra finished school. We asked the Reverend to officiate.

"If the good Lord still gives me strength to travel, I'll be here. I'd be honored to bless your union together."

On Monday morning, Ezra and I walked to the textile mill for my first day at work, and one of his final few days. Tonight, he'd teach the adult class alongside Mrs. Tomlinson. He'd work in the mill until Thursday. Then on Sunday, following services, Ezra would leave with Reverend Platt to begin his two years at the Payne Institute. I could already feel the hurt of missing him.

When we reached the factory, the ominous black smoke belched from the chimney tower. I went inside to give Mr. Collins my information and Ezra went to the loading dock where huge bolts of finished fabric were loaded onto a train car. I wouldn't see him again until we finished work for the day.

~~*~~

Aunt Imani managed a rare treat for dinner. Jem and Tyrone had been fishing in the Saluda River and came home with a load of bass. They shared it around camp. She cooked it along with three ears of corn. I had no energy to help with dinner or clean up. She saw my fatigue and waved me away. The heat of the mill and standing all day with no break and too little water zapped my strength like I was a ninety-year old. And I'd need to do it again tomorrow. And the next day, and the next. Aunt Imani said my body would adjust, but it needed rest tonight.

Ezra had worked the same hours, yet was full of vigor. He loved teaching and hurried off to school while I nursed my aching feet. About an hour later, I had sprawled onto my blankets when I heard the commotion. Deborah came bursting through the door.

I sprang up from my reclined position. "What's wrong?"

"I came from town. I heard two men talking. I wasn't supposed to hear, but I had ducked into the underbrush to take care of my needs." She stopped to catch her breath, pulling in gasps of air. "They talked about the Klan meeting tonight. Meeting at the school. Said they need to stop the white teacher."

Ezra was there. And men from the village who were learning to read. "Did you tell the sheriff?" I was already pulling my shoes on.

She looked aghast. "Me? No sheriff's gonna listen to me."

"Deborah, you've got to run back. Find Sheriff Beltzhoover. He'll listen. Honest. He will." I ran past her but Aunt Imani grabbed my arm. "No, child. You're not going there. Leave this to the men. There's plenty here. Help me spread the word."

I'd help spread the word, but there was no way she'd keep me from going. Not when my Ezra was there. I ran from door to door calling. Some men grabbed their guns but they waited to gather into as big a group as possible. Safety in numbers, someone said.

When they were gathered, I figured there were about twelve men, and about half of them had firearms. I had waited long enough. I ran ahead, down the road that would lead to the school, the posse of townsmen behind me. Pain shot through my aching feet with every strike of the path. Only the burning in my chest slowed me down. I was halfway there when I heard footsteps—many of them. The thunderous sound wasn't from the posse behind me. They were coming toward me. Would white robes and hoods come around the next bend? No. That made no sense. They wouldn't come to the village. I moved forward despite the fear filling me up. The first face I saw was black. Mr. Jackson from the village. Then the others came into view. All of the adult learners were running back to camp. I searched the faces but didn't see Ezra. One of them grabbed me.

"No, missy. Turn around."

I scrambled out of his hold. "Where's Ezra?"

More hands reached me, pulling with more strength than I possessed. "You don't wanna go there, Charlotte."

"I have to find Ezra." With a kick that hit the target and a lunge that took all of my strength, I broke free and ran. Others followed. I didn't know if I heard the armed posse headed toward the school or the men who were fleeing from it. The school was near and I kept my feet in motion. A cacophony of clomping hoofbeats sounded. When I turned the final bend toward the school, I saw the white robes, the cowardly hoods hiding evil faces. Some had mounted their horses and others were in the process of doing so. They began to disperse into the woods. That's when I saw him.

Ezra dangled like a lifeless baby doll, his hands tied together behind his back. His head turned at an odd angle, separated from his body by a noose.

I screamed and fell to my knees. Then I lost consciousness.

~~*~~

I was told that the men carried me back to the village. I don't remember anything after seeing Ezra. I woke with Aunt Imani standing over me, weeping and trying to revive me. When I regained consciousness and remembered, a sob came out so loud and long, I barely managed the next breath. It came with a moan that I didn't recognize as my own voice. Aunt Imani held on to me and we cried, but couldn't cry out the hurt. It was too deep. Ezra. My love. My future. Gone.

Some village folks sat around us weeping openly. I recognized the man I had kicked. Together they told what happened.

"We was sitting there learning our sums and how to count out change. We heared the sound of horses approaching and Ezra looked outside. Them white hoods surrounded us. They hollered in that everyone should leave 'cepting for Mrs. Tomlinson and our own teacher. We would'a stayed to fight 'cepting we had no guns and there was too many of them white hoods."

Another man finished the story. "We tried to stop you from going in, missy. We knew it had come to no good. They let Mrs. Tomlinson go, but told her this was only the first. If she kept on teaching, they'd come back and another one of us would see the noose."

247

James Pearson. A sour taste rose from my stomach almost choking me. He was behind this. He wore a robe and hood that night. It might have been his voice giving the warning. His hands looping the noose over my sweet Ezra's neck. A hatred so strong surfaced inside me. He had to pay. I would avenge the life of my Ezra and the future James Pearson stole from me. This time, he would not get away with it.

35

Annie

Annie swiped away the tears that gathered in her eyes for Charlotte and Ezra. They didn't see the fulfillment of their dreams. No love for a lifetime like the teenaged Charlie and Patty, Lillian and Michael. No chance to make a difference in a broken world. At least not for Ezra.

Was it true that the sins of a father are visited on his offspring? Was Charlotte's life condemned from the beginning because of her father's evil act? If so, what hope did Annie have?

~~*~~

The magazine hit the newsstand without fanfare. Without any cover pictures of Annie. As Peter suggested, the cover alluded to the surprise inside. However, he didn't manage to have the name Miriam as an emblazoned headline, only a subheading that no one would notice without picking it up and intentionally reading the menu of items inside. Annie bought a copy at the checkout line of the Piggly Wiggly, surrounded by groceries so no one would take too much notice of her purchase.

She hid away in the privacy of her bedroom to assess the damage. Peter may not have gotten the headliner on the cover, but he managed to get the most damaging pictures inside. The bikini shot, the beach cover over a tan suit that gave a nude appearance, the off-the-shoulder top that exposed enhanced cleavage. The worst part of the two-page spread was in the script. "Known to the world as Miriam, the supermodel has returned to the name Ann Gentry." Annie slammed the cover closed and held the heels of her palm over her eyelids to stop the tears. Crying helped nothing. It was out of her hands.

~~*~~

Lillian completed her rehab and returned home. Twice Annie tried to talk about Charlotte, but her grandmother's energy had been depleted. Any mention of the journals seemed to tire her out. Weeks had passed since the art show. Annie's days were filled painting, taking care of Lillian, and spending time with Seth.

Life as a model had been busy enough to obscure the emptiness. Annie's time with Seth filled a nascent yearning, one that hid in dormancy for years. They hiked Chimney Rock, searched for the Mice on Main in Greenville, toured the Biltmore House in Asheville, and planned his new home. He wanted Annie's input on all aspects. She couldn't help but wonder what that said about the future. Did he see them together in this house? The foundation was laid and the builder began the framing. Estimated completion was six months, start to finish.

Their first real kiss came a week after the art show. Seth had kissed her cheek a few times when leaving. This time, he lingered on her cheek, then turned until their lips met. There was no repulsion. No nightmare memories of those days as a child. It was a tender act of love, so natural, so beautiful.

When they weren't together, Seth occupied Annie's thoughts. She frequently scanned the property behind the hardware store hoping for a glance. At night, she'd lay in bed thinking about the touch of his lips, remembering the warmth of his eyes staring into hers. Is this what it felt like to fall in love? She knew Seth felt it too. So often, he'd breathe her name, rich with emotion.

One evening, they stood by her back door under the light of a full moon. Seth drew her into the circle of his arms and whispered the words. "I love you, Annie."

Annie breathed in the wonder of those words. Words that bound them together, gave her life a purpose. A place where she belonged. She never imagined it really happening.

He loosened his hands and cupped her face. Warmth rose through her body when their lips met. Her flesh quivered when one kiss melted into another. When their lips finally parted and he rested his forehead on hers, Annie whispered, "I love you too."

When they reluctantly allowed the night to end, Annie closed the door, watching Seth trek across the lawn to his apartment above the hardware store. Unadulterated joy lasted only a moment. Her latent fear came creeping in to steal the moment. Dalton. The catalog. Her immense wealth. She had to tell Seth everything, including Kurt Gentry. He deserved the truth. She'd need to pick the right time. The right setting. It absolutely must be this week.

As Annie readied for bed, the journal on her nightstand stared at her. She reached for it but then remembered. *Ezra.* She quickly dropped it back to the wooden surface not wanting it to spoil her joy. She felt a kinship with Charlotte. Both experienced the joy of new love. An awakening of the senses. Hope for the future. Charlotte had no idea of its brevity.

~~*~~

Most mornings, Annie would start her day at The Coffee Grinder. She and Seth met up for coffee and to share the plans for the day. Annie crossed the street with a knot in her stomach. The discussion would not occur at the coffee shop, but she must set up a time. Seth's wide smile met her. Margie called out a greeting. "Morning, Annie."

When she had her coffee, Annie sat across from Seth. His smile hadn't diminished. Annie allowed the casual conversation to ease her into the question. "Are you free tonight? I thought maybe we could hike up the hill and see what's been done on the house."

"Well, I don't think much has changed since we looked two days ago. I have a meeting with the HFSBA."

Annie knew he met monthly with the Hickory Falls Small Business Association.

"You know you can go up anytime you want."

"I know. Mostly, I just wanted some time to talk."

"How about Wednesday evening? We can check out the progress then grab a bite to eat? Simone's or the crepe place?"

Wednesday. It had waited this long. What difference could two more days make?

~~*~~

Wednesday morning, as Annie crossed Main Street, she saw the signature red hair through the window. Simone. She and Seth sat at the front table. Seth's back faced the window but Simone saw her. Even through the glass, Annie noticed the smug jut of her chin, the brash tilt of her head. Annie couldn't imagine why. Everyone in Hickory Falls knew that she and Seth were dating. As her steps took her closer, Annie saw the reason. The magazine lay opened in front of Seth. Simone stood, gave a condescending pat to his shoulder, and strutted out the door. She threw a triumphant look in Annie's direction and sashayed down Main Street toward her restaurant.

Annie stopped short of the door, torn between the decision to run back home or go inside and face Seth. He hadn't yet seen her so she could flee unobserved. But there was no benefit to delaying the inevitable. Seth loved her. She'd make him understand. Moving one foot and then the other, Annie took tentative steps in the direction of the coffee shop door, her heart fluttering like hummingbird wings. She lowered herself into the chair across from Seth, reached her hand over the table, and the closed magazine.

His stony expression held a mixture of hurt, disappointment, and anger. She met that with a pleading look and breathed the words. "I can explain."

He shook his head slowly. Was he attempting to remove the images from his mind, or did his head shake in disbelief? "Some things are self-explanatory."

"Seth." Annie reached for his hand, but he withdrew it, moving out of her reach. "Seth, not everything in life is black or white. There *is* an explanation."

"A reason for lies? I don't think so."

"There are things I haven't told you, but I never lied."

His laugh was derisive. "It seems we have different definitions of the word *lie*. When you live in two different worlds, have two different names, and neglect to tell me, I call that a lie."

"*Lived*, Seth. Past tense. I told you I had baggage in my life and you said the past didn't matter."

Seth leaned forward, his voice a notch louder, anger winning over hurt. "Past?" He jabbed the magazine. "This is the current issue. These pictures were taken recently. Can you honestly tell me this wasn't in the last few months?"

"I was under contract. I had no choice."

"You had a choice to tell me or not tell me. Honesty's the issue here, Annie. Or do I call you Miriam?"

Hearing that name come from Seth sent a rush of adrenaline through her body, her pulse pounding. "No, you don't call me Miriam. I intended to tell you." Annie tried to soften her tone. "I'm sorry this came first, but Seth, not everybody's life can be like yours. Neat and tidy, wrapped up

with a big bow. Some people have junk in their lives."
Annie's chin trembled. "People make choices based on their
paradigm—what they think, feel, and know at the time. You
can't understand where I was, what took me to that world,
what brought me here."

"That's what hurts, Annie." He jabbed a finger, like
she'd hit the mark. "You never trusted me enough to share
anything with me. I've been upfront with you since day one.
I am who I am. And I've told you what matters to me.
Integrity. Character. Honesty. That's all I asked of you."

"Really? You let me believe you worked for Charlie."

His jaw fell open. "Big difference. And I wasn't
responsible for your assumptions."

Margie stepped into view and set coffee on the table
for Annie. "Skinny vanilla latte." Annie reached for her
wallet, but Margie shook her off. "On the house." She placed
one hand on Annie's shoulder, then other on Seth's and
leaned in to whisper. "I don't know what's going on here, but
I don't think either of you want to be today's entertainment.
Why don't you kiss and make up?"

Seth apologized. "Sorry, Margie." She walked back to
the counter and Seth pushed his chair back. "I have to open
the store." He spun around and left the coffee shop.

Annie watched Seth cross Main Street. She could see
him pull his keychain from a pocket and unlock the hardware
store. She followed his movements as he flipped the sign to
open and hit the switch that brought light to replace the
darkness. Normal movements, hiding the hurt she had
caused. She had to make him understand. She'd give him
time to stew, then she'd tell him everything.

Annie scooped up the magazine, took her coffee and
crossed the street. The November morning was comfortable
so she sat on the porch swing. She wasn't ready to talk with
her grandmother or the nurse. She wanted to be alone with
her thoughts.

Charlotte had lived in two worlds. When her mother came to the village to see her, those worlds collided. That's how Annie felt this morning. Her past, her present, and possibly her future just crashed together. She prayed that the damage wasn't irreparable.

The day passed and brought the evening. No word from Seth. Annie avoided The Coffee Grinder the following morning, but she peered out the window, watching to see if Seth kept his routine. It appeared that he, also, avoided the coffee shop. A second silent day went by.

After dinner, Annie watched from her studio window. Seth left the hardware store through the back door. He climbed the stairs to his apartment. He'd had plenty of time to cool down. She'd give him a chance to settle in, then she'd make the first step to restoring what she'd broken. A look in the mirror showed her short hair gaining length. Despite her care, a dash of blonde began to show at the roots, a telltale sign of her deception. No time to deal with that now.

Annie scaled the steps and knocked on Seth's door. She had only been here once when he brought her up to show blueprints and computer images of his house. He answered the knock, his hair damp from a shower, pulling a T-shirt on as the door opened. He tugged the shirt down and stared at her, his eyes hammered steel.

"May I come in?"

Seth stepped aside and gave a grudging nod.

She walked in and Seth closed the door. "What do you want, Annie? I'm tired."

"We need to talk."

His brows rose. "I don't need to talk. Maybe you do."

"Okay. *I* need to talk. Will you listen?"

"I've googled you. I know all I need to know."

Annie's pulse hammered. Time hadn't mellowed Seth. He was filled with anger and it fueled her own. "No, you don't. You know nothing. You said you loved me. Are you not willing to work through this?"

The word *love* seemed to curb the anger. His tone softened. "I love the you I thought I knew. But if I can't trust you, it's over, Annie. I need to protect my heart."

It's over. Her knees weakened under the weight of those words. Why had she let her guard down? Miriam never allowed emotions to enter. Emotions pave the path to hurt. She reached for the nearest surface to steady herself.

Seth had to see the effect of his words. But he continued his cutting attack. "Answer one question for me. Is this why you and your dad don't get along? Was he upset that you posed half naked?"

Her dad? Seth dared to blame her? An image of that thirteen-year-old girl dashed through her brain. A raw fury surfaced from somewhere deep. Deeper than Annie had delved in a decade. Something snapped and every nerve screamed. Her body reacted without warning as she lunged at Seth, her fists pounding.

"Whoa." He grabbed her arms but she wrested loose and struck him again.

"How dare you! You know nothing, you and your arrogance." She was shouting now, pummeling while he tried to contain her. She shoved him hard, but he managed to catch his balance. Annie's shouts morphed into an enraged whisper, inches from Seth's face. "He raped me! He raped me for two years." Words she'd never spoken turned the rage into a guttural moan, then sobs erupted as Annie lost all strength. She fell to her knees sobbing a decade of latent tears. "I was thirteen years old."

Seth dropped down to her level. "Oh, Annie," he whispered as he reached for her.

Annie's arms flailed, shaking him off. "You're so self-righteous." She made a stab at his chest with her closed fist, but it held no strength. He captured it and held it to his lips.

"I'm sorry, baby. I'm so sorry." Seth shifted from his knees and sat leaning against the wall. He pulled her close and stroked her head while she cried.

Words came through broken gulps of air as Annie attempted to breathe. "I've never told anyone."

When her sobs subsided, Seth pulled her to her feet and led her to the sofa. He settled in beside her and wrapped her in his arms. "Annie, he should be in prison. Why didn't you turn him in?"

"You won't understand."

Seth handed her a tissue and she blew her nose until she could breathe again.

"I'll try. I promise. I'm sorry if I was judging you. Can you forgive me?"

Annie was slow to answer. "You mean like you were going to forgive me for not telling you?" They both knew the answer.

"I'm sorry, Annie. Can we start over?"

Annie touched the swollen space beneath her eyes. "I never cried like that. I thought I was strong enough to block out the hurt. My face must look like puffed marshmallows."

Seth leaned close and softly kissed the swollen spots. "Talk to me, Annie."

"I never posed half naked. I modeled fashions. Some of those happened to be beachwear. It's a work of photography to make it look so suggestive."

"You said I didn't know what your life was like; what took you there. Help me understand."

He had to hear the whole story, the one that began long before her memories. Bits and pieces weren't enough.

36

"I was abandoned when I was one year old. Selah's age. I look at her and wonder how a mother could do that. What was so wrong with me that she'd leave me on a safehouse step, tied to the railing. I could understand her giving up a newborn but she'd had me for a year."

Annie had witnessed a mother's love in Darlene. She'd read of that same love in Charlotte's journals—about a mother who couldn't bear to let her go, even knowing the hardship ahead.

"At four years old, I was adopted." Annie continued, talking about the pageants, the lack of education, her mother's determination to succeed. "It's the only life I knew. I had no school and no friends. There was no one in my life but my two parents and my grandmother. Nana was always the bright spot, but only when my mother allowed time for me to see her. Even as a child I recognized my hunger for love, a base need that drives us all. I'd do anything to please my parents.

"My mother was on the local pageant committee and had a standing meeting every Monday night. One of those Mondays when I was thirteen, my father decided to join me … in my bed. He said it wasn't wrong since he wasn't really my father. He told me this was a normal part of growing up. Something all girls go through."

Annie couldn't look at him. She didn't want to see the disbelief he must feel. It sounded implausible that anyone could be so naïve—even a young teenager.

"I know what you're thinking, but you have to remember, I knew nothing of the world. I lived my life in a bubble created by my parents. That was my paradigm. Every Monday night when she went to her meeting, I squeezed my eyes closed and endured what he said was right. It always hurt. I hated it and soon began hating him. That hatred peaked when I was fifteen. Maybe it was teenage rebellion. A part of me always knew it was evil and I suddenly realized I had the power to say no. That's when I said no to him and no to my mother. I fought him and threatened to expose him. Then I refused to do any more pageants.

"I wasn't sure what I'd do since I didn't go to school. My mother was furious. She even threatened to take me back to the orphanage. I'd been offered modeling jobs even as a kid. At fifteen, I took one. It was all I knew to do. I didn't know any other life. My dad—well, when I said no to him, he found someone who said yes. He left my mother. It was a relief for me, but it hurt her badly. Still does. In some twisted way, I felt responsible that he hurt her. My life was a failure. I'd let everybody down.

"So, for the next few years, I modeled clothing for advertisements. Then I caught the eye of Peter Dalton. He hired me with a four-year contract and my modeling career soared. I traveled to places I didn't know existed. After three years, I was tired and wanted out. A quieter life. I wanted to bring my grandmother home. The modeling had always been about fashion, some sleek and revealing, but not to the extreme. What you saw was Peter's vengeance. He was mad and made me pay."

Annie needed a glimpse into Seth's thoughts. Was he understanding or condemning? "Does any of this make sense to you?"

Seth's arm still embraced her. "There are two things I don't understand."

He sounded more puzzled than judgmental.

"When you said no to your dad and realized it was child abuse, why didn't you turn him in?"

Annie laid her head back, staring at the ceiling. "Nana. He's her only son. It would kill her if he went to prison."

"If Lillian knew what happened, she'd agree that he belongs in jail."

Annie sat up straighter. "You're seeing black and white, Seth. Of course, it would grieve my grandmother to know he'd hurt me. But seeing her only child in prison? I can't do that to her."

He seemed to mull that around in his mind for a moment. "The other question—when you left modeling, why the big secret? Why not go public and say goodbye to the world of fashion? Why the elaborate ruse to hide?"

What had he seen when he googled her? "I was labeled a supermodel. In simple terms, that means world-wide recognition. In practical terms, it means multi-million-dollar contracts. Can you honestly tell me I'd have blended in the Hickory Falls community if people knew that?"

Seth let out a low whistle. "Nope. There'd definitely be no blending in."

He said what Annie already knew, but it brought a trickle of tears anyway. She'd never fit in. Never be able to call this home. She had no choice but to move from Hickory Falls. Her grandmother had ample support here. People would watch out for Lillian. Annie would sign the house back to her grandmother and leave the place she'd come to love. And the man she'd grown to love. The sins of the father. Happiness didn't belong to her.

"You and Simone know the truth. When two people know, it becomes four people, then eight, and so on. Hickory Falls will offer no refuge for me. I'll stay with my grandmother through Christmas, then I'll be leaving."

Seth sat up straighter. "Leaving? What about us?"

"There is no *us*. You said it's over."

"Annie, I was angry. It's not over. It never will be."

The thought of losing Seth had made her knees weak. Yet somewhere in the midst of telling her story, something changed. Everything became crystal clear. The absurdity of a relationship with any man once they knew her history. Especially a man like Seth.

"Thank you, Seth, but you don't have to say that. I always knew deep down it couldn't last. Our lives have been too different. I tried to tell you a long time ago when we had a picnic in your future kitchen." The memory of that day brought Annie a smile filled with regret.

"I won't accept that. Love bears all things. We can work through this."

"I wish that were true. You deserve more than my soiled past. And frankly, I don't want to live in the shadow of your goodness."

Annie stood and moved toward the door but Seth caught her arm. He turned her toward him. "Annie, I'm sorry I didn't listen to you earlier. Don't go."

The scene had turned upside down from her tentative walk up the outside staircase. He'd been angry and she had come to work through the hurt. Now Seth pleaded while Annie's determination grew stronger. She loved him, but he'd never see her the same way. And she needed to find out who she really was. Who was Annie Gentry without Eleanor, Kurt, Dalton Designs, or Seth Walker?

~~*~~

The connection between Annie and Charlotte haunted her. One mother adored her child while the other threw her away. Yet both girls were flung into a life where they didn't belong. Both girls were abused by a father who wasn't really a father. Neither experienced a normal childhood. No school. No friends. Both Annie and Charlotte longed to breakaway.

To be free. They each found solace in painting. An outlet to capture life's beauty and pain.

Charlotte and Annie both loved a man they couldn't have. Ezra had been cruelly taken from Charlotte. Seth? He'd once said, "Stay sweet." Annie loved when he'd seen her that way. Sweet and innocent. She couldn't bear him looking at her differently. Seeing her soiled and used. Once he knew, everything changed.

~~*~~

Living in a town like Hickory Falls allowed little concealment. Despite Annie's efforts to avoid the hardware store and the coffee shop, their paths still crossed. She'd made her intentions clear. Seth didn't pressure her, but neither did he try avoiding her.

Lillian slept and Annie sat on the front porch. Dusk arrived earlier each evening and fireflies became scarcer. Hickory Falls began closing shop for the night. Annie watched lights dim and cars vacate the parking spaces.

From her peripheral vision, she saw Seth step from the hidden view of the hardware store to look in her direction. Then he moved toward her. As Seth sauntered up the front walk, Annie's pulse raced. Despite her decision, it happened every time she saw him. She willed herself to breathe deeply, calming the senses.

Seth sat on the first step, turned toward her leaning against the post. "Hey, Annie."

"Hi." That was all she managed to say.

"Are you doing okay?"

Was she? She nodded, then swallowed the lump lodged in her throat. "I'm fine." The universally correct answer. "And you?"

He stared at a speck in the distance, then shook his head. The weight of sorrow rested heavily.

They sat in tense silence before Seth's slow grin appeared. "I heard an anonymous donor covered the Crowley's fire damage. Don't suppose you know anything about that?"

"I ... I barely know them."

"Funny how we've seen an upsurge in generosity around here. Someone's doing a good thing." He sent a probing look her way.

Annie had no intention of rising to the challenge.

"Just thought I'd say hi. Guess I better head on home."

"Goodnight, Seth."

"Goodnight, Annie."

They were back to being friends, chatting on the front porch. But now memories were tucked between each word; unasked questions hidden behind every look.

Charlotte's journal waited in Annie's lap, filled with sorrow and loss. Pages of anger and hatred that Annie fully understood. The teenage love never saw adulthood. Charlotte and Ezra were denied the chance of love for a lifetime. Once more, their stories met. Annie told herself that her loss couldn't compare to Charlotte's. The hardship of her own life paled in comparison. Yet the connection remained, pulling Annie 150 years into the past.

37

Charlotte

I still don't know how Reverend Platt heard the news, but he was at the village the following day. The townsmen worked together to dig Ezra's grave. He'd be buried alongside others from Coltrane Village. A community gravesite. Roughhewn wooden crosses instead of etched gravestones. It took many hours and many men to dig deep enough. When it was ready, they took Ezra's body from that tree of death and laid him in the ground.

Aunt Imani was inconsolable, weeping and wailing. My eyes were dry. My face rigid. Anger's an emotion so big that it doesn't leave room for anything else. It swallows up the hurt and presses it deep inside. Even Reverend Platt couldn't console me. I heard words. Phrases. Platitudes. *Let go of bitterness. What Ezra would want. Need to forgive.* I shut them out. When James Pearson was dead, I'd deal with my bitterness. Until then, my mind held only one thought. He must pay.

We stood around the gravesite with folks singing Deep River. I heard the words *walking into heaven* and *crossing the Jordon.* They brought me no comfort. I didn't want Ezra crossing that river or walking anywhere when I wasn't beside him. I wanted to hear the richness of his voice, smooth as a glassy lake, soft as silk. A new wave of anger surged. Everyone around me sang of the everlasting but the words in my head were different. *Find a gun. Hide in the barn. Wait until he's alone.* I imagined my finger pressed on the cold metal trigger. I pictured the fear in his eyes right before I squeezed it.

The community came together and prepared a lunch. They shared a time of food and fellowship, much like each Sunday after services. I couldn't eat and stole away to the spot behind Aunt Imani's house where Ezra first kissed me. Lowering myself down, I sat in the grass leaning against the house. I began to work out the plot. I had to steal a gun. I'd never fired one before, but I could figure it out. I tried to remember which of the townsmen had guns that night, and who's house was often empty so I could search for it. I examined the picture in my mind of men carrying firearms. I never heard Reverend Platt approach. His voice startled me back to the present.

"Charlotte, may I sit?"

I nodded and he eased himself to the ground. I could tell that wasn't easy for him. His hair had turned white, but somehow, I had never thought of him as old. Maybe I confused his wisdom for energy.

"I know you're hurting. I've been praying for God to be your comfort. I'll keep on praying until you can feel it. God sees your pain, Charlotte."

"Sees but doesn't act." My response sounded as biting as a winter wind.

"He acts, child. Even when it's hard for us to know how He's acting."

"Don't call me child." I spit the words out, wanting him to remember how close I came to becoming a married woman.

"I want to talk to you about something. I know you're hurting badly, but I have something for you to be thinking about. Do you know the name Mary Jane Patterson?"

"No." My answer was curt, showing my disinterest. I wished to be left alone.

Reverend Platt began an explanation that sounded like it would be a long, drawn-out tale, like Sunday messages. "Mary Jane Patterson—one spunky lady. Along about fifteen years ago, she earned herself a bachelor's degree. Unusual for a woman, right?"

I hated that he had sparked my interest, and I refused to show him. I didn't look up when I answered. "It's becoming accepted for women to be educated."

"You're right. Absolutely right. But what if I told you that Mary Jane Patterson's a black woman?"

My head sprung around to face him. I didn't speak but he saw my questions.

"Yes, ma'am. She was the first black woman to earn a college degree. 1862 Oberlin College. A few years later, another black woman, Vivian Malone Jones, earned a degree. 1865 University of Alabama. There have been others since then."

I resumed my detached position. I hadn't known of those two, but it had nothing to do with me.

"Mrs. Tomlinson's not going to continue teaching. It's too dangerous for our folks. But she still has a heart to help our people receive an education. Still looking for someone to sponsor. She asked me to help choose."

Was he suggesting I might be the one? "So why are you telling me?"

"You know why, Charlotte. Let's get your name among those others. You're the only one in this village equipped for college."

Another dream. I wanted to be the one to do something big. Something meaningful. But I couldn't accept this. I'd made two promises. "I can't, Reverend. I promised Ezra I'd take care of Aunt Imani."

"Aunt Imani's got a village to take care of her. Ezra knew that. Even before you came, he planned to leave for Payne Institute."

I knew that to be true. But I had another promise to keep. My promise to myself. James Pearson must pay.

"Even so, I have to decline. There are things I need to take care of."

Reverend Platt stared at me, like he could see inside my brain. "You sure those aren't things God should be taking care of?"

My anger resurfaced. "Should be, but He doesn't."

"Charlotte, Charlotte. Don't let bitterness eat away the sweetness. Remember, everyone will have their day of judgment."

"We need judgment now." Where did the tears come from? Why did they choose to return now?

"So, you planning to stop someone? How you going to do that? Kill him?"

"He's an evil man."

"Well then you best have a lot of bullets because there's a lot of evil men out there. Might take you a lifetime."

I stared forward and didn't answer. He didn't understand. Suddenly, I wanted everything to come out. Words I'd never spoken in my entire life. They came, laced with hatred. "You don't know what happened to me. You know nothing about spending your whole childhood hiding in an attic. Knowing you're a shame to your own mother because a black man accosted her. Being treated like some vermin running across the floor. I grew up as part of a family, but they wore finery while I wore scraps. I had meals alone in my attic instead of sitting at the table with my family. One wrong word and I got the whip. The first time it lashed my bare skin I was five years old. I didn't even know what I'd done wrong." Years of unshed tears began to fall. "When I was old enough, I came out of hiding to be their housemaid. They told folks I was an orphan they rescued. I couldn't call my own mother *Ma*. I had to call her Mrs. Pearson."

Reverend Platt sat stoically, listening to the secret of my lifetime being told. "Mr. Pearson hated me. Hated all blacks. He wanted to take me to the Negro orphanage. I wish he had. I'd have been treated better. I wouldn't have had whip lashes at five years old."

When I paused, Reverend Platt shifted, lifting himself to his knees. I could see the pain of the movement. "I grew up in a Negro orphanage." He lifted his shirt to show me his back. A pattern of stripes crisscrossed, showing healed-over scars, raised so high it looked like a nest of snakes. There were scars on top of scars. I tried to imagine how many beatings it would take to cause that. "I ran away one too many times. Got myself caught and sold into slavery."

He pulled his shirt down and sat back, rubbing his knees. "Sorry. These old knees have been clubbed a few times."

I was aghast. "How can you be so … so hopeful when you've been through so much? How did you learn to read and become a preacher?"

A contented smile formed. "Little nuggets of gold God sent along the way. He was always there. I suspect you've had nuggets of gold too, Charlotte. Someone taught you to read. You've been well-fed. Your mother didn't discard you. Sometimes we have to look real deep to see, but God hasn't abandoned us. The Bible tells us the eyes of the Lord search to and fro throughout the earth in search of those whose hearts belong to Him."

I buried my face in my hands and cried. "But why did he have to take Ezra?"

The Reverend's sigh was deep. He grieved for Ezra too. "Some questions have no answers. Why did he allow me to be sold and moved far from my family? Did you know I have three little boys and one daughter?"

I moved my tear-soaked hands and looked at him. He half chuckled. "Oh, I suspect I'll always see them as little boys. Guess they're grown men by now. And my little Esther, she's probably a mama herself, God willing."

"Did you look for them?"

"Course I did. I still do. But the looking has come up empty, same as Ezra's search. I had to make a decision, Charlotte. Was I going to dwell on my past or my future? Was I going to keep putting all of my efforts into a futile search, or was I going to use my life for kingdom work? That's the same decision you have to make. Those nuggets of gold in your life—they've made you a strong person. A special person. That's why Ezra chose you."

Ezra. His name refreshed my tears. "Do you think he can see me?"

"Can't answer that one. But I can answer this. He'll see you again one day. You can be sure of that."

Could I lay aside my revenge? Could I walk away and allow Mr. Pearson to go unpunished?

"Charlotte, there's a better way. If you don't believe me, believe Ezra. He knew that education is the answer. The timing's too late for this term, but a new one begins in three months. Think about it. I'd like to see you enrolled and moving to Hodges. Let's beat evil with knowledge."

Was this God acting? Was this His nugget of gold? I felt the change happening inside me. I'd do this for my Ezra. "Okay, Reverend. What do I have to do to enroll?"

38

I didn't go back to the textile mill that week. When I returned the following Monday, I no longer had a job. I had to find other work so I could take care of Aunt Imani. I'd need to earn as much as possible to leave with her once I was gone, and I'd have to secure a promise from townsfolks that they would take care of her.

When I left the mill after learning I'd been terminated for not showing up, I went into town. Ezra hadn't wanted me to take a housemaid job, but that's all I knew how to do. Hiram was acquainted with folks from Hickory Falls. He could give me a few leads. I walked the main street looking for Hiram's carriage without success. The street felt so familiar, it's dusty pathway and the shops I had entered many times. I passed the general store where the City Gazette was sold. The front cover boasted about the post-war progress. They aimed to lay cobblestone and officially name this road Main Street. The dusty old path would have a real name, but not me. I'd never be Charlotte Williams.

Horses and carriages traveled up and down the street, and finally, I saw the carriage belonging to Hiram's employer. I scurried to catch up, but with Mr. Danville seated in the carriage, I didn't dare call out to him. I waited, watching for the moment when Hiram was alone. Then I hurried over to him.

His wide smile crinkled his eyes. "Well, hey. Ain't seen you around."

"I know. I've had to make some changes. I don't work for the Pearsons anymore. I've moved to Coltrane Village, and I need a job. Do you know of any townsfolk needing help?"

"Yes'um. I sure do. Times, they's getting better with the federals gone."

He rattled off the names of three homes looking for domestic help. "Thank you, Hiram. I hope to be seeing you more often." I hurried off.

On Mondays, Mr. Pearson always had a council meeting, and Zachary had been away for school for the past few months. I aimed to see Ma. When I approached my old home, I went around to the back door. It felt awkward knocking but this big, beautiful house was no longer my home. I waited for Ma to come to the door.

The door opened, but there was Mr. Pearson. When he saw me, his eyes widened before becoming two slits in an angry face. "What do you want? I thought you were gone."

Common sense calmed my defiance. I didn't want to see his fists again. Not on me nor on Ma. "I'm not staying. I'd like to see …" I bit back the word *ma*. "I'd like to see Mrs. Pearson."

"She ain't here and I haven't forgotten you back-talking me."

I took a step backwards, but he grabbed my wrist. He pulled me inside and closed the door. I looked at my wrist and imagined the same hand slipping a noose around Ezra's neck. I yanked my arm from his grip and turned for the door.

Suddenly his arms grabbed my waist from behind me, lifting me from the floor. "You don't walk away from me, wench."

I kicked my feet but only found air. My arms thrashed, hitting their mark and leaving a scratch on his face. He carried me to my pantry bedroom and threw me forcibly on the bed. "Well aren't you the little wildcat!" His fist connected with my stomach, taking all of the fight out of me.

Pain stabbed my midsection, and I knew a rib had been broken.

When I caught my breath, I looked up to find him staring at me, his gaze moving from my head downward. "So, the wench has grown up." He reached and began to tug at the hooks on the bodice of my dress. I scrambled, swatting him away. He placed his hand on my ribcage and pushed right where he had punched me. Right where I figured the rib was broken. I screamed in pain while he opened my bodice. Once the top hooks were freed, he grabbed and yanked it, causing a rip clear down the front. I wore pantalets, but no corset, so my breasts were exposed. I tugged the fabric with one hand and pushed him with the other, but was no match for his strength. His hand found my breast and covered it. I screamed again, but this time in outrage, not pain. I kicked and thrashed, then bit his upper arm. He cursed and punched my jaw, jarring my head to the side. Blood spewed from my lip, trickling down to my neck. When he had taken my breath away once more, he used that moment to pull my pantalets down, exposing me from all but the ragged clothing I managed to yank back.

"This is what your pa did to my wife."

He began to climb on me with his hand working loose his belt. I heard the door and screamed again before I took another punch to my midsection.

"Get off of her!"

Ma's voice.

He only paused a moment to say, "Get out of here, woman."

That paused allowed me to bite his arm again. He cursed and smacked my face with his open hand.

"I said, get off of her."

Ma's arms tried to pull him, but his rage was too great. One strong push and she was on the floor. I saw her climb to her knees, then her feet. Then she left the room. She left me.

He started to climb on me again when I saw the shadow behind him. Ma raised the fire poker and lifted it high over her head. With more strength than I ever saw from Ma, she swung it down. When the poker cracked Mr. Pearson's skull, he immediately went limp, falling on top of me. I kicked and pushed at the same time, and James Pearson fell to the floor.

Ma stood there, her mouth agape, still holding the poker. I scrambled, tugging torn fabric to cover my bareness, then looked to the floor. Blood seeped from his skull, a growing puddle surrounding his lifeless body.

The poker clattered to the hardwood floor as she let out a gruff wail, probably thinking what I suspected. If he wasn't already dead, he would be soon. There was too much blood.

Then Ma took charge. "Charlotte, go to my bedroom and put on one of my dresses. Then hurry back to the village." I didn't move. I sat there, holding my painful rib, looking at both of the Pearsons.

"What's going to happen, Ma?"

"I don't know, but I don't want you here. Go. Now."

I still didn't move. "Ma?"

She breathed deeply. "They'll arrest me, but I'll tell them he was beating me. Some folks saw my jaw last week. It will be okay. They'll believe me."

I stood with my torn dress. "Ma, I can't let you do that. We'll tell them I did it."

"And you'll hang from a noose."

"Can we tell them we found him like this?"

She looked stunned, like she was half in shock. "Yes. Yes, that's what I'll tell them. But you must be gone. Really. Please go."

But that wasn't to happen. A banging on the door sounded before the door opened and Sheriff Beltzhoover let himself in. "James? Davina? Someone said they heard screaming."

Ma stepped from my room into the kitchen. "You better come in here, Otis."

The sheriff looked at Mr. Pearson. Then at me trying to hold my clothes together. Then at Ma and the poker at her feet. The scene explained itself. He leaned down and felt for a pulse, but shook his head. There was none.

"Davina, I wish I could tell you something different, but the courts may not be sympathetic. Some folks around here will think you should'a let it alone. Let him have his way. I ain't saying that's what I think. I'm just telling it like it is."

Quiet filled the space that moments earlier held screaming. We stood that way, each knowing what was coming next. Then Ma took charge again. "Charlotte, it looks like I'll be going with the sheriff. Please go to my bedroom and change into one of my dresses. Don't forget you still have some belongings here. Make sure you take what's yours."

She wanted me to have my treasures. My paintings. My journals. But the sheriff halted that. "I'm sorry, Davina, but I can't allow that. This is a crime scene. Nothing can leave the house." He looked at me. "But I don't see the harm in you changing into something decent."

I scurried up the stairs and opened the armoire, choosing the plainest dress I could find. A brown and tan print with a stiff collar and buttons down the front.

Otis looked as somber as Ma. "I see no need for cuffs. Let's walk peaceably down to the station. I'll send some officers here to ..." he glanced at the body, "to take care of things."

I sent a question to Ma with my eyes, but she swished her chin toward the door, telling me to go. I walked back to the village thinking about what almost happened. Almost. But Ma stopped it. No one had stopped it years ago when she was attacked. Had she kicked and screamed like I did? Was my real Pa evil like Mr. Pearson? I kept wondering what would happen to Ma and if I'd ever see her again. I wanted her to know about Ezra. We both lost our man this week.

Mr. Pearson? Well I guess God took care of my revenge. But why did He use Ma to help? Like Reverend Platt said, some questions have no answers.

39

Except for telling Reverend Platt, I had kept my ma's secret all my life, but after Mr. Pearson died it all came out. In a trial, you have to tell the truth, the whole truth, and nothing but the truth. That doesn't leave room for hiding. Ma said it was best to tell her lawyer everything before the trial began. Now folks in Hickory Falls knew Davina Pearson was my mother. They all knew a black man had his way with her, and that Mr. Pearson tried to have his way with me.

At least I had some time to talk with Ma before I left for school. They let me see her for short visits. I told her about my Ezra and that Mr. Pearson was probably behind everything that happened. I told her we would win the lawsuit. A jury would never blame her. We smiled like we were both sure, but neither of us believed it. I could see it in her eyes.

Zachary came home to see Ma. He blamed me for his pa's death. Guess he figured I should have stayed quiet and let him beat and rape me. But Zachary had to return to school. He was studying the law and would be an attorney one day, like my Ezra would have been. But Zachary would never fight for civil rights. Not since his own pa indoctrinated him against everyone black.

"Charlotte," Ma said when I visited her. "The house is no longer a crime scene. If I don't make it home, it will belong to Zachary. I want you to go there, now, while he's away. Take what's important to you, and take whatever you need. Food. Clothes. Household items. I can buy more. And take the money in my bedroom drawer. I think there's about $22.00."

"I'm not stealing from your house, Ma."

"No, sweetie. It's not stealing. I'm giving it to you. It's your birthright."

This was the last I'd see her until I returned for the trial. I looked at her in her course cotton prison clothes. I thought of her eating alone in an isolated cell, not able to breathe the scent of flowers or feel the sunshine on her face. I knew as well as anyone how hard that was. "Ma, thank you for keeping me. And for trying to make things better. Reverend Platt says God sends us little gold nuggets that help us through the trouble times. You've always been my gold nugget."

We hugged and cried, and I left the jail, ready to go to Hodges and start college. All because she schooled me well. The next time I'd see her would be during her trial.

I stopped at our home on the corner. Our big beautiful house that would now belong to Zachary. The spot where Mr. Pearson poured his blood onto the hardwood had been cleaned, but the stain remained. It was fitting. Some things shouldn't be erased. I decided I would take two things—the money and some food. No sense the food spoiling. And the money? Well, it was a gift from my mother and it would help me to take care of my aunt.

I went to the attic, pulled a cardstock from the shelf, and placed it on my old easel. It had been a while since I'd painted anything but my hands were desperate to capture this picture. There was no hurry in me. No one would be coming home, and the picture needed to be perfect.

Hours later, satisfied with my painting, I sat down at the child's table, making the final entry in my journal. I recorded the last of the recent events. Now I would leave it with my other journals. I couldn't take my treasures. I had nowhere to store such things as books and paintings. Maybe someday, someone will read them and know about the life of Charlotte Pearson.

40
Annie

Annie swiped at her tears, then gathered the journals and carried them downstairs. "Nana, can I come in?" Lillian startled awake from the recliner in her bedroom. "Sorry. I didn't know you were sleeping." Annie climbed up on her grandmother's bed, sitting cross-legged.

"That's alright. I sleep way too much." Lillian readjusted the oxygen tube that had fallen askew while she dozed.

"Nana, I've finished the last journal. I know Charlotte lived in this house. I know this was the house you grew up in. I'm trying to do the math to figure where Charlotte fits into the genealogy. Can you help me?"

"I'll tell you what I know and what I don't know. I didn't want to talk about it until you finished reading. It was important to me that you read to the end."

"I did, but the end isn't really the end."

"No, child. It isn't. I'm a Pearson. My granddaddy was Zachary Pearson."

"I suspected that. Then Charlotte would be your great aunt."

"Yes, but I never knew about her. My parents never told me and by then, the town gossip had long since died down. I only learned about Charlotte when I moved back home after Daddy died. My mother knew nothing about her, either. When I found the journals and told my mother, she dismissed it as someone's work of fiction."

"Do you think it could be a work of fiction?"

"I considered it. Two things convinced me the journals are true. First is the picture. Who would set up a playroom and stage a tea party simply to paint a picture? The other thing that convinced me is the use of true facts. Real names and circumstances. My dad told me he'd never met his grandparents. My great-grandfather, James Pearson, died when my grandpa, Zachary, was in law school. My great-grandmother, Davina Pearson, died in prison. She was incarcerated for murdering her husband." Her sigh held the relief of a burden finally yoked. "She died of dysentery two years after the trial. That's all I know. My grandpa never wanted to talk much about his parents."

"So, she was found guilty. That was one place where the journals didn't tell the ending. I didn't know if they convicted Charlotte's mother."

"They did. I figure Charlotte never came back to this house after leaving that final journal entry. My grandfather was a racist. Not as bad as what I read about his dad, James Pearson. When I was a young girl, society began shifting. Blacks were viable members of our community. Some old school folks, like my dad and my grandfather never accepted that. Zachary Pearson would never have allowed Charlotte to come home."

"What happened to her? Did she go to college like she planned? Did she ever marry or have children?"

Lillian lifted her palm-out hand to halt the questions. "Slow down, child. Those questions are part of the ending that we don't know. An ending I'm hoping you'll find out. I always knew those journals would burn your curiosity as they did mine."

"How do I find the answers?" It was more a question to herself than her grandmother.

"I was never computer savvy like your generation. I figure you can start there."

~~*~~

Lillian said she suspected that Charlotte never returned to the house. The journals indicated she didn't take anything, except the money that Davina gave her. That meant any early paintings should be here unless they'd been discarded. That made no sense. Anyone who discarded the art would have discarded the journals.

Annie hadn't thoroughly searched the dusty attic. She gave the door a tug and it scraped against the threshold to open. Dust particles danced in the artificial light. Annie stood, hands on hips, scanning the attic. A few unopened boxes remained. She started with the ones closest to the child's furniture. The second box she opened held the treasures. A few paintings were on paper from a linen sketchpad, but most were on cardstock. None were framed nor matted.

Annie leafed through them seeing a variety ranging from amateur drawings to quality works of art. One cardstock painting showed a carriage on a dirt-packed road. The driver, an older black man, smiled widely, showing gaps between teeth, one missing completely. Hiram. Charlotte managed to capture light in his eyes that matched the smile. Behind him, the store sign said *apothecary*. The drug store that had a soda counter forbidding blacks, was now her beloved coffee shop. Charlotte managed to capture the leathery wrinkles of Hiram's forehead and on the sides of his eyes.

A few more juvenile pieces depicted toys painted with too much negative space behind them, clearly the work of a younger Charlotte. Annie found the three musicians from the church service and a painting of the hillside with worshippers. When she picked up the next picture, she held it reverently. She somehow knew it had been that final painting—the one that Charlotte painted the day she left her last journal entry. Ezra. Stark white teeth contrasted with ebony skin. Charlotte managed to capture the man's character. She'd created the illusion of wisdom, honesty, and pain. Pain and loss. How could anyone rip a five-year old from his mother's arms? Ezra had told Charlotte their love must honor God. A man of integrity. A man like Seth. How could James Pearson, her great, great, grandfather, dismiss the value of this man? How could he so frivolously take a life? Nausea and anger filled Annie's belly. She understood Lillian's reference to shame.

The portrait of Ezra carried the best artistic quality of all. This collection must be preserved. It fared well in the dark of the attic without the fading of sunlight, but needed separation and climate control. Annie carried the box downstairs, determined to pack them correctly.

~~*~~

Annie cursed her lack of education. Her computer literacy extended to simple searches and checking e-mails. A search of Charlotte Pearson brought up two results. Her name was mentioned in a court judgment against Davina Pearson in the murder trial of James Pearson. Charlotte's name was also mentioned as an alumnus of Payne Institute, an historically black school located in Hodges, SC which is in Greenwood County. The school relocated to Columbia, SC and now goes by the name Allen University. The school document offered no information. Only Charlotte's name tucked in a list of other names.

How do you search for a person who lived 150 years ago? Where else should she look? She could ask Darlene, but she suspected that her level of computer literacy may not exceed Annie's. She considered asking Nadine. Even though it was outside her field of expertise, a cardiac nurse would have a well-rounded education. Pride restrained Annie.

Anyone in her generation with minimal education should know. Seth studied business management. And he already knew her background. He'd understand her limitations.

Since he'd reopened the door for friendship, Annie would ask him for help.

~~*~~

The following day, Seth and Annie sat side-by-side at her kitchen table. He plucked keys faster than Annie could keep up.

"We have a number of resources we can go to. Census info. Vital records. Ancestry websites. Vital records may be the best starting place. They keep track of marriages and births. If we find information there, we can check land ownership. But first, I'm ordering a book for you. It's a Hickory Falls historical publication. Even if there's nothing about Charlotte, you should find it interesting."

With a flourish, he hit *send*. "There. You should have it in a few days."

"Thank you, Seth. Do you think those sites you mentioned will take us back 150 years?"

"Yep. It's harder to find info before 1850, but post-civil war will have better records."

Vital records proved to be a windfall. It offered no birth record for Charlotte, but that came as no surprise. In 1886, an African American woman named Charlotte Pearson, married Vincent Arthur. They had one son, Tyrone, and one daughter, Bessie. Charlotte died in 1920 at the age of 57.

A search of Vincent Arthur resulted in a few hits. Vincent worked as teacher at Shaw University in Raleigh, NC. He outlived Charlotte by twelve years. Further searches showed that their son, Tyrone, died of a childhood illness, but their daughter, Bessie, lived to have three children. Seth found death certificates for two of them. Charlotte's grandson, Gerald Robinson may still be living.

Seth sat back, rocking on the two back legs of his chair. "Okay. What's the plan?"

"Can you help me find his location?"

"Yep. Shouldn't be hard since he lived in the Raleigh area. Looks like the whole family stayed close to that region."

A few more clicks of the keyboard showed that Gerald's home had been sold three years ago. "The trail stops here, but I'd say he either moved in with one of his kids or is in a nursing home."

"How can we find out?"

"If I was FBI, we could track the money, but that's out of my league. What are you planning to do with this information, Annie?"

"I want to find him. I'd like to go and meet him. Ask him about Charlotte."

"Are you sure that's a good idea? By my calculations, he's nearing 90 years old."

Annie pondered that. Two years older than Lillian. He could have a weakened heart like her grandmother or perhaps be mentally impaired. Besides, they had no current address.

"Who did you say is his oldest child?"

Seth re-opened the tab. "Dr. Lisa Pendleton. Looks like she's a Tarheel. Teaches at UNC. Professor of Music with a concentration in …" Seth squinted looking at the word, and pronounced it slowly. "Ethnomusicology. Sounds like she specializes in ethnic music."

Annie jotted notes as Seth read the information. She finally had a starting place.

"Thank you for your help. I couldn't have done this without you."

He smiled the easy grin Annie had grown to love. She quickly turned away so it didn't melt her resolve. He touched her shoulder, bringing her eyes back toward him. "There's not much I wouldn't do for you, Annie Gentry." Their eyes held for a moment before she lowered hers. Seth pushed his chair back and stood to leave.

Annie watched each step as Seth strode through the backyard to his apartment. When he was gone from her view, her gaze moved to the hillside where workers were pounding wood that would become his new roof. It struck her that she'd never see it finished. She'd be leaving after Christmas, hopefully before the pictures of her LA photo shoot managed to reach the rest of Hickory Falls.

Miraculously, no one seemed aware of her fame and fortune. She could believe that Seth would avoid spreading that news. But Simone? She'd do anything to bring Annie down. Why hadn't she broadcasted it all over town? What might she be planning? Annie remained guarded.

41

The semester would be ending with the approach of Christmas. Annie shared her findings with Lillian. "Will you be alright if I'm gone a few days?"

She waved Annie off with a flick of her hand. "Heavens, yes. These nurses hover over me like an old mother hen. And Iris? She's here every morning and reminds me she's a holler away."

"Okay, Nana. I'll leave in the morning. If all goes well, I'll be back the following day."

"It's a long drive, Annie. Seth might like to join you."

Her grandmother had asked what happened between them only once. With Annie's reluctance to share, Lillian didn't bring it up again. Yet she frequently dropped little suggestions like this one.

"Thanks, but I enjoy driving."

The following morning, Annie packed up and left early. She arrived in Chapel Hill at 10:30 and went directly to the university. Signage made it easy to find the School of Fine Arts where she'd locate the music department. Annie asked at the reception desk and learned that Dr. Pendleton had a class ending at 11:15. She was invited to wait in the student lounge.

Annie waited, re-reading passages from Charlotte's journals when a voice interrupted her.

"Excuse me. I'm Lisa Pendleton. You wanted to see me?"

Annie looked at this descendant of Charlotte Pearson, then stood and offered her hand. "I'm Ann Gentry."

"Is this okay?" The professor motioned to the table where Annie had been sitting.

"Yes, thank you." She was beautiful and stylish in tapered dress pants, heels, and a jacquard blazer with a subtly woven floral pattern. When they sat and she had a closer look, she realized the professor was older than her initial impression. If her father was 89, she'd be in her 50's or 60's. Yet she was striking. Slender. A contagious smile. A gentle demeanor.

"Are you interested in our music program?"

"No. Dr. Pendleton. I'm not a student."

"Please, call me Lisa."

"Thank you, Lisa. And please call me Annie. I'm here for a more personal reason."

Lisa's eyebrows rose slightly in question.

"I believe we're distantly related."

That widened the professor's eyes, bringing a glimpse of amusement.

"Is Gerald Robinson your father?"

"Yes."

"And your grandmother was Bessie Robinson?"

"Yes." Lisa's interest was definitely piqued. She pulled her chair in a tad closer.

"I may be going back too far, but do you have any knowledge of Charlotte Pearson? She would be your great-grandmother."

"Charlotte Arthur," Lisa corrected. "Vincent and Charlotte Arthur were my great-grandparents. I didn't know either of them, but I know *of* them. They both left their mark."

Charlotte wanted to leave her mark. She longed to do something important.

"Where do you fit into this picture?" Lisa held her coffee brown wrist next to Annie's white flesh. "I don't recall hearing of any Caucasian ancestors."

"It's a long story and I warn you it's not pretty. Charlotte's mother was white, I'm adopted but my family's ancestor is Charlotte's half-brother, Zachary Pearson. These are Charlotte's journals." Annie shifted them toward Lisa.

"And you're giving these to me?"

"I think they rightfully belong to you." It was the only right decision, yet Annie felt like she offered a slice of her heart. "And I have something else for you. There's a box in my car. Charlotte was an amateur painter. I have paintings from when she was a teenager. I've brought all of them, but I made a print of one that's special to me. I'd like to respectfully ask your permission to keep the print."

"My great-grandmother wasn't an amateur. She was a renown painter. Her works are on display in many prominent museums."

Chills tingled up Annie's arms. "I'm an artist. Not well-known, but I've sold a number of pieces." She wanted that kinship with Charlotte. Something positive that connected them.

Lisa flashed a brilliant smile. "Well, Annie, I guess it runs in our family."

They began the trek to Annie's car when it hit her like a steam roller. She stopped in her tracks. "Charlotte Arthur? Did she use the name C.P. Arthur?"

"Ahh. You know her work?"

"Only one piece. The Gardener."

When they reached the car, Annie opened the box to reveal the treasured paintings. They now carried a new value. The early works of C.P. Arthur. The tea party painting didn't hold near the artistic quality of Hiram's carriage or the portrait of Ezra, yet it was endearing. It started Annie on the journey. "This is the picture I had printed." Even prints now had greater monetary value than when she assumed Charlotte to be an amateur. "I'm happy to purchase it from you."

Lisa crossed her arms to mock an offense. "I can't take your money. Aren't you my first cousin three times removed?" They both laughed. "Annie, our family would never have these if it hadn't been for you."

"These paintings have a story they want to tell. They'll mean so much more to you when you read the journals." Annie took a final glance at Ezra's portrait. She suddenly saw him dangling from the tree, Charlotte on the ground wailing. So little time they had. Her eyes flooded with unshed tears.

Lisa's hand reached to Annie's. "Are you alright?"

Annie's attempt at a smile fell short. "I will be."

Lisa's head tilted in confusion. "Why is this so personal for you?"

"You can't read these and remain detached. Charlotte's life was different from mine, yet there are so many parallels. I have some big decisions to make."

Lisa set the painting down and turned her full attention toward Annie. "Are you seeking help for those decisions?"

Annie faltered. Did she mean counseling? Probably not a bad idea. "No, but perhaps I should."

"I don't make big decisions before taking them to God."

Annie never expected much of God. Not after the way she had lived. "I have a lot of junk in my life. I have to deal with that first." She had no intention of going into detail, but wanted Lisa to know things aren't always easy.

She lifted both hands in the air. "Well praise the Lord for that."

Now Lisa totally confused Annie. "For the baggage I carry around? Why would I be happy about that?"

"Honey, some people go all their life without knowing what they're carrying. I say *praise the Lord* because

289

you know. That's a big step. He can take all that junk and wash it white as snow. First chapter of Isaiah. He'll toss your baggage as far as the east is from the west. Psalm chapter 103. I could go on, you know. The Word's filled with promises."

A wave of bitterness washed over Annie. "Promises like the sins of the father being visited on the offspring?"

Lisa's smile faded to sadness. "Oh, honey, that's not a promise. That's all of humanity. Adam sinned, now all mankind sins. That's the reason for the cross. Here's what you need to know. You are a beautiful, one-of-a-kind miracle, uniquely formed in the image of God, beloved by the Father, heir with His Son Jesus, and created for a purpose. Don't spend so much time looking at the scars that you miss the purpose."

Annie tried to digest that, to own it. "Thank you, Lisa."

"Hey, that's what first cousins three times removed are for."

~~*~~

Annie hit I-40 westbound for her trip home, thankful for the four-hour drive alone so she could examine her life. She told Seth that decisions are made based on our paradigm. Based on what we think, feel, and know. For most of her life, she felt ugly despite outward beauty. Unlovable even while fans vied for her autograph. Used and abused without purpose.

What does that look like now? Can God truly cleanse her from the inside? Could she be with a man like Seth and not feel lesser? Lisa told her not to focus on the scars and miss the purpose. What was her purpose? When she studied art in New York, if she erred, her instructor always told her, "Don't start over. Start from where you're at," and would point to the part that needed to be repaired.

Paint can't be erased, but it can be repaired. Annie couldn't change the past. If she'd had a different childhood, she'd have a different starting point. But she had to start from where she was today.

With the droning sound of tires spinning on the interstate, Annie talked with God, awkwardly at first, until it became natural. By the time she neared Hickory Falls, she'd made some decisions. She pulled into a rest stop, made a few phone calls, and booked a flight to New York.

Thanksgiving was less than a week away. Lillian and Annie made arrangements for a quiet day and a simple meal. Seth was heading to Florida to his parents' home. Charlie declined Annie's dinner invitation. He planned to have a meal with Patty, but said he'd be right pleased to stop in for dessert. Annie would fly to New York after Thanksgiving.

~~*~~

Seth deserved some feedback after helping to locate Charlotte's descendants. Annie wanted to tell him about Lisa. Since the fateful day of finding Seth with the magazine, Annie had made her visits to The Coffee Grinder late morning. Seth had returned to his early morning routine. Their paths didn't cross on a daily basis but she decided to make an early morning visit across the street. That was more comfortable than seeking him out at his apartment or the hardware store. Annie watched to make sure she saw no flaming red hair seated with him.

"Good morning, Margie. Skinny …"

Margie finished her words for her. "Vanilla Latte. Got it."

"You have me pegged. I'm going to need to add some variety to keep you on your toes."

Seth looked amused as he listened to the banter. "Morning, Annie."

"Hi. I wanted to thank you for the historic Hickory Falls book. It arrived yesterday."

"Good. How'd things go in Chapel Hill?"

She sat across from him. "That's why I stopped this morning." She proceeded to fill him in about Lisa, handing over the journals, and learning that Charlotte was a famous artist. Seth hung on every word. Annie had missed these mornings. Missed sitting across from Seth, having casual conversations. He looked happy. His relaxed posture. An easy smile that made his eyes dance. An occasional glance at the clock reminded her that work waited. He'd need to open the store.

"I'm sorry. I'm jabbering away and you have work."

"No harm if we open a few minutes late."

"I'll let you go. I'm glad I caught up with you before you head to your parents. I'll be gone when you return."

Seth's whole demeanor changed. A hard line replaced his easy smile. He thrust his chair backward and stood. "Then I guess this is goodbye."

He misunderstood. "No, I'll be back for Christmas. I have to make a run to New York. There are some things I need to take care of. A few things I have to put in order."

He stared at her with eyes angry as a thunderstorm. "Have a nice Thanksgiving." He spoke as he moved past her nearing the door, never looking back.

42

Annie greeted the doorman outside of her Manhattan apartment, then took the elevator ride up. When she opened the door, a deafening quiet met her. It was almost tangible. How had she lived in the solitude all those years? She wanted to throw the windows open and let noise and air flood the stuffiness, but New Yorkers can't do that in late November. Annie turned on the radio and set about the task of cleaning out her closet. Her first appointment would be with her financier tomorrow morning.

Annie stuck to her agenda, and a week later, everything was falling into place. She and Eleanor met for dinner. Her mother declined Annie's invitation to spend Christmas in Hickory Falls. A new love interest won out over a Christmas with family. Annie had one last hurdle before returning to Hickory Falls.

~~*~~

As a model, Miriam had been the major attraction on many occasions during the past few years, yet stepping onto the set of a live TV talk show brought a new wave of nerves. A stage hand smoothed the soft blue skirt of her Dalton dress. A silver cross pendant hung centered in the keyhole neckline. She whispered a prayer and, using her modeling poise, stepped onto the set. Cameras were off during the commercial break. Her host, Lana, sat front and center of the main camera.

"Watch for the signal from Geoffrey and then we'll be live." She motioned toward the director.

When he signaled, Lana began. "Our next guest is none other than supermodel Miriam, the face of Dalton Designs." She turned toward Annie. "And I understand you've had some interesting changes in your life."

Annie flashed her brilliant smile, the one the audience would know from TV and magazines. "Yes, I have."

"Am I correct that you're now going by the name Ann Gentry?"

"Actually, Ann Gentry is my real name. Miriam is the name I used during my years at Dalton. Other than those three and a half years, I've always been called Annie."

"Well, Annie, you've earned the coveted status of supermodel, and now you're leaving that life behind to pursue other interests. Will you tell our listeners why you've made such a drastic life change?"

"Sure." Annie turned toward the camera. "Life as a model has been exciting. I've had opportunities to travel the world, to meet interesting people, to wear beautiful clothing. Actually," she motioned toward her dress, "this is a Dalton Design. I'm grateful for the opportunities they gave me. Yet, after a few years, I realized I wanted to do something more. To make a difference somewhere in this world. But I wasn't sure what that was.

"A friend talked about an assignment from his college ethics class. They were to write their own obituary. Now, that may sound morbid, but it gets you thinking. How do I want to be remembered? What accomplishments would be attributed to Annie Gentry? I've always had a love for art, and I enjoy painting. Art is something that lives on longer than we do, hopefully bringing pleasure to people in generations far beyond ours."

Lana interjected. "And you're quite talented. We have copies of two paintings to show our audience." The camera paused while digital copies of Tranquility and Stormy Sea were displayed.

"Thank you." Annie continued. "The lucrative side of modeling has also allowed me to enjoy a little philanthropy. I've seen needs where I was able to offer financial help, something I'd like to continue doing."

Lana stepped in again. "Now listeners, let me jump in here before our phones start ringing. Annie, will you tell our audience how this started and what it will look like in the future."

"I'd be happy to. It actually started by accident. I heard of a hardship and wanted to help. I didn't want to step forward personally and make someone uncomfortable, so I had my financial administrator send funds anonymously. After doing this a few times, I knew I needed to establish some type of foundation. With the help of my financier, we established The Ezra Foundation. If you have a need beyond the scope of your ability to manage, you can apply for assistance. No strings attached. All we ask is that, someday, at some point in your life, you pay it forward. Help someone else in need. This is not for those who can't manage money well or those who want lofty purchases. It's for someone with overwhelming medical bills, for someone who has suffered a tragedy through fire, flood, or other natural sources. A board of directors will review all requests and determine if it meets our standards for offering assistance. All requests must be approved unanimously from the board of five people. It's designed to be self-sustaining, based on interest income. Hopefully, the foundation will outlive all of us."

"The Ezra Foundation. Does that name carry some significance?"

Annie expected the question. She'd give the simple answer, not the details. "The name Ezra means *help*. That's the purpose of this fund—to help people."

"And what will you do if people come to you personally?"

"I'll direct them to the foundation. I've provided a livable income for myself that is not to excess. It's likely I wouldn't have the means to assist people personally."

"Well, that's indeed a rarity in today's culture. Why would you lock up your fortune and choose to live a simple life?"

"I live in a small town where everyone knows everyone. I love it there and want to truly belong. No celebrity standing. No financial status. I want to be a friend and neighbor."

After thanking her, Lana turned to the camera. "Ladies and gentlemen, we've been visiting with Ann Gentry, former supermodel, Miriam."

They held their smiles as the cameraman counted down with his fingers and said, "It's a take."

~~*~~

By the time Annie returned to Hickory Falls, the town was buzzing. Even if Seth didn't see the broadcast, he'd certainly have heard about it. YouTube offered the clip of Annie's interview making it easy for anyone to view.

When a ding from her e-mail sounded, Annie set her paint brush down and opened the message from her phone. *Well done, Cousin. You must be in the King's council. I sent you a Christmas gift. It should arrive sometime today.*

Annie resumed painting until she heard the doorbell. Lisa's package? She darted downstairs to see a man and young boy at her door. The boy held a cookie tin with a red Christmas bow stuck on top.

His father spoke. "Not sure if you remember me. I've seen you around town a time or two." The man stuck his hand out in greeting. "Buck McCann. This here's my son Mikey."

Annie reached to accept the handshake. He closed his left hand over hers, enveloping her hand between his, and gave it a squeeze. "You ever need anything, anything at all, give me a call." The gesture was filled with unspoken words holding a tangible message.

The boy lifted the cookies toward her proudly. "Merry Christmas, ma'am."

"Thank you, Mikey. Merry Christmas to you."

Annie watched them walk away, then took the tin to the kitchen and opened it. Examining the variety, she chose a thumbprint, before putting water on for tea. She needed a fifteen-minute break from painting.

"Cookie, Nana?" She held the tin open. "I'm making tea. Would you like some?"

"No. You give me that make-believe tea. I never developed a taste for it."

"Chamomile tea, Nana. You know you can't have caffeine." Annie turned the tin towards Nadine. She shook head as well then excused herself to do some paperwork.

The doorbell sounded before Annie had a chance to settle in. This time it was a package. Annie carried the box to the living room. What would Lisa be sending her? Brown packing paper hid the contents inside the cardboard box. A white envelope had been taped to the top of the wrapping.

"Thank you for the precious gift of our family history. I've read every word and wept. Our numbers are many and I, alone, don't have claim to the journals or the paintings. Therefore, I've had Charlotte's journals made into books for my siblings, cousins, nieces, and nephews. I'm honored to share a copy with you.

"You will also find prints of Charlotte's early works. I had them made for family members, of which I count you one. The originals will be donated to the Raleigh Historic Center, never to be sold.

"As we celebrate these gifts together, may we be ever mindful of the greatest gift. *God so loved the world that He gave his only son.* True love gives itself away, sweet cousin."

Annie unwrapped the packing and lifted the books from the box. The two-book set contained a compilation of Charlotte's journal entries, not typed but copied in her own script. Beneath them she found professional prints of each painting she had delivered to Lisa. Hiram's Carriage. Ezra. The Church on the Hill. The Three Musicians. Each named and matted.

Charlotte's legacy. She made a difference.

43

With few breaks, Annie stayed holed up in her studio, obsessed with the painting on her easel. She employed some techniques that she hadn't used for a while. Vanishing point for perspective. Cross-hatching for shading. Sgraffito, the art of scraping paint to reveal glimpses of the color beneath. It worked beautifully for creating brick.

Annie hadn't seen Seth since her return from New York. She debated whether to wait until she saw him out somewhere, or be intentional and knock on his door. The last time she saw him ended badly. He still thought she planned to leave. Annie hoped the TV interview softened him, that he could see the changes in her.

Charlie's visit forced her decision. He stepped in to say hello to Lillian, his face dejected. "We lost Useless this morning. Seth's hurting real bad. The way he tells it, that pup was little as a skinny minute when Seth found him, hobbling on up the road. He scooped the little feller up and carried him home. His mama said the little guy was a load of extra work, but let Seth keep him anyway." Charlie shook his head, like he could shake away the sadness. "He went down to feed him this morning and couldn't rouse him. Useless was gone. Seth loaded him on the golf cart and hauled him up the hill. He's up there now, digging a final resting place."

Annie didn't wait. She left Charlie and Lillian behind and ran to her car. She turned from Larkspur onto the gravel path the builder had cut to eventually be Seth's driveway. The golf cart was parked near the end of the cleared property, next to the wooded trees. Seth stood there, bent over with a shovel in his hand. Annie left her car by the framed house and headed toward him. Useless was spread out on the back bench of the cart, wrapped in a blanket.

When she drew closer, Seth heard her and looked over his shoulder. Scrubby growth that had not been shaved away shadowed his face. Glassy eyes met hers. Seth dropped his shovel. "I guess you heard."

Annie stepped toward him and opened her arms as he'd done for her when Lillian fought for her life. "I'm sorry, Seth."

He held her close. Annie didn't want the moment to end, but Seth pulled back first. "Thanks, Annie. I needed that."

"Can I help?"

"I think I've dug enough. He's heavy as a load of concrete. I've backed the golf cart close thinking I can push him directly in. Does that sound like a disrespectful end?"

"It sounds like a practical solution. How'd you lift him up here?"

"A few guys from my landscape crew helped. They offered to come with me but I needed time alone."

Annie scanned the solitude surrounding them. "I'm sorry. Am I intruding?"

Seth took her hand. "You could never intrude." A gust of wind blew through. He freed her hand. "I guess we better get this done. Winter's reminding us it's coming."

Seth peeled back a corner of the blanket to see the dog's face. The coonhound looked the way Annie had always seen him. Mustard brown fur, eyes closed, floppy ears, like he was asleep near the hardware store register. Seth stroked his fur. "Hey, Duke. Sorry about the nickname. It just kind of stuck. No one's useless when someone loves them. No matter what I called you, you've always been loved." He closed the blanket and tucked the edge in firmly "I guess we push."

True to the expression 'dead weight,' pushing the coonhound into the newly dug grave took all of their strength. When he fell, he proved gravity well, landing with an unceremonious thud. Thankfully, the blanket still cocooned him.

Seth had unshed tears and stepped forward where he'd be out of Annie's view. She gave him a moment, then stepped behind him and wrapped her arms around his waist. He covered her hands with his.

"Are you leaving, Annie? Are you leaving Hickory Falls?" His voice was heavy with sadness.

Annie laid her head against his back, her arms still fastened around him. "I'm not leaving. Everything I want is here."

He turned so he faced her. "I miss you, Annie. I have this empty space where you belong. Nothing's right without you."

"I've been through a lot in the last few weeks. You once said I wasn't dealing with my past and you were right. I stuffed it somewhere deep inside thinking it was gone. Thinking that I'd dealt with it. We both saw what happens when that explodes." A breeze chilled her, carrying the scent of freshly dug earth. "I've started counseling—something I should have done years ago."

Seth's slight smile began to form. "Good for you. It's a first step."

"Even with a few sessions under my belt, I've realized some things. When I told you the truth, the problem wasn't how you saw me. It was how I saw myself. Once you knew the truth, I felt inferior beside you. I knew I couldn't live my life feeling that way. Every time you'd touch me, I'd imagine you thinking about those two years. That you'd see me as stained."

"Oh, Annie. I see you pure and beautiful."

"But I don't. I never have. I'm trying to believe what God says—though my sins may be as scarlet, he washes them white as snow."

Seth backed up. "Wait a minute. You were a victim. Those sins belong to your father, not you."

She screwed her eyes shut, thinking back. "They belong to both of us. There was something within me that knew it was wrong."

"But you were a child. You had few resources."

"Those are the things I'm working through."

Seth rested his forehead against hers. "Is there room in your life for me?"

"There will be, if I can have time. I want to heal completely."

"I can be patient."

"My therapist also suggested that I go to the police. I still can't, Seth. Not while my grandmother lives. I love her too much to do that to her."

"I understand. Lillian's easy to love."

"I suppose I should tell you—I'm going back to my natural hair. I'm tired of coloring it. And it's part of the therapy. I don't want to hide anymore."

He caught a lock of wind-blown hair dangling near her eye. "I think I can get used to that."

"There's one thing I don't understand. Ever since the magazine came out, I keep waiting for the whispers, the snide comments and knowing glances. Why hasn't Simone spread the pictures around town? I expected her to take pleasure in sullying my name."

Seth shifted slightly to block the wind from Annie's face. "I asked her not to. It took a little convincing, but she agreed. I'm sure she was hoping to please me. Hoping for something more between us. It doesn't matter now that you've told everyone. She has no leverage. It would make her look bad. People around here love you."

"Thank you for doing that." A shiver shook her body. "I'm freezing."

"So, the New Yorker's become a true southern gal. Go home and get warm. I have a job to finish." He glanced toward the hole and the pile of dirt. "I guess this wasn't the most romantic setting to talk about us."

"No, but it was apropos. Emotions laid bare. May I stop over later? I have something I want to bring you."

"Yep. Give me an hour."

~~*~~

Annie wrapped the painting, then tied a red ribbon around the corners. She carried it up the staircase to Seth's apartment—an apartment that he'd leave empty in a few months. Seth answered her knock. He had shaved and changed clothes since coming back from burying his dog. Seth held the door open wide, eyeing the wrapped painting.

"Merry Christmas." She held it out for him to take.

One eyebrow rose "You're a little early."

"I couldn't wait."

"It's that good?"

"Probably not. But I had fun painting it."

Seth set it on the table and removed the wrapping. Before he turned it over, Annie stopped him. "Wait. Step back and let me hold it up." He lifted his hands from it and took a step backwards. Annie hoped he hadn't seen her title, *House on the Hill,* scrolled on the back of the frame.

Annie lifted the painting and watched his eyes. His mouth began to open but decided to turn into a wide smile instead. He stood back, as he knew she wanted, placing hands on his hips, as his eyes traveled back and forth, taking in every detail of his new home. The red brick house sat at the plateau of a small hill, mountains for a backdrop. Annie added details that would someday become a reality. A paved driveway lined with crepe myrtles. Lights in the window of furnished rooms. Lush landscaping with a rose-draped arbor. Deep violet clematises climbing a mailbox post at the end of the drive. Rocking chairs on the front porch. By the time Charlie came with the news, it had been too late to debate the wisdom of her details. She'd already painted Useless curled up on the porch beside the rocker.

Seth's head bobbed in slight nods of approval as he scanned each detail. "It's perfect. Exactly how I want it to look. Annie, how did you create brick to look so real? I can practically feel the rugged edges, the smoothed mortar joints."

"Trick of the trade. I ... I'm sorry about Useless. I mean, if it's a hard memory. He was already part of the picture."

"He belongs there." Seth finally took his eyes off the painting and looked at Annie. "You belong there."

"Seth, ..."

"I won't rush you, Annie. I told you I'd be patient. But I've always planned it with you in mind. I just want you to know what I'm thinking. When you told me you were leaving, the house lost its importance."

"Seth, you know I'll never sell my grandmother's house."

"Of course not. Who would sell a treasure like that? We've seen a glimpse of its potential to be an art gallery."

An art gallery. Annie breathed in the dream. Isn't that exactly what drew her here in the first place? An art gallery in small town USA. "We're getting way ahead of ourselves. This is a discussion for another time. I'm sorry you still thought I was leaving. After the interview, I figured you knew I'd never leave Hickory Falls."

"I heard about the interview but didn't listen. It was too hard when I thought you were moving. The town's been buzzing, but most of the talk is about the Ezra Foundation. That's a good thing you've done."

Annie laid the painting down. "It's still on YouTube. Listen to it, Seth. I talked about Hickory Falls, how I love living here. I'm not going anywhere. I'm here for the long haul. Hickory Falls is home."

His eyes sparkled. "*O glistening, perfumed South. My South.*"

Walt Whitman's Longings for Home. Would Seth Walker ever cease to surprise her?

He caught her hands and held them.

"And now that you're not moving, you'll be around in January. I have something for you." He tugged her hand and went to his laptop. A few clicks later, he motioned for her to look. "The Columbia Museum of Art. They'll have a C.P. Arthur display for the month of January."

Annie gasped when she saw it, her hands flying to her chest.

Seth chuckled. "I take it you'd like to go."

"Yes. The first day of January. I can barely stand to wait."

"I believe that's New Year's Day. I'm afraid you'll have to wait until the second day of January."

44

January in South Carolina can be blustery cold, or a sunny, jacketless day. Annie was grateful for the mild temperatures and bright sunshine. After parking the Thunderbird, she and Seth walked to the entrance of the Columbia Museum of Art. Boyd Plaza, adjacent to the museum, had early morning coffee drinkers, starting their work day with a newspaper or iPad. The beautiful brick plaza was complete with fountains and flowers. But that's not why they were here.

They passed beneath the red awnings to enter the art museum. Signage led them to the room designated for the C.P. Arthur collection. At the room's entrance, Annie saw her. The three-foot high banner proudly displayed her photograph. C.P. Arthur. Annie gazed, taking in every detail. She'd seen one other photo of Charlotte, a teenager in coarse gray maid's attire. That distant and scratchy photo barely revealed the details of her face. But this professional display showcased her in living color.

Charlotte's full mouth, painted a soft mauve, blended with the warm mocha skin. Her lips opened a slight crack as if she attempted a smile. Annie figured smiling didn't come easy for Charlotte since it reached no other part of her. Guarded eyes in a deep chocolate brown showed intensity. Tension held her jaw taut. Charlotte's short hair had the distinction given only to the African American culture. Untamable afro-textured hair, cut close but not sheared.

Annie searched Charlotte's hands. The photograph kept them visible, cropping her image at the waist. The elongated fingers were spread wide, showing work-worn callouses. No polished fingertips. Charlotte wore two pieces of jewelry—a thin gold band on her left hand and a dainty cross at her neck.

Seth placed a hand on the small of Annie's back. "You ready?"

Annie nodded, then walked through the cordoned-off pathway with reverence. She had a respect for the collection that would be denied to most visitors. They had no backstory. Charlotte's early paintings depicted a walk through her life. Annie quickly realized that the pictures she now viewed also had a story to tell. The story of life after James Pearson. Life when no one beat her or hid her away like a dirty secret.

The story in paintings showed a classroom filled with black faces, seated in worn and mismatched chairs. Others showed a teacher, a wedding, a baby, and faces Annie may never identify. Annie found The Gardener and wondered how he fit into Charlotte's life.

Other museum visitors came and went. They viewed the gallery, but Annie drank in every brush stroke, every blend of color, every technique. Seth followed with the patience of Job. When she had exhausted details of every painting, she gave him a nod. "I'm ready."

As they left the room, Annie stopped once more at the banner with Charlotte's photograph. She longed to lay a hand on the image, to touch Charlotte in some esoteric way, erasing the years between them. "I'm sorry for what we did to you." Tears clouded Annie's eyes. "Thank you. Thank you for sharing your story in words and pictures." Annie's voice cracked, rich with emotion. She glanced at the crowd beginning to form at the satin ropes that created a walking path distanced from the art. "You did it, Charlotte. You made a difference."

Book Club Discussion Questions

1. The lives of Annie and Charlotte have many parallels. What similarities do you see from their young childhood? What differences?

2. How did early childhood change with their 'coming of age'?

3. We meet three mothers in Arms of Freedom—Eleanor, Davina, and Darlene. How did each approach motherhood? Describe similarities and differences.

4. Why did Miriam so quickly agree to her grandmother's suggestion of a move to Hickory Falls?

5. Annie allowed a transformation from Annie to Miriam, then three years later, converted back to Annie. Describe how each journey changed more than just her name.

6. Annie had decided that romance would never happen for her. Why, and what changed her mind? What characteristics attracted her to Seth?

7. When Annie had a meltdown, she called Seth arrogant and self-righteous. She accused him of seeing only black and white. Would you agree with her accusations?

8. Why would Davina Pearson allow Charlotte's abuse to continue and turn a blind eye to James' Klan activity? Was her love for Charlotte sacrificial or selfish?

9. Charlotte's longing for a friend took her to Coltrane Village. She described herself as 'living in two worlds.' How did those worlds differ? Why would Charlotte give up living in a comfortable home with plenty to eat and move to the impoverished village?

10. Davina visited the village. Why was that scene pivotal?

11. Secondary characters contribute to a story. What key contributions do the following characters make?
    - Charlie
    - Reverend Platt
    - Aunt Imani

12. Everyone loves a *Happily Ever After*. How would Arms of Freedom be different if Ezra had lived to marry Charlotte?

FICTION—Hickory Falls is a fictional town. However, I've placed it north of Greenville, SC and south of Asheville, NC. If you check your map, you'll find a delightful little town called Traveler's Rest. It was my inspiration for Hickory Falls.

FACT—In 1871, 500 KKK members attacked the jailhouse in Union County, SC. Eight black prisoners were killed during the attack. This occurred one year before Charlotte's journals began, but Sheriff Otis Beltzhoover made a reference to the historic event. (https://www.britannica.com/place/Union-county-South-Carolina)

FACT—Otis also reminded James that confederates were required to formally pledge their allegiance to the United States after their failed attempt to secede. This was indeed a post-war requirement. You can view a copy of the document at https://digital.lib.ecu.edu/37256#?c=0&m=0&s=0&cv=0&xywh=-1%2C-102%2C3027%2C2318

FACT—During a fictional KKK attack, Otis's deputy was arrested. His punishment was a $100 fine and six months imprisonment. While the character and that particular incident were fictional, the consequences were typical to those received during that historic timeframe.

FACT—The emancipation proclamation was a presidential order, not enacted into law until two years later when the thirteenth amendment passed. The chaos of emancipation was a key factor is Charlotte's birth.

FICTION—The report that the governor's mansion had been attacked by the KKK is purely fictional. But let's look at some governmental facts.

FACT—The governor at that time was Franklin Moses. He came from a prominent Jewish family. Although initially supporting secession, he became a forerunner in Jewish and African American alliances. He later was indicted for misappropriation of funds. The charge to indict him was driven by allies of Wade Hampton who would later become governor.
(https://digital.lib.ecu.edu/37256#?c=0&m=0&s=0&cv=0&xywh=-1%2C-102%2C3027%2C2318)

FICTION—James and other KKK members plan an attack on two black men who are rallying support for Chamberlain in the governor's race. Charlotte is able to intercede by slipping a note to the sheriff. These are fictional characters created for a fictional scene.

FACT—The election race between Hampton and Chamberlain was highly contested and required a Supreme Court decision. Historical findings report that Hampton's supporters were active in their attempts to suppress the black vote.
(https://www.digitalhistory.uh.edu/teachers/lesson_plans/pdfs/unit6_5.pdf)

FACT—Fictional character, Ezra, was accepted to Payne Institute in Hodges, SC. Payne was indeed a college for blacks, founded in 1870 and located in Hodges, SC in Greenwood County. It has been renamed Allen University and is now located in Columbia, SC.
(https://www.indexjournal.com/news/cokesbury-birthed-one-of-scs-earliest-black-colleges/article_1d1350f9-8603-5418-a6e4-f395445e0845.html)

About the Author

Kathleen Neely is the author of THE STREET SINGER, BEAUTY FOR ASHES, THE LEAST OF THESE, and IN SEARCH OF TRUE NORTH. She is a former elementary teacher. Following her years in the classroom, she moved into administration, serving as an elementary principal. Kathleen is an alumnus of Slippery Rock University in Pennsylvania and Regent University in Virginia.

Among her writing accomplishments, Kathleen won second place in a short story contest through ACFW-VA for "The Missing Piece" and an honorable mention for her story "The Dance". Both were published in a Christmas anthology. Her novel, THE LEAST OF THESE, was awarded first place in the 2015 Fresh Voices contest through Almost an Author. She has numerous devotions published through Christian Devotions. She continues to speak to students about writing. Kathleen is a member of American Christian Fiction Writers.

She resides in South Carolina with her husband, two cats, and one dog. She enjoys time with family, visiting her two grandsons, traveling, and reading. You can contact her at www.KathleenNeely.com .